Hong Kong Noir

EDITED BY
Jason Y. Ng & Susan Blumberg-Kason

BROOKLYN, NEW YORK, USA
BALLYDEHOB, CO. CORK, IRELAND

Published by Akashic Books
©2018 Akashic Books

Series concept by Tim McLoughlin and Johnny Temple
Hong Kong map by Sohrab Habibion

Paperback ISBN: 978-1-61775-672-6
Hardcover ISBN: 978-1-61775-730-7
Library of Congress Control Number: 2018931224

All rights reserved
First printing

Akashic Books
Brooklyn, New York, USA
Ballydehob, Co. Cork, Ireland
Twitter: @AkashicBooks
Facebook: AkashicBooks
E-mail: info@akashicbooks.com
Website: www.akashicbooks.com

ALSO IN THE AKASHIC NOIR SERIES

CHINA

HONG KONG

SOUTH CHINA SEA

LANTAU SOUTH
COUNTRY PARK

CHEUNG CHAU

Kam Tin
Ma On Shan
Ma On Shan
Country Park
Hong Kong
Diamond Hill
Mong Kok
Yau Ma Tei
Tsim Sha Tsui
North Point
The Pottinger Steps
Tin Hau
Lan Kwai Fong
Wah Fu
Repulse Bay
Lamma Island

TABLE OF CONTENTS

PART III: FAMILY MATTERS

PART IV: DEATH & THEREAFTER

For my fellow Hong Kongers, alive and dead.
—JYN

For Tom, for bringing me back.
—SBK

INTRODUCTION
BEHIND THE NEON LIGHTS

Fourteen.

That number is about as bad as it gets in Hong Kong. Pronounced "sup say" in Cantonese, the city's lingua franca, the ominous word sounds like "sut say"—which means certain death. It is so universally avoided that buildings have no fourteenth floor and people stay clear of cell phone numbers, license plates, and hotel rooms with that inauspicious combination of digits. Think about the myth surrounding unlucky thirteen in the West, amplify that a thousand times, and you'll start to get the idea.

So when Akashic Books suggested that we put together fourteen stories for a Hong Kong noir volume, we cringed. *Choy!* as older folks in Hong Kong like to say when they hear something sacrilegious, before they spit on the floor and shoot the offender a dirty look.

Then it clicked. Of course. It has to be. What would the city's first noir volume be without the most forbidding of all numbers? A collection of dark tales set in Hong Kong must have fourteen stories—no fewer and no more. Call it foresight or blind luck, the publisher had gotten it dead right.

But unlucky numbers are hardly the only ominous thing that Hong Kong has to offer. Going back two centuries when it was a sleepy fishing village on the underbelly of imperial China, Hong Kong was rife with pirates roaming the South China Sea. Once the British snatched Hong Kong—after not one but two wars with the Middle Kingdom—they built it up with opium money. Conglomerates in modern-day Hong Kong like Jardine, Swire, Wheelock, and Wharf started out as drug pushers to a country that never wanted opium in the first place. With checkered beginnings like this, it is little wonder that Hong Kong has always had a dark side that persists to this day.

Sun Yat-sen, the father of modern China, spoke Cantonese as his mother tongue and spent his formative years in Hong Kong in the late nineteenth century. It was there he and likeminded rebels plotted an empire-ending revolution against the Qing Court. Soon, with its laissez-faire environment, Hong Kong became home to Jews, Russians, Parsees, Gurkhas, Hindus, and other foreigners seeking new starts and business opportunities. When the Second World War reached East Asia, Hong Kong became a refuge for mainland Chinese fleeing Japanese invaders. And on Christmas Day in 1941, the city fell and so began one of the darkest chapters in its colonial history. During the occupation, Japanese collaborators and the Allied resistance played dangerous games of espionage in Hong Kong, risking it all to outlast and outmaneuver each other. It is against those tumultuous times that Brittani Sonnenberg set her haunting story included here, "The Kamikaze Caves."

Hong Kong began to recover and thrive after the war ended, as mainland migrants from wealthy businessmen to skilled artisans and poor peasants continued to pour into the British-governed city, while the Communists fought the nationalist government in a bloody civil war. It was then that monikers like the Fragrant Harbor, the Pearl of the Orient, Shoppers' Paradise, and Asia's Little Dragon were coined. Feng Chi-shun describes the 1950s in his story, "Expensive

Tissue Paper," which is set in a neighborhood of mostly Shanghai immigrants aptly called Diamond Hill.

Hong Kong continued to benefit from the southern migration, as refugees swam across the Shenzhen River in search of safety and opportunities. Mainlanders overran the border during Mao Zedong's epic land reform and the Great Leap Forward, a man-made famine that reportedly took forty-five million lives between 1958 and 1962. Enter Hong Kong's "Belle Epoque." The West learned about this exotic southern belle through Hollywood romances like *Love Is a Many-Splendored Thing* and noir films such as *Hong Kong Confidential* and *The Scavengers*.

Hong Kong's "Golden Age" was a period of rapid urbanization. Infrastructure projects began with the construction of public estates, subsidized apartment blocks in which hundreds of thousands of hillside squatters—as seen in Hollywood's *The World of Suzie Wong*—were resettled. It was one of the colonial government's most ambitious and proudest campaigns. Carmen Suen's story, "Fourteen," takes place in the first public housing estate to have its own bathroom and kitchen in every unit.

The fifties and sixties were also an era of R&R mayhem during the Vietnam War, which comes alive in Xu Xi's "TST," about a young girl in the world's oldest profession. James Tam writes a dark yet comical account of another lady of the evening in the gritty and populous Mong Kok district. Sexual exoticism came to a halt in 1967, when leftist riots broke out in Hong Kong shortly after the Cultural Revolution began to ravage China. Shen Jian writes about those eight months of bomb scares and street violence in his story, "Kam Tin Red," and how one local family was torn apart.

The early 1970s saw the peak of police corruption, which

resulted in the Independent Commission Against Corruption, an agency created to investigate dirty cops and bring order to law enforcement. At the same time, the Royal Hong Kong Police Force began to hire more local Chinese and fewer British cops to address widespread discrimination and improve public relations with the hoi polloi. Charles Philipp Martin's story, "Ticket Home," brings the reader into the last few years of the Royal Hong Kong Police Force, before the word *Royal* was eventually dropped in 1997, when the city was handed back to the Communist regime under the promise of "one country, two systems."

We relive the handover in Rhiannon Jenkins Tsang's story, "One Country, Two People," which takes place in Ma On Shan in the New Territories, while Tiffany Hawk flashes back between the handover and the present day in "You Deserve More," set in the rowdy expat enclave of Lan Kwai Fong. And on the subject of expats, Christina Liang writes about domestic drama in Hong Kong Island's luxurious Repulse Bay in "A View to Die For."

Hong Kong's sordid history notwithstanding, the city remains one of the safest in the world. In a place that never sleeps and barely even blinks, violent crimes are a relative rarity and people feel safe hanging out on the street at all hours of the day. When Hong Kongers do commit murder, however, they do so with plenty of dramatic flourish. Dismemberment, cannibalism, a laced milkshake, and a severed head tucked inside a giant Hello Kitty doll—Hong Kongers have seen it all. The media always has a field day with homicides, splashing gory photos and fifty-point-font headlines on the front page. Shannon Young sensationalizes a grisly murder in "Blood on the Steps," set on Hong Kong Island's fabled Pottinger Street. Marshall Moore memorializes gruesome suicides on the outlying island of Cheung Chau in his story, "This Quintessence of Dust," and Ysabelle Cheung's story, "Big Hotel," takes place at an eerie funeral florist shop in North Point.

As coeditors, we come from two very different backgrounds. Jason was born in Hong Kong and spent his formative years in Europe and North America before moving back to his birthplace to rediscover his roots. Susan was born and raised in the United States and lives there now, but spent her formative years in Hong Kong and mainland China. What brought the two of us together was our love of Hong Kong and its history, culture, and freedom. The city may be far from perfect, but there is a bounty of quirks to make writers like us constantly feel like kids in a candy shop.

All across the city, for instance, you can find little shrines dedicated to Tudigong—the God of the Ground—placed in front of retail shops and outside residential homes, complete with burning incense and a pyramid of Sunkist oranges. Religious holidays such as Buddha's birthday, Christmas, and Yulan—the Taoist Festival of the Hungry Ghosts—are observed in secular Hong Kong with equal zeal. Jason brings alive Tudigong, Yulan, and other elements of the local folk belief system in his story, "Ghost of Yulan Past."

Jason's story also takes us to the present day, Hong Kong's darkest era yet. His tale alludes to the Umbrella Movement in 2014, during which student activists occupied large swaths of the city for months on end to demand universal suffrage and oppose the Chinese government's increasing interference in local politics. Since then, many young activists have been jailed for their involvement in the movement, and publishers of books critical of the Communist leadership have been kidnapped, only to reappear on the mainland in staged confessional videos. The city's future is murky and the rights enshrined in the Basic Law—the constitution governing Hong Kong for the first fifty years after the handover—are being chipped away by the day. Twenty years into the handover, the Sword of Damocles that hangs over the city's heads is inching ever closer.

So what will Hong Kong look like in five years, ten years, or thirty years—when the "one country, two systems" promise expires? It's impossible to foresee. Hong Kong's future may not be within our control, but some things are. We can continue to write about our beloved city and work our hardest to preserve it in words. When we asked our contributors to write their noir stories, we didn't give them specific content guidelines other than to make sure their stories end on a dark note. What we received was a brilliant collection of ghost stories, murder mysteries, domestic dramas, cops-and-robbers tales, and historical thrillers that capture Hong Kong in all its dark glory. The result is every bit as eclectic, quirky, and delightful as the city they write about.

So bring on the fourteen.

Jason Y. Ng & Susan Blumberg-Kason
September 2018

PART I

HUNGRY GHOSTS & TROUBLED SPIRITS

GHOST OF YULAN PAST

BY JASON Y. NG

Tin Hau

C hoi gives the faded red door a hefty push and it creaks like a rusty old ship. He puts one foot across the granite threshold and pokes his head in.

"Hello?"

A thick whiff of burning incense hits him before his eyes adjust to the temple's dark interior. A giant statue of Tin Hau—the Taoist Goddess of the Sea—snaps into view, her calming face drenched in the altar's crimson light and her commanding figure flanked by a pair of porcelain guards.

"Anyone there?"

"We're already closed," a woman's voice echoes through the airy hollow of the foyer. "Come back tomorrow. The temple opens daily at seven a.m.," she says with a practiced apathy.

"Well, the door was ajar and I thought the temple might have extended its hours for Yulan."

Yulan is Choi's favorite day on the lunar calendar. The annual Festival of Hungry Ghosts, celebrated on the fifteenth day of the seventh month, is Halloween without the goofy costumes and free candy. The only trick-or-treaters are the ghosts, who for one night every year get a free pass to mingle with the living and help themselves to offerings of barbecued pork, roast duck, and free-flowing rice wine.

"Come back tomorrow, *lah*. The temple opens daily at

seven a.m.," the woman repeats impatiently as she approaches the door to close it. "Have a good night."

Choi gets a better look at the woman as her face comes into the amber streetlight. He is surprised to see how young she is—no more than two or three years older than he. She has large downturned eyes, high cheekbones, and squeaky-white teeth. A veritable Maggie Cheung if it weren't for her petite stature.

"Wait, is that an HKU sweatshirt you're wearing?" Choi cheers. "I'm a freshman there. Poli-sci. What a small world!"

"It belongs to my older sister," the girl explains. "She's a journalism major. We wear each other's clothes all the time."

"My name is Choi. Do you work here? Do you *live* here?"

"Look, I'm closing up . . ." She demurs, grits her teeth, and continues, "You can call me Suze. I don't live here, but my family runs this place. We all have to pitch in and take a few shifts a week. The temple closes at five p.m."

"Then why are you here so late?"

"I . . . Well, today is Yulan and we had loads of visitors. It has taken me forever to finish up, that's why."

Choi senses an opening and offers, "Is there anything I can help you with? It's only nine thirty and I'm already finished. I've got tons of time to kill."

"Finished with what?" She sizes him up. "And what's the deal with *that?*"

"Oh, this?" He shows her his flashlight and starts to flick it on and off. "I was in Tai Hang earlier to check out the famous nullah before I started wandering around and ended up here. The nullah is—*was* supposed to be haunted and I wanted to see it for myself."

"You wanted to visit a haunted place on Yulan of all days?"

"That's the whole point, *ah!* Years ago some children fell

into the water and drowned. Since then, kids can be heard laughing and weeping in the middle of the night. At least that's what I read when I googled it."

The nineteen-year-old is a thrill-seeker. Every year, he visits one of the well-known haunted sites in Hong Kong, like Tsat Tsz Mui Road in North Point, Bela Vista Villa in Cheung Chau, and Hung Shui Kiu in Tuen Mun. Why pay money to go to those fake haunted houses at Ocean Park when he has free access to the real ones across the city? Last Yulan he snuck into the defunct psychiatric hospital in Sai Ying Pun and got a real adrenaline rush.

"So did you manage to run into any weeping children tonight?"

"Fat chance! Tai Hang has been gentrified beyond recognition with all those high-end restaurants and pretentious bars. The poor old nullah was paved over by the government and turned into a regular street. I should be the one weeping tonight!"

The girl chuckles. "Next time, perhaps you should check out Park's Tower down the street. It was a movie theater before they tore it down to make way for an office building. I was told a couple of construction workers died in an accident during the redevelopment. Now the landlord has a hard time finding tenants because businesses are too scared to move in."

"Is that right?" Choi chirps as he puts his other foot over the threshold. "Well, this place is pretty spooky too. Do you mind if I take a quick look around?"

Suze considers the request for a moment and relents. She gives the boy a half smile and ushers him into the dimly lit main hall. Inside, the air feels musty and ancient, but the overpowering smell of incense soon takes over as they approach the altar.

"So this is the famous Tin Hau?" Choi marvels at the sheer size of the statue. "She mustn't be very busy these days considering how few fishermen are left in Hong Kong for her to protect."

The two settle into a corner that looks like a makeshift home office: a wooden desk, a telephone, and a pile of ledgers to keep track of donations. The naked lightbulb hanging from the ceiling swings to and fro, making every shadow on the walls rock like roly-poly toys. She offers her visitor a wooden stool before sitting cross-legged on the floor, leaning against a life-size statue of Guan Gong—the God of Justice.

"You said your family runs this temple. How did that happen?"

"A long time ago, my clan raised money to build this place after my great-great-great-great-grandfather supposedly witnessed a miracle when a red incense burner was washed ashore by a typhoon. Believe it or not, the temple used to look out toward Victoria Harbor. The shoreline wasn't far from where we are until a huge land reclamation project created all this new land."

"So your family *owns* the temple?"

"Yes and no. It's our temple but we have to hand it over to the government eventually. We spent years negotiating with the bureaucrats and finally got them to agree to let us operate it for a few more years. Who knows what they'll do once they get their hands on it. Tin Hau Temple Road is such prime real estate, and property developers have been salivating over it for decades."

"I'm sure it'll be fine. Isn't the temple an official monument? No one will be able to touch it."

"Don't be so sure. You know what the name Tai Hang means?"

"It means a big ditch."

"Precisely. The area is named after the famous nullah—the one you wanted to check out. But did the government care? Did it stop them from filling the ditch with concrete and turning it into a sidewalk? They even renamed the site—Tai Hang Nullah is now called Fire Dragon Path—as if to erase it from history. From our memory."

"You're worried that the same thing might happen here?"

"Wouldn't you be? Who is to say they won't sell the land underneath the temple to the highest bidder and relocate us to the boondocks, just like . . ."

"Just like what they did to the Star Ferry Pier!" Choi finishes her sentence. He likes a girl who has strong opinions and is a little feisty. He knows exactly what Suze is chafing against. Since the handover twenty years ago, landmark structures in Hong Kong have been dropping like flies to make way for new development. Heritage conservation is a joke.

"This neighborhood, this street, and even the subway station are all named after this place. Tin Hau wouldn't be Tin Hau without the temple. But what can we do? We're just taking it one day at a time."

"How's the temple doing these days? You said you got lots of visitors today, so you must be doing all right."

"Most months we're lucky to break even. The temple is busy only a few times a year—on Tin Hau's birthday, Chinese New Year, and Yulan. Donations are way down. Ask yourself: when was the last time you visited a Taoist temple?"

"Let's see . . . Not counting tonight, the last time was probably when my mom took me to Wong Tai Sin Temple when I was seven. Wow, that was twelve years ago!"

"You see my point? And when people do come, they donate a pittance and ask for the world: men pray for pretty wives and women pray for rich husbands. Just about everyone wants to win the lottery."

"I guess when the government doesn't look after its people, they have to look to something else."

"Nowadays most of our visitors are tourists who read about us in their guidebooks. Lots of mainland Chinese and Koreans. The only regulars are old folks from the neighborhood. Some even pay for our upkeep and bring me food. They know my favorites—fuzzy peaches and steamed buns." She flashes a smile and looks up at the soaring ceiling.

Choi looks up too. He is struck by how tall and cavernous the temple is. He glances around at his surroundings, at the dozens of lifelike sculptures and busts in every corner and recess. Many of them are glaring straight back at him, the weight of a hundred eyes producing an uneasy feeling of both protection and consternation.

"Doesn't it creep you out being here all by yourself?"

"I thought that's what you like—creepy places." She winks. "I grew up here. I guess I've gotten used to it."

"Speaking of creepy, have you ever seen anything unusual around here?" Choi's eyes light up, waiting for his new friend to regale him with a ghost story or two.

There is no reply. She shifts her weight on the floor and looks straight at the Tin Hau statue as if to seek her advice.

"Come on, Suze, throw me a bone here!" He nudges her shoulder with one knee.

"I . . ." Suze bites her lip for a good five seconds before she finally says, "Let's just say I have a talent. I see what most people don't."

"*Wah*, are you serious? You mean you have *yin yang* eyes?"

She nods reluctantly, already regretting saying too much.

"That's crazy! I don't know anybody like you. Do you see *them* all the time?"

"It's not what you think. I don't see them as much as I *sense* them."

"Sense them how?"

"There are always signs: things get knocked over when nobody's around. Dogs bark for no reason and cats hiss out of the blue, those sorts of things. Animals have good instincts— the same way rats and snakes head to high ground before a tsunami hits."

"Do you see them right now?"

"Not right now, but who knows?" She teases him with another wink. "I'll be sure to let you know if one shows up."

"Hmm, how do you know I'm not one of them?" Choi winks back. He is tempted to spook her by putting on a raspy voice and making a scary face but decides against it. That's no way to impress a girl he has just met. Instead, he asks, "More importantly, how do I know *you* aren't one of them?"

"You'll just have to take your chances, won't you? Look over there," she says, pointing at the wall. "Those are our shadows. Ghosts don't have shadows. Besides, they can't enter most homes because of Tudigong, let alone a temple with so many deities around."

"So that thing really works, huh?" Choi's parents have a small Tudigong shrine outside their front door, as do most traditional households in Hong Kong. The Taoist God of the Ground is supposed to protect the home and keep evil spirits away. Choi promises himself that from now on he will stop practicing soccer with the shrine and kicking garbage into it.

"It works except for today," Suze says. "On Yulan, the gates of the underworld are flung open and even Tudigong will look the other way."

"I wish I had *yin yang* eyes too. It's like having a superpower!"

"Be careful what you wish for, Choi. Occasionally, even people without my sight can see things they don't normally see—if they are mentally vulnerable, like after a traumatic experience or when they hit a low point in life. If you actively seek them out, you make yourself vulnerable too."

"Really?" The adrenaline junkie is excited again. "When they show up, do they try to talk to you? And do you talk back?"

"That depends on them. But sure, we have conversations just like what you and I are doing now. People think I'm crazy when they see me talking to myself. My family knows about my abilities and they're used to it."

"What do they want from you?" Choi is completely intrigued. This Yulan is shaping up to be one hell of a night.

"Frankly, they're a lot like people: they just want to be heard. Some of them have been wronged or betrayed by a friend, a spouse, or a family member. But most of them linger around because they have unfinished business to take care of. I listen to their stories and tell them what I think."

"But aren't you afraid? Don't they scare you?"

"What about you? You seek out haunted places. Aren't *you* afraid?"

"I dig the rush. It makes me feel alive. I guess it's the same reason people go on a roller coaster or bungee jump. Besides, it takes my mind off all the depressing stuff happening in Hong Kong. But I don't want to bore you with that; most people get bored when I talk about politics." He heaves a sigh. "You still haven't answered my question. Aren't you—"

"Hush!" Suze's face stiffens, suddenly on guard.

"What? What's going—"

"Sssh!" Suze turns her head to the arched doorway that opens to a dark den. "You're back, Mrs. Ling."

Every muscle in Choi's body tenses up. He is in shock and can't even turn his head to see whom Suze is conversing with.

"Yes, Mrs. Ling," Suze speaks, her voice much deeper than before. "I'll tell your husband to bring extra white lilies to your grave on Valentine's Day. I promise."

A stream of cold sweat runs down Choi's back. His face is as white as a sheet of joss paper.

Just then, a loud bang pierces the silence and sends Choi jumping from his chair and screeching three octaves higher than his talking voice. It was his flashlight—it had slipped from his hands and hit the ground.

Suze picks it up and hands it back to its owner, before bursting into a thunderous laugh.

Choi is confused. "Is she . . . is she still there?"

"*Aiya*, I was just messing with you. You're too easy!" She is now rolling on the floor, laughing herself to tears. "So much for digging the rush!"

"Oh, that was very mature . . ." Choi is more embarrassed than angry, his face turning from paper white to a bright lobster red. But he has to hand it to Suze—she got him good and it was pretty funny. He starts to laugh with her, at the same time regretting not spooking her a few minutes ago when he had the chance.

"Awww, you're a good sport." Suze slaps his leg playfully while wiping tears from her eyes. "Consider that a test, my friend. How else would I know if you could handle the real deal? But seriously, you should've seen the look on your face!"

"I'm glad one of us is amused," Choi pouts, certain that any girl would find his mock anger endearing. He absently straightens his T-shirt, which now has wet patches around the underarms, and gingerly checks the doorway to make sure nothing is lurking there. "What were we even talking about before your third grade prank?"

"All right, I'm sorry. Before I nearly scared you to death, you were asking me if I was afraid of *them*. Believe me, there's nothing to be afraid of." She looks Choi in the eye and says, "Sometimes I find people much more frightening."

He stares back at her, bewildered and wanting to understand more. His embarrassment has melted away, forgotten and forgiven.

"You don't know the half of it. As soon as people find out about my abilities, they flock to me asking for help. Sometimes the line stretches outside the temple."

"They want you to help them communicate with loved ones who have passed away?"

"Some do, like parents who have lost their young children and can't let go. It's tragic and I do what I can to help them. But those cases are few and far between. Oftentimes, family members are quite happy to see their aging parents and grandparents go, to be finally rid of the financial burden. This is Hong Kong, after all—people are too busy to be sentimental." She shakes her head. "But still they come to me, not to talk to the departed but to look for things."

"What things?"

"Money, of course. They want to know where the dead husband has stashed his secret wealth, or why the rich grandmother has written them out of her will. The worst are people who treat dead relatives like fortune-tellers and ask them for lottery numbers. I don't understand what's with Hong Kong people and their obsession with the lottery! It's ridiculous."

"And incredibly sad."

"People fear ghosts because they're afraid of what they can't see and don't understand. But if you want to know what

I really think? I think they're afraid of seeing their own ugly selves. The dead merely hold up a mirror on the living and reveal their greed and bad hearts. On the other hand," she continues, "most of *them* are harmless and good-natured. I see sadness on their faces, especially the ones who died young. There's so much they haven't experienced: falling in love, seeing the world, making a difference in the city they love. The life that's not yet lived and never will . . ."

The conversation is getting a little depressing and Choi tries to lighten the mood: "You mentioned an older sister? Does she work here too?"

"Not anymore."

"She's a journalism major at HKU? How is she liking it?"

"You might have read about her in the news." She bunches up her sweatshirt. "My sister is in jail. She was sentenced to two years for unlawful assembly. Her picture was all over the papers."

"For Occupy?" Choi's interest is piqued again. He was sixteen years old when the Umbrella Movement erupted, when student protesters occupied large swaths of the city for nearly three months to demand universal suffrage. He wanted to join the protests but his parents wouldn't let him, for fear that their only son would be injured or arrested. To Choi, the movement was a culmination of everything that had gone wrong since the handover: a widening income gap, sky-high property prices, a tone-deaf government that citizens had no part in choosing, and, above all, the gradual disappearance of Hong Kong's unique character, epitomized by the demolition of heritage sites and other collective memories. He is now writing a research paper on the movement for one of his poli-sci classes.

"My sister and I both camped out in Admiralty and fought the police on the frontlines. I'll never forget the sting of tear gas and pepper spray. But that's not what got her into trouble. She was arrested last year during a protest against the government's rural redevelopment plan. She was upset about the land grab and threw paper effigies at the police. They got it all on video and she was convicted and thrown into prison."

"That's terrible. I'm sorry to hear that," says Choi with genuine empathy. He lives in Tai Po with his parents, not far from the villages that were facing forced resettlement. "How's she holding up?"

"Better than I thought. I bet it's boring as hell being locked up, given how hyperactive she always is." Suze glances at the wall calendar. "In fact, I just saw her today. That's why I need to stick around—someone needs to watch over her."

"Stick around? Were you thinking about leaving Hong Kong? So many of my friends have already left because they don't see a way out. Anyway, I'm glad you decided to stay."

"We can't all leave, can we?" She smiles, before getting serious again. "We need to stay here and guard this place—we need to be our own Tudigong. I complain about Hong Kong a lot, but the truth is, I love this place. It is my home."

Choi is touched by Suze's earnestness and her feelings for Hong Kong. It's not every day that he finds a kindred spirit. Even at HKU, he has a hard time meeting people who are as passionate about political issues as he is. He recently set up an online group to monitor free speech on campus, but friends think he is becoming "politicized" and "radicalized." Most of his classmates care only about grades and summer internships and job offers, oblivious to the slow death that his city is suffering. But not Suze—she is different from the rest of them. Stumbling into Tin Hau Temple is the best thing that has happened to him since he got admitted to college. *Thank you, Tai Hang Nullah!*

Euphoric, Choi suddenly realizes it's getting quite late and he hasn't had dinner. He musters his courage and asks, "Do you want to close up and grab a bite with me around here?" Not to appear too forward, he adds, "I mean, I haven't eaten and I assume you haven't either. There're tons of places in Tai Hang that are open even at this hour. They're mostly really overpriced, except for this chicken hot pot joint tucked behind Wun Sha Street. It's a bit of a hole-in-the-wall but it's definitely worth trying if you've never—" He realizes he is rambling and cuts himself off, blushing.

Suze gives the invitation a thought and says, "You're sweet. But look, I don't eat much these days. Besides, I have all that to finish." She points to the plates of fuzzy peaches and steamed buns next to the incense burners on the altar, the food rotting and covered in a heavy layer of dust.

Choi doesn't know what to make of this. For a second, he thinks Suze is messing with him again, except this time she looks dead serious. She gets up from the floor and signals to walk him to the door. He is too confused not to comply.

"Thank you for the chat," Suze says with tenderness in her voice, "but you should go now. If fate will have it, we'll see each other next year."

As they walk, Choi notices his shadow on the wall moving with him, but not Suze's. It stays where it is. In that instant he realizes the shadow isn't hers—it belongs to the Guan Gong statue she was leaning against.

Just then a dog barks loudly from the courtyard outside. "Keep your eyes on the road when you cross," she says. "Drivers can't see you when they make the sharp curve. I found out the hard way."

Choi starts to hyperventilate. It all adds up: the shadow, the dusty offerings, and the unfinished business to look after—a sister in need of protection. Or is it a cherished neighborhood under threat?

Suze gives her ashen friend a knowing nod, as if to remind him of everything she has said about her kind. *Believe me, there's nothing to be afraid of. Sometimes I find people much more frightening . . .*

Choi is back at the granite threshold by the faded red door. The midnight moon has turned the peeling stucco of the temple a shade bluer. He wants to run but his knees have betrayed him. There is too much to process and his head is drawing a blank. He closes his eyes and takes a deep breath. He knows Suze is right: there is nothing to be afraid of, and he knows exactly where he will be on the next Yulan.

TST

BY Xu Xi 許素細

Tsim Sha Tsui

L*isten to me, it's not too late.* On quiet nights, you will hear us speak. At the end of the last water snake year, the year that *autre* calendar brackets between February 10, 2013, and January 30, 2014, our storytelling began. During that lunar year, the Seven Sisters Club vanished for good. Once upon a time, a perfect geometry of white smoke against dark pistachio and rust that was almost vermilion graced its facade. Remnant tiles, like torn evening wear, barely cover the gunmetal wall now, but under streetlight, the colors still glow. I watched the building disappear. Each year, a little more deterioration—a sign gone, a door off its hinges, a window-pane shattered—until finally the wreckers appeared, and now we might never have existed at all.

The girls, they were all there, most idling in doorways along Minden Row, others squatting along the uphill path toward what had been the Royal Observatory, some loitering at the crest of the hump toward Middle Road. They all came to tell their stories to anyone who would listen, and once they started, they wouldn't shut up.

But the first time they came it was because I called. Our home was gone and we needed a way to come together. We were like that, you see, undeniably sisters in eternity's muddle. The Milky Way swirled through our story every 乞巧節, that Chinese heavenly *Romeo and Juliet* story for thwarted lovers all girls adore. Occasionally, we gathered in the forgotten village in North Point, along the shoreline where bathing pavilions later stood, although even those are gone now, remembered only by a street named 七姊妹道, meaning Seven Sisters, which correctly transliterates into English as Tsat Tsz Mui Road. Unlike our own mistranslated Minden, named after a Royal Navy ship to recall the 1759 Battle of Minden, our street's name in Cantonese is Myanmar, formerly Burma. Our club on Minden Row, we have nothing to do with Burma. Even if it is possible to cross over a hump to get here, this isn't the "over-the-hump" air route of that long-vanished airline, the one that ferried legal and not-so-legal cargo to and from Burma during and after the second war.

Our only crime was being bar girls at Seven Sisters.

And girls like us are better off dead, at least while we still answer to *girl* instead of *woman*, the way I did. The way I still do. I'm not old enough to be forgotten. None of us are. Which is why they all come when I call, these girls who were not privileged to ever become women, no matter how old they are when they die.

* * *

Men don't lie to whores. I once had a lover who had been MI5. He was gentle, though, and sometimes cried after he fucked me. The man who killed me was rough and never cried. He kept two fierce Alsatians in his bathtub. That's the trouble with Hong Kong flats—too small for dogs, especially large ones, but some people insist on having them. This man, an English police inspector, he was vice. Those dogs were hungry the night they ripped me apart and almost tore his left hand off in the process. He still has the scar. The photo in the newspaper caught it when he put up his hand to cover his face the day he was arrested, although that happened years later, long after I was gone. Jail ended his career, but he just went to the mercenaries. There's always a place in the world for the rough ones.

About my death, though, that was an accident. He lost control of his hounds and they savaged my jugular and feasted on my flesh until he muzzled them. Afterward he hid my corpse because what else could he do? First, however, he cleanly sliced off my hands and feet to be found with no canine teeth marks, separated from the rest of me. It saddens me that the American sailor was wrongly accused. He, the police inspector, pinned it on him. Easy because the other girls saw me go off with sailor boy. They didn't know Alistair came by after he left and took me to his home with the dogs. So that's my story. And now I have no feet to walk or hands to cradle my favorite *fleurs*. All I can do is talk my story till someone hears me.

"Kowloon, Hong Kong" was silly pop, sung in our day, with its choppy chop-chop 2/4 or 4/4 time, like the impossible waltz that is "Chopsticks." We didn't say *TST* back then, since we were mostly Cantonese and said 尖沙嘴, Tsim Sha Tsui; the impossible English of our district's name confounded foreigners who showed up later, in the eighties and nineties amid rampant nightlife (and daylife as well), and our neighborhood was abbreviated to TST, an acronym better suited to a parasitic bloodsucker, the tsetse fly.

We were poorer then, during the four decades before and after the second war, even though wealth lined some of the lanes, avenues, streets, and roads of TST. We came to TST because of that wealth and the men who haunted the district, trolling for love, gluttonous with desire. But we were happier then because any money is better than being impoverished. After all, we were young and pretty enough, smart and hungry enough, sad and desperate enough to go away and stay away in TST, far from the shanties or villages or homes of our birth. Those homes where love was absent and our desire for more translated into lust for a future that could be our own. We came in droves during war and peacetime, hunting out a perch to land on for what passed as a lifetime.

So here I am beginning at the end, or what you out there think of as the end. I am dead, have been dead since the mid-seventies. Alistair scattered my hands and feet in some kind of perverse ritual. My left hand propped by the back entrance to the Peninsula Hotel, the one where we sometimes used to enter the kitchen where his friend Gaston the chef served us scrumptiously gourmet dinners for free. It surprises me Gaston did not recognize my hand when he found it. After all, I was sometimes payment for those meals, jacking him off in his office while Alistair waited outside. My left foot he tossed in the harbor, late one night, from the Star Ferry Pier in TST. It didn't sink to the depths and landed on a ledge where it wavered precariously, never tipping into the sea. Someone found it and turned it in to the police, and it was preserved as evidence for a while until the case was closed and it eventually rotted away. My right hand and foot were never found.

We girls don't mind, though, where a story begins. We have, as we like to say, all the time in the world, so sometimes we begin in the middle, other times at the beginning, and often enough at the end. It doesn't much matter how you tell a story, as long as you tell it. This is my story so I'll tell it however I want.

I don't like the beginning of my story. Remembering myself in long pigtails when I really was a girl just makes me miserable. I had a cloth doll Ah-Ma sewed for me and I hung onto her and called her Little Miss, the polite form of address for a young lady. *Siu jie,* I'd admonish, *where have you been? Don't you know it's dangerous out there at night? You stay with me and I'll take care of you.* It was what Ma used to say before she died, TB or something, I'm not sure, but I remember she coughed a lot. Pa sold me. I was twelve with buds for breasts and had only just begun menstruating. It was summer. He dragged me out of bed in the middle of the night and hosed me down like one of the pigs. A woman undid my pigtails and combed out my hair. She put me in a thin dress, stuck a pair of sandals with plastic flowers on my feet, and took me away from the village. I was too scared to speak or even cry. The last memory I have of Pa is a vision of his back to me, walking away toward our hut. He never even said goodbye.

And then for a while—I'm not sure how long, maybe three or four months—it was a cyclical blur of sleep, food, nights, men, men, men, and more men, until nothing they did could ever hurt again.

Until Monsieur Autre.

That wasn't his name but it was what we girls called him. He was French, but he spoke our language very well, had lived in Taiwan where he said he studied Mandarin, and was in Hong Kong teaching French, and he spoke Cantonese too. He visited Auntie Lam, our mama san, once a week, always asking for her freshest flower. Usually he chose Little Pear or Night Blossom—they were sixteen and eighteen but dressed to pass for younger—until I arrived at Seven Sisters.

So this is the real beginning of my story, when I became Monsieur Autre's "Little Cabbage," his special *amour*.

I met him the night of my debut at Seven Sisters. It's a fancy word, *debut*. Some American sailor taught me that. *It was my sister's debut*, he said, and when I asked him what it meant, he said that where he came from, young girls were presented to society at a ball for debutantes to make their de- but. His sister wore a pretty white dress like all her girlfriends and young men escorted the girls so everyone could check them out and see how special they were, and one day one of those young men would make her his bride. The sailor was a gentleman, soft spoken, whose English swayed like a willow in a typhoon. He didn't wear a naval uniform but from the haircut you knew he was one of them. *An officer*, Auntie Lam whispered when she assigned me. *Treat him nice and he'll give you a big tip, maybe even buy you something special.* He kept me a whole weekend. *Did one of them marry your sister?* I wanted to know. *No*, he said, *she died.* He was silent after that and I didn't have the heart to ask what happened. His name was Jefferson, *like the president* was what he said.

But Jefferson was during Vietnam, long after Monsieur Autre, a time when Tsim Sha Tsui was flooded with boys who waddled like ducks. Those were good days, when all us girls made money, when Seven Sisters was busy every night. Even that was a long time ago, and now TST is all about jewelry stores and designer boutiques for mainland tourists or massage parlors where the girls make a pittance for their slavery. The flower markets are gone, along with the food markets and 好好, our favorite won ton noodle haunt. The good days are over and we, despite all our talk, are forever dead.

You see what I mean about our talk-stories? We have so many middles there are no beginnings. Monsieur Autre, though, he looked after me for a time, so I suppose he was a kind of beginning.

The day he finally left, he told me his real name. It was difficult and he laughed when I tried to say Archambault. *So long*, I complained. *Why do you people make such long names? Chinese so much easier!* I've always wondered, after he left, why he told me his name. He didn't ask me to remember him like some johns did. Nor did he tell me to look him up if I was ever in Paris the way others occasionally would. As if I'd ever go to Manhattan, Kansas, which is where one john was from. He wrote down his address and phone number, insisted I keep the torn slip of paper. I threw it out the minute he left. Such a boy, sweet-faced, told me he wanted to show me off to his friends, to introduce me to his mother. *Dor yu! Many fish!* as Monsieur Autre would say, making us all laugh at his deliberate mistranslation by mispronouncing the tones for 多餘, meaning something superfluous or a pointless endeavor. He taught me a lot of English words and phrases, and a little French, although sometimes I think he was poking fun by teaching me deliberately wrong words and phrases. *Don't make me look like a fool*, I'd complain, and his answer always was, *You could never be a fool.*

Was I a fool? Now that I have all the time in eternity, it is the only question that still vexes and nags. All those sexy clothes and bright shiny things, just to earn a few dollars from so many johns I lost count. Wasn't there anything else I could have done? Monsieur Autre, he often said: *Why don't you go back to school, learn something?* But honestly, that would be *way* too many fishes! He was just as much to blame, don't you think, because he liked fresh girls? And I was young and fresh and even though my hymen was already torn and too many cocks had come before his, he could still pretend I was his baby girl. Pedophile, that's all he was. It doesn't matter now how nicely he treated me, all he wanted was to fuck a child, and there's something so vile and wrong-headed about that, so . . . *unnecessary*, this burning desire of his. Don't you think?

You know, I don't even know to whom I'm speaking anymore. Look around, it's always only the girls who come when I call. Many of our johns are just as dead as us, but do you see them here? No. Bang, bang, thank you, ma'am, as the sailors used to say. And then they get to sleep the sleep of the dead. Meanwhile we're wandering, exhausted, famished ghosts with no hope of rest. What we're looking for to appease our restless spirit we'll never find, and what we need to still our hunger pangs is lost to that heaven where emperors rule and girls must remain girls forever.

Listen to me, it's not too late. You can still fix things. Girls are not pigs to be hosed down and sold. We all return to where Seven Sisters once stood, because it's the closest thing to home. But the club's long gone, and even the abandoned space that stayed vacant for so many years has been transformed into a third-rate restaurant, famous mostly for its rat population. Maybe it's just as well it's gone, although for every Seven Sister who dies, a new one is born elsewhere in TST. You'd think one of those johns would at least come back and visit, maybe look for one of us? Like Manhattan, Kansas, and his earnest plea that I should come visit? Oh sure, they've had their wives and daughters or girlfriends and maybe even other younger, fresher girls. But I can't go very far because my feet are gone, and I can't reach out to strangle the ones who are still alive because my hands are gone as well. It's a hell of an eternity, and if you had any sense you'd do something to turn this world around, find some way to right the wrongs, figure out a better way for me to die.

Listen to me, it's not about fate. We girls love to chatter on about fate because it's a small comfort to think that really, there's nothing to be done so why not just shut up and die the hand you're dealt? But look at us, we're all here, and we haven't shut up, not like those johns whose dead-to-the-world sleep is peacefully silent. There's only one thing I'm sure of and that is that I have to keep talking-story until you hear me, until you truly listen, until you fix this mess you call life. Fix things so that girls like me can become women, need not always be enslaved, stripped, beaten, fucked, or treated like dolls, created just to satisfy impersonal lusts. You *will* hear us, me, one of these days, because I know you can if you try.

Listen, it's never too late. Just listen.

THIS QUINTESSENCE OF DUST

BY MARSHALL MOORE

Cheung Chau

1

I couldn't tell where the jet lag ended and the hangover began. They fused into each other like the stairs in one of those Escher prints where the only way is down. I had been back in Hong Kong for two days. The swelter of late summer here is a physical assault when you're not used to it. The noise too: taxi horns like air-raid sirens, old ladies bellowing in their raspy banshee voices, relentless. I remembered in the abstract but my body had forgotten.

I could have stayed on the island. Hong Kong Island, that is; not Cheung Chau. There's no lack of serviced flats in busy districts like Causeway Bay and Wan Chai. But in its peculiar way, Cheung Chau is home. My mother grew up there. She left when she married my father; I grew up in Mid-Levels and a couple of international schools. The old ties are still there, though: a tangle of distant uncles and aunties and cousins, a familiarity I felt as deep as my own bone marrow and saw about as often. I knew them mostly as names. After so long abroad, what's left of my soul wanted to come *back* to something, to hear the seagulls and smell the diesel from the fishing boats. Where the rest of Hong Kong defines itself by its chaos and right angles, Cheung Chau is about silence and curves. There are no proper roads: it's all narrow sidewalks and winding brick lanes. No cars bigger than the scooters the police and the fire service use. The only horns you hear are on bikes.

Like many Hong Kongers of their generation (never mind the fact that Dad's an American who washed ashore in the 1980s and stayed), my parents bought property. When there's no social safety net, you have to weave your own. Back in the nineties, my parents got a good deal on a house on the forested hill above Cheung Chau's single town. They renovated it and moved in the same year I left for Roehampton. Cashing in on the suicide binge that drove prices here down two decades ago: not what I'd have expected of a respectable sociology professor, now retired. Mom talked him into it. Investing on Suicide Island took a certain sangfroid unique to the Chinese. She was a bank manager. Death could be lucrative.

Why I thought the house would be empty and waiting, I don't know. They're in Christchurch now. With every new quake that hits the South Island, there are deals to be had. Mom being Mom, the house had to be rented out. It was too good a source of income to sit vacant, and no one thought I'd be back so soon, if ever.

I'm staying in a wretched little flat in Bela Vista, the same seaside cluster of buildings where people took their one-way vacations twenty years ago. Rent one of these apartments for the weekend, enjoy one last sunset, drink a few beers, and then burn charcoal in one of the rooms. This form of suicide is one of Asia's worst clichés, much like jumping from a high window or a slow death from drink. Even the reasons can sound trite if you're not the one enduring them: a crash in the property market, so much homework you only get three hours of sleep a night, parents unwilling to settle for anything less than Oxbridge and a doctorate. If the apartment were dirty, I'd consider a briquette exit too. But no, it's immaculate. Mom has her standards. Tidiness above taste: its drab kitsch feels somehow worse. It's meant to look like what it is, a short-stay rental for locals in their twenties who can't afford a dirty weekend at the Mandarin Oriental. There's a little too much pink. Furniture mass-produced and made in China, more garish and less sturdy than IKEA's budget best. At least the fridge works.

The instant udon noodles I choked down around two are long gone. From my walk yesterday, I remember there's a little restaurant/pub on the next beach over. More of a spot for the local expats, there's a pretty good selection of beer, and I saw fish and chips on the menu when I passed by. Some protein, some grease, and some hair of the dog. I'll get over this.

Cheung Chau's funny. The town center occupies a narrow strip of land that connects the island's three peninsulas. This isthmus is just six blocks wide. The ferry pier and promenade on the other side are so packed with tourists you can't move at times. Over here where it's quiet, you might as well be in some sleepy beach town on an island off Vietnam or Cambodia, the ones the tourists haven't ruined yet. This side's all residential and rentals—the faded kind, tarnished by superstition. Cotton-candy blues and pinks bleached almost white by sun and neglect. Most locals avoid this side of Cheung Chau now. They believe there are ghosts. Hence the quiet.

There are people out strolling, just a few, so different from the jabbering throng only a few blocks away. I stop and pet a friendly golden retriever on a leash after its human says it's okay. A couple of very tan guys are kicking a soccer ball back and forth. One's in tight biking shorts, and his friend's shirtless, hallelujah. Another couple, obviously mainland Chinese, are walking just ahead of me. It's easy to tell where they're from: she's in heels, and her jacket and skirt are different patterns; and the waistline of his jeans must be nudging his navel.

A pier of sorts juts out over the sand. Just a single large concrete block walled off from the sidewalk by a low fence, it looks like an accident somebody liked. If you jump up from the beach or climb over the railing, you can sit there. Two boys have. I stop to watch them.

Side by side, their backs are facing me. I'm pretty sure they're university students. Nineteen or twenty. Any younger and they'd be in school uniforms. The one on the right's resting his head on the left one's shoulder. I'm smiling even as the sight of them pierces me. I don't have to talk to them to tell their story: they go to different schools, and I'd bet their families and most of their friends have no clue they're gay. High school sweethearts, maybe. They've been together awhile, or else they wouldn't be affectionate out in the open. I silently wish them good years, better ones than my last few have been. As I'm stepping away, I bump into someone. She's been standing next to me, maybe half a step back, watching too.

"*Gau chaww*," she mutters. Cantonese slang, no direct translation, it's what you say when you've seen or heard about something kind of fucked-up. A bit of anger, a bit of disgust. If she's got more to say, I don't want to hear it.

I don't really get a close look at her. Maybe she's their age; maybe she knows them. Generic shoulder-length hairstyle and black glasses. Almost pretty, I'd say, based on a glance. Too much makeup. Then my stomach growls and I need to get going. It's getting late.

The pub's the sort of place you only find in expat enclaves in Asia. Chairs and low tables on the beachfront terrace so spavined that secondhand shops wouldn't sell them. Sand underfoot. The dogs of people who've known each other for years yelp and sniff each other's butts. The menu features fish and chips and mac and cheese. But the drinks list features

Belgian Trappist ales on draft and good sauvignon blanc from New Zealand. The facade of cheap, cheerful seediness is only as deep as a worn Gucci loafer.

With a pint of something I'm not sure how to pronounce, I read e-mail on my phone and wait for my food. The first sips of lager dispatch the last shreds of the hangover. I won't get hammered again. I don't want my time here to be a black cascade of days where I can only keep track of the passage of time by using shaving cream to write a number on the bathroom mirror before I pass out for the night.

There are five messages from Adrian. About what I expected. He understands why I left but not why I did it so suddenly. No goodbyes, I just packed my shit and cabbed to Heathrow. Four years, gone just like that. This was how I wanted to thank him for putting up with my craziness while I worked on my thesis? And what the hell, I fucked off back to Asia the day after I submitted it? I skim through the rest of his *Reuben, I miss you, come back* bullshit, delete the message, delete the others. Done.

My food comes. While I'm waiting for it to cool, I order another beer. Hell, I've earned it. Two sips in, and I get a message. It's from my uncle Tsz Lam. In English, he goes by Charles. *Do you want to have dinner tomorrow?* He names one of the seafood restaurants on the promenade. Says it's good. Of course I say yes; I'm not busy. I spend a couple of hours at the beachside pub, drinking more than I planned to. It hurts less than thinking. I chat with a couple of Australian backpackers, watch kids romp on the sand, nurse beers. The Aussies invite me to throw a Frisbee with them down on the beach. I have to decline. The cast is off but the bones still ache and my grip isn't great.

I tell them it was an accident. The wince when I cut my

fish with the side of my fork is sincere. Even after a couple of beers, there's an arthritic ache in my wrist. I tell myself one more pint of Flemish unpronounceable. Then I won't feel anything.

2

Today's better. Overcast, like my head, but still better. That bender from two days ago didn't get Adrian out of my system. Only time will do that, or drastic measures. But that's for later. For now, I just need coffee.

Sometimes people compliment me on my Cantonese. This is funny. I grew up speaking it with my mother and her side of the family. Even my dad can twist out basic sentences. There's no reason why I wouldn't be fluent. It's my appearance: on the dark side of white, I've been taken for Italian, Portuguese, even Polish. In England I tend to feel Chinese. And now that I'm here, I feel transparent. While I'm eating, I watch the local news. Might as well know what we'll talk about over dinner. More than that, it's for language. Like any language, my Cantonese recedes when I don't use it.

I tune out the weather and politics. They're both more of the same: heat, haze, and bullshit. The last story catches my attention, so I sit back down on the awful little sofa and watch. A university student's gone missing. A girl. Third year at CityU. Last seen two days ago. The reporter is saying something about boyfriend trouble. No known history of mental health issues or drug abuse. There's a part of me that marvels: this is actually on the news here. Hong Kong is safe and orderly enough that on a slow news day, this story warrants airtime. Then I realize where I've seen her—where I *think* I've seen her. I bumped into her yesterday, glaring at the two boys at the beach. By the time the story ends, I've convinced myself I'm imagining things. It might have been the same girl. But even if I were to go to the police, they wouldn't believe me. It was just a glimpse, after all.

The day advances with minor agendas. I left London in such a hurry that I need clothes. I enjoy shopping almost as much as I enjoy biopsies, and I don't have the right clothes for this climate. I'm always sweaty. I'm not sure there's such a thing as living in London too long, but if there's a next destination for me, it'll have to be cooler than this. I'm also running low on clean boxers. Like coffee and toilet paper, underwear isn't negotiable.

Arriving back on Cheung Chau after a few hours on Hong Kong Island is like arriving into a different country. The low row of shops along the modest harbor bring Vientiane to mind, a modestly sparkling flatness along the north bank of the Mekong. Decades fall away. Everyone troops off the ferry, rattled after an hour on choppy waters. Down the ramp with its lateral ribs to keep people from slipping when it rains. To the right, a row of hawker stalls under canopies and big umbrellas: stacks of vegetables, fresh cuts of meat, seafood caught earlier today and still twitching in beds of ice. There are little pyramids of fish balls and tofu puffs. I feel like a tourist for noticing; I feel like a displaced local for wondering which stall has the best food; I feel like a foreigner again for worrying about hygiene and MSG; I feel like a lazy bastard for being grateful I'm eating dinner with my uncles so there'll be no dishes to wash up afterward. It's early evening, so lines of commuters form at the hawker stands. People picking up dinner. The waterfront promenade isn't as chaotic at this time of day. The day-trippers have gone home and the folks who work in Central are trying to do the same thing. Here, there are no blaring taxi horns, only seagulls and a few squalling grannies.

I stop at the apartment—hard to think of it as home when my parents' house is so close by—to drop off my bags. The creaking dehumidifier needs its tank emptied. The groaning air conditioner just needs to be taken out and shot. Quick spin through the shower to wash off the sweat. There's time for one beer.

The news again. Background noise. Just loud enough to keep me company in this rank little flat, not so loud as to assault my ears like the crowds and the car horns in town. It's just starting. The lead story: the body of the girl who vanished has been found on one of the Lantau Island beaches not so far from here. She must have waded out to sea to end it all. She didn't leave a note behind, and her friends and family would like to ask the community what happened. I can't shake the feeling I've seen her before. Maybe I'm not meant to. After this comes the weather report: more of same. Politicians making speeches. You can almost see the not-so-invisible hand of Beijing overhead, pulling their puppet strings.

In the shower, so narrow I bump my elbows against the wall when I turn around, I'm thinking of Adrian. How we'd both fit into this space. He's bigger. He drinks. Bit of a beer belly. It's not unattractive. The shower curtain keeps blowing in and sticking to my ass. This would annoy him. He'd complain about it but he wouldn't know how to fix it and wouldn't try. It would all come back on me somehow in the end: how I have a hundred ways to make him the bad guy, how I look down on him, how he puts up with me even when I hurt him, how I'm spoiled. Spoilt. He'd spit out that British *t* at the end.

To make myself stop thinking about him, I hurry. It mostly works. So what if I rack myself pulling clean boxers up my legs too fast or bang my hip against the nightstand, or drop my keys instead of putting them in my pocket? In the moment, they erase Adrian.

Charles stands up to greet me when I arrive. There's a surprise: Gideon, my other uncle, is with him. Charles and Gideon were more like cool older cousins than uncles when I was a kid. They didn't mind buying me beer now and then. It's been years.

"Did you put on insect repellent?" is Charles's first question.

"I forgot."

Gideon hands me a spray bottle, and I thank him. We take a seat and Charles signals the waiter to bring me a pint while I mist my exposed skin and rub the stuff in. Now I smell like a grapefruit. It's essential, though. Like the other restaurants on this part of the waterfront, the dining area's outdoors under a retractable roof. The mosquitoes are bloodthirsty little vultures and dengue's making a comeback.

They've already ordered. Razor clams in black bean sauce. A steamed fish. Hainan chicken rice, which Charles tells me this restaurant does well. When the waitress comes back with my beer, Charles asks what kind of vegetables I want. *Gai lan* is the default, the one people tend to order. Black bean sauce, garlic, or *belachan*? In Britain, I missed these restaurant conversations. Here, the waitstaff will tell you what's good today. She reminds him the clams have black bean sauce, so we should opt for the garlic. Skip the *belachan,* it's too salty and too fishy. She doesn't understand how Southeast Asians can stand the stuff.

"What brought you back?" Gideon asks. He speaks slowly as if he's not sure I remember Cantonese. Before I can answer, he has more questions: "You're doing a master's, right? Or a PhD? Are you finished?" I'm swallowing some beer and before

I can answer, he's at it again: "When's your graduation? Do you have to go back to England for it?"

"I haven't had my viva yet. Someone in my department will e-mail me when they've decided on the date."

"Will you pass?"

"I think so. I don't know why I wouldn't."

"And then you'll graduate?"

"That's how it usually works, unless the examiners want me to change some things in my thesis. They might. But I've been thorough. My supervisor said I'm a little bit scary."

I said this last part in English: *a little bit scary*. Gideon blinks and looks to Charles for clarification. Charles obliges. I could have, but I'm used to this. Unlike the rest of the family, Gideon left school in form five, went to a technical college, and became a mechanic. He's a wizard with an engine but words are a challenge.

Our razor clams come. We dig in. The chef has put just enough chili oil in the black bean sauce to give it a bite. A couple of times, I catch Charles looking at me in a thoughtful way: he can tell there's something I don't want to talk about. Some*one* I don't want to talk about. I stay vague about why I came back: I've been away for so long, I missed Hong Kong, I needed a break after I turned in my thesis. Maybe later I'll tell him about Adrian. Something tells me he'll get it. But it's a relief when talk turns to food, as is axiomatic in Asia. The black bean sauce is perfect but the clams are a little on the rubbery side. The fish, though: it's perfect, tender without falling apart. It's a real skill, knowing when to be done.

Have I heard from my parents? An e-mail yesterday or the day before, I mumble to Gideon through a mouthful of *gai lan*. They bought some land outside of Christchurch and are driving down to Dunedin to look at property there. Charles asks about this week's political storm in a thimble. I haven't paid much attention. Some politician did something. There's always some politician doing something. It's a scandal. Somber legislative council members are giving interviews nonstop. It's the kind of thing I tune out. Besides, I was on a plane when it was all happening.

"What about the girl?" Gideon asks. "You must have heard about *that*."

He's on his third pint now. The third one that I've seen, that is. His face blazes sunset red. Like many Asians, he lacks the enzyme to metabolize alcohol completely. He's not drunk but he looks like it.

"It's pretty sad," is all I know I can say safely.

"Last year, there was a suicide epidemic. High school students, university students . . . even some younger ones. I heard it was worse than we saw in the news," Charles says.

"How can that be?" I ask.

"I know a psychiatrist. He said a lot of his colleagues reached out to the newspapers and the TV stations. They convinced them to cover it up, to stop the copycat suicides."

Suicide's a touchy subject here on Cheung Chau, the site of Hong Kong's last string of publicized suicides. For a time, you couldn't buy charcoal here. Even braziers were banned, but that didn't keep people determined to die from buying them on Hong Kong Island and bringing them over on the ferry.

"Her note said her boyfriend was gay," Gideon blurts.

"I thought there wasn't a note," I said.

Charles shrugs, sets his beer down on the table too hard. It's a fresh glass—a waitress just brought it. Foam splashes his hand, and he looks around for a tissue. "*Ki-hong*," he says quietly. Gideon's name in Cantonese.

"Do girls still kill themselves over that?" I ask. "I thought the world had moved on. Today they're like, *Let's be besties and go shopping?*"

For the record, I fucking hate shopping. Did I already mention that?

Gideon sinks into an odd silence. After all that beer and food, we're slowing down. The waitress brings the last dish, fried rice with prawns, and we share a final-course groan. There seems to be no choice at this stage but to order more beer and dig in. Our talk turns back toward safer subjects: the weather (cooling down for the season), politics (heating up), and the family (same as usual). Once we've eaten so much that one more bite will be fatal, Charles asks for the bill.

There are no knowing looks, no dark undertones, no double entendres. Maybe we're all just too drunk. But I'm pretty sure there's something my uncles aren't telling me.

3

Thomas keeps checking his phone. This isn't surprising. I met him on an app. We're at a coffee shop in SoHo. It's a million degrees and he's wearing a scarf to show how European he is. He was working in Milan until a couple of months ago doing something I've forgotten already. Fashion? Finance? Now he's back in Hong Kong, adrift like me, trying to belong while holding onto a measure of difference. We're supposed to connect.

Adrian's a thing of the past, or he would be if I could make myself filter his e-mails; it's time to try dating again. I've had it with white men for now. When you're outside of Asia, they have preconceptions. You're passive, a geisha with a dick. You're good at math. Your parents don't know you're gay and would be appalled to find out. What about the family name, the bloodline, the grandchildren? Asia's not that simple. Now that I'm back where I came from, I want to touch skin that looks like mine. I want to wake up and see someone else's black hairs on the pillowcase.

It's been nine or ten days since that dinner. I met Charles a couple of days later for a beer, but he didn't mention the dead girl and neither did I. He told me he was going to Bangkok and Phuket, a long-delayed holiday. For the first time, something occurs to me: I don't actually know what he does for a living. I assume he flips properties, or he once did. He owns shares in a couple of restaurants, I think. And stock. I think he's one of those Hong Kong guys who made good investments back when you still could, and now coasts on the rents and the dividends. As for Gideon, he has some on-again, off-again thing with a woman over in Macau. Once or twice a month, he spends the weekend there. This is one of them.

There's nothing more on the news about the girl. I wasn't expecting much. No matter where you go, the news is the same. Reporters break stories and milk them for drama. If it bleeds, it leads. But half the time, you don't know how they end. I can fill in the blanks for myself. The family wants privacy. They had her cremated over in Hung Hom. There's a memorial service, an interment. Best to bury the story as well as the girl. Too many kids kill themselves as it is.

Thomas sets down his phone and looks at me for the first time in what feels like twenty minutes. "Is this . . . working out?" he asks.

"I think the question suggests the answer," is all I can come up with.

"I'm sorry. I was texting my friend Jerry. He's telling me not to be so damn shy. You're . . ." Here, he stops, seems to be hunting for the right words, and switches to Cantonese for an idiom that means, *You're out of my league,* more or less.

"I'm just a guy who lives in Cheung Chau and doesn't know what he wants to be when he grows up."

"It doesn't show," Thomas says. "You seem . . . very together."

"I fake it," I assure him.

Is he expecting me to compliment him in return? I scramble for something that won't be a cliché. Mostly I'm grateful. He's being real now. The locals' self-loathing can be problematic. There's a sort of flustered charm I didn't see before, and my urge to shake his hand and take my leave has gone.

"Don't you feel nervous, living out there? Or just bored?"

"Why would I be nervous?" I ask.

"Cheung Chau—the suicide capital of Hong Kong? Aren't you superstitious? I would be."

"I don't think I believe in ghosts." Besides, there are other ways to be haunted. But I don't say this part. "I've never seen one, anyway, and I live in one of the buildings where it happened."

"You're braver than I am, living there," he says.

I wonder if he'd feel this way if he were to have witnessed what happened with Adrian. I'm not proud of it. I won't tell him.

"A distant cousin of mine killed herself out there. I think it was two years ago, maybe three? I was in Italy then." He looks down, gives the ice cubes in his empty glass a stir with his straw, takes a last sip of his liquid dessert. He's a slender guy, which must mean he has the metabolism of a blast furnace if he drinks these sugar bombs often. "We weren't close, and I couldn't come back for the memorial service."

"I'm sorry to hear about that," I say, a reflex.

"You know what the funny thing was—*funny* in the sense that it was weird? She was seen boarding the ferry to Cheung

Chau. But something happened after that. I mean, obviously it did. She killed herself. But you know where they found the body? Lamma."

"You're right, that's weird."

"The cops said she swam out to sea, but it didn't make sense. Aren't there currents between the islands?"

"I've never thought about it much." I have, actually. We don't need to talk about why. "I suppose so. You're saying they should have . . ."

It seems unseemly to finish my thought, but he does it for me: "Should have carried her away? Yes." He shrugs. "It was a long time ago. Kind of a funny story, but it's Hong Kong. It's not as lawless as a lot of other places, yet . . . things happen."

"Things happen," I repeat in agreement.

He has to leave: an appointment at a friend's art opening at some gallery in Sheung Wan. He invites me to join him. I'm about to say yes. Then I check the messages I've been ignoring. There are four from Charles, all variations on the *Call me, it's an emergency* theme.

Thomas's disappointment when I decline feels like a small hand pressing gently against the center of my chest. After Adrian, I wasn't planning to like anyone. It's not good for them. When I propose dinner tomorrow night or Monday and even mean it, his smile—which he tries to hide—is enough to make me reconsider my emergency. What could be more urgent than having some kind of life here?

Another message from Charles comes: *Where the fuck are you?*

"Fuck. It really is some kind of emergency."

Awkward goodbye. What are we supposed to do, shake hands? Hug? Kiss? We fidget our way through the first two options. I'll text him later. We'll sort something out.

Out on the street, where there's no one to overhear, I call Charles.

"Finally," he says when he picks up.

He lays it out for me: normally he and Gideon look after the family's properties—the house on Cheung Chau, the holiday rental flats, and others. I don't know how many there are, or where, only that there's a lot of money involved. Gideon's in Macau with his lady friend, though, and Charles is in Bangkok. Something's wrong at my parents' house. He got a call from a neighbor. How soon can I get there?

Quick calculations. If I can get a cab and traffic's not bad, I'm ten minutes away from the ferry pier. The next boat departs in half an hour. I've just missed one. The crossing takes an hour. The walk up the hill to the house, ten minutes if I hurry?

"I'm in Central. Two hours, give or take?"

"Fuck. Okay. But one thing, Reuben. This is important. If you find something there, if there's a problem with the tenant, call the number I'm going to send you. He's a friend on the police force. Then call me back right away. Got it?"

I assure him that I do.

The number comes as I'm climbing into the back of one of Hong Kong Island's red taxis. There's that moment of awkward surprise, the cab driver chat I'd rather not have: "You speak good Cantonese for a white guy." "I'm not white, my mother's Chinese." I think he's from the mainland. Somewhere in nearby Guangdong province like Foshan or Zhuhai. Mercifully, he shuts up and bullets through traffic, perhaps to save face and get rid of me sooner.

This is the great disconnect of Cheung Chau: when something goes wrong, you can't speed back home in a taxi or on the MTR. There's only the ferry. They leave every half hour.

After midnight, there are only a few sailings. The boats leave on time. You spend the hour-long trip checking your messages obsessively and muttering, *Fuck fuck fuck*, under your breath if the news is bad or the waves are.

I'm not in a panic just yet. I haven't been back in Hong Kong long enough for that. There are old ties but few connections. I'd be alarmed if the house was on fire and my parents were in it, but they're in New Zealand investing in rubble. Social media is the best anodyne, so I spin through various updates and feeds without seeing them. All I accomplish is draining the battery.

Cheung Chau at twilight is a place of shadows. Although it lacks Central's architectural canyon walls and false sunsets, the narrow streets of the town seem to contract. Dusk comes early here too. I make my way through a couple of lanes that shouldn't be crowded at this hour and almost miss my turn. Old cement walls the color of oyster shells and stippled with years of rain. A clan hall, ground floor open to the street, walls covered with black-and-white photos of someone's long-dead ancestors. Redbrick road twisting up the modest hill. Darkness under the low canopy of trees. Random shapes of deep turquoise sky visible through the branches, incongruous next to the salmon-amber glow cast by the streetlights.

The house, when I get to it, is a dark monolith. It faces the sea. To go inside, you open the garden gate and head down a paved ramp. Turn the corner at the edge of the property and the view opens up, a sudden tree-framed vista: water the color of denim, the sky slightly lighter. There's a walkway through a stand of fruit trees, and beyond that, a screened wooden deck.

There's no need to go inside, though. I can see the problem through the living room windows. On this side of the house, a few lights are on. I believe the tenant was a professor at HKU. Irish, if I remember. It's dark enough that I can't see details, just the outline. A human form and the rope he used to hang himself. So much for tenure.

It was like this after things blew up with Adrian, this numbness. If I'm honest with myself, it hasn't retreated. I have nursed it on wine and it's thriving.

The policeman answers on the second ring. I tell him who and where I am, and why I'm calling. He listens, responds with terse instructions to wait outside, says he'll be there in ten minutes.

I call Charles back, and when I've got him on the phone, I almost yell, "What the fuck?"

"It's bad?"

"It's a dead tenant, Charles. In my parents' house. Yes, it's fucking bad."

"Did he leave a note?"

"The cop told me not to go in."

"That's fine. Wilson's thorough. If the guy left one, he'll find it."

"What the hell are you talking about?"

Charles is silent for so long that I hold the phone away from my head to look at the screen. Did the call drop?

Finally: "You really don't know?"

"No."

"The suicides . . . they never stopped, Reuben. They were going to wreck business on the island. Remember, it got so bad that some asshole even tried to offer a one-way vacation package for people who wanted to kill themselves? A suicide theme park? Bargain rates at his rental flat and a charcoal brazier they could use?"

I mumble something about having heard of it before.

"The only reason people in Hong Kong think they stopped is because we've been . . . handling it. For years."

This isn't the time for logistics. I don't ask how the moving parts work and he doesn't offer to explain. Instead, he asks me to wait for the cop, who'll tell me what to do.

"And Reuben?"

"What?"

"Don't talk about this. I'll be back the day after tomorrow. We'll talk then, okay?"

Talk about it? I don't know anyone here. Not that well, anyway. I try to imagine a Skype call to one of my friends back in London: *So, guess what my family does for a living?* No, that's not going to happen.

When the cop comes, he needs my help cutting the noose. The knot's too tight. The tenant hanged himself from a bar he'd installed in a doorway arch. He used rope, the nylon kind, and it's cut into his throat and the sides of his neck— almost like gills. He'd put a plastic bag over his head first too. A thin sauce of blood and foam sloshes around the ligature. The reek of shit pours off him.

I rummage in the storage room off the kitchen to see if there's a tarp or some plastic sheeting. There isn't. But I'm relieved to find cleaning supplies. After the body's been dealt with, I'll mop the floor.

Back to the living room. The cop tells me I can go home. He's talked to Charles and made a few calls. It seems there's a network. In a way, we've been lucky. If this were a local Chinese man, there'd be an extended family to deceive. But with a dead expat and no ties other than his job and a couple of friends, there are options.

I'm about to ask how they're going to move him when I realize I already know. An ambulance would draw attention.

But there's a path at the end of the garden leading down to the sea. There's no pier, but you can get an inflatable dinghy pretty close to the shore, drop anchor, and wade the rest of the way in.

"You're quick," says the cop.

"Do you need help?" I ask.

He doesn't. People are on their way. I look out to sea. Three immense cargo ships are out there, visible only as arrays of orange lights at the horizon. A haze has rolled in, hiding the stars and the moon. Apart from the ships, all I can see in the distance is black.

4

It's the waiting that kills you. The waiting for purpose and clarity. For a watched pot to boil. For the results of a blood test. For proof you've left the past behind once and for all. Like everyone else my age, I've lost the ability—if I ever really had it—to inhabit my own skin for more than thirty seconds at a time. I've heard of stillness. I've even seen patches of it here on Cheung Chau. Yet I check my phone every ten minutes for updates about scattered friends and grievous exes.

No one said, *Welcome to the family business*, made me swear a blood oath, or handed me the keys to a black ambulance. After Charles and Gideon returned from their respective trips, they talked to my parents, to whoever else made up this organization, to me. Even now, after . . . how many weeks? I still don't know what to call it. It's a protection racket without the extortion. Insurance without the paperwork. Business owners on the island pay Charles and Gideon a certain amount of money each month to make suicides vanish. I'm not sure how much. A lot, apparently. I'm on the payroll now. Somebody transfers a respectable five-digit figure into my account every month. Although I have questions, I won't ask them.

First there was the tourist. Doughy Mitteleuropäisch angst even before the sea took her. German or possibly Swiss, she OD'd on kava, codeine, and Cointreau. Waded into the sea so fucked up it's a miracle she could walk. Maybe she crawled. We found the empty bottles in her rental bedroom. No note, but she left an iPad on the bedside table, the passcode on a sticky note next to it. Gideon took a look because he does that, said, "It's in German," and switched the thing off. Afterward, we dropped it into the sea in the same burlap sack as its owner, weighted down with cinder blocks from one of Cheung Chau's few construction sites. It was a grand night to dispose of a body: borderline chilly, foghorns in the night, lights from nearby ships, and islands' surreal blurs in a filthy dense haze.

The very next day, a Korean. Just sixteen. No note, but when a jogging expat found him on the beach at Repulse Bay, where we left him, the news said he had killed himself rather than moving back to Busan with his family. Hong Kong kids have it hard; Koreans have it harder. Cram school till midnight. Teachers not shy about administering beatings. And then, at the end of it all, military service. From what I've heard, it's two years of cheap kimchi, pushups in the snow, and anal molestation. I didn't blame him.

Two weeks later, there was a group suicide. College kids, for the sweet love of god. Four of them. Two boys and two girls. They rented a room in one of Cheung Chau's few proper hotels. Sneaked the charcoal brazier in somehow, maybe in a suitcase or in a backpack. Two boxes of cheap red wine, the budget Australian kind. I had a sip afterward. It tasted like rancid grape juice.

The night manager suspected. Four college kids, probably looking mopey and scared and relieved. You work in a hotel on Cheung Chau, you've seen it before. More than once. Black T-shirts, unwashed hair, no overnight bags, and at least one kid who doesn't look convinced it's a good idea.

Three were dead when we got there because they tend not to get on with it. A few beers first, or bad whiskey. A walk around the island. Maybe a joint if they've got a connection. Straight or gay, the couples want one last fuck. These are the preliminaries. In this case, they wasted no time. Finals must have been coming, or midterms. All the night staff have a number to call, not Hong Kong's standard 999. It's taped to every reception desk; new managers are expected to memorize it. Most of the time, Gideon answers. That time, it was Charles.

The night manager, a frump with a mop of oily hair and a mouth that wouldn't shut all the way, unlocked the door for us. Smoke from the burned charcoal rolled out of the room. It was a slow weeknight or else there'd have been complaints, the scared kind, not on account of who might be killing themselves in the next room but on account of exposure to ghosts. No one wants that.

In the room, four bluish undergrads. The two girls were dead drunk before the party got started, if the number of empty beer cans and the bottle of convenience-store vodka was any indication. Lipstick on the mouth of the bottle, half an inch left standing inside.

"Four," Charles said under his breath.

The word *four* sounds like the word for *death* in Chinese. Only the tone is different.

One of the boys reminded me somehow of Adrian. The cheekbones, the bristly haircut, the shape of the jaw. Unlike the other three, who'd dressed up a bit, this kid had on Nike track pants and an unseasonal windbreaker. Choosing active-wear to die in: something Adrian would do.

I looked closer. "Is he still breathing?"

"Fuck," said Charles and Gideon at the same time—Charles in English, Gideon in Cantonese.

There were things I couldn't tell them. A flurry of e-mails from Adrian saying he needed to talk to me. Urgently. Please let him call me or Skype. The guilt I felt throughout all of this. I hadn't looked him up when I went back to England. Passing my viva hadn't made me feel smarter. I've done plenty of stupid things and am likely to keep doing them. But it was the out-of-the-blue Facebook message from my replacement, a Terrence Kong, earlier that day—that's where my mind was.

> *Dear Reuben, you don't know me. You don't even have to trust me. But there's something you need to know about Adrian. He's got HIV. And I don't think he got it from you. When I met him, I didn't know he had a boyfriend. I must say, I understand why you beat him up when you found out about me. All I can do is apologize. But you should get tested.*

In bed we used protection, but the beat-down I gave him when I learned about Terrence broke the skin. His. Mine too. The Cantonese slang term to describe my build translates as *steel stick*. Thin, and cabled with muscle. I don't look like much. Then I hit you.

"Reuben? What's up?" Charles asked.

"Just thinking," I said. "I'm a little freaked out."

"What do you think we should do?"

In Cantonese, Gideon said, "This can't get out. That's what we're here for."

I looked down at not-Adrian.

"Hand me a pillow," I said.

And that brings us up to the present. I'm in a clinic in Jordan, waiting. This morning I sent Adrian an e-mail: *Come to Hong Kong and let's talk.* Thomas isn't completely out of the picture, but there's nothing there. He's just a rebound. We've been careful, and that makes him safe from me. If Adrian has to vanish, it'll be a little more complicated. He is traceable. Plane tickets, a paper trail. But Charles and Gideon have years of experience. I don't even know the extent of the network.

Glance down at my watch. Five more minutes and I'll know how our story will end.

THE KAMIKAZE CAVES

BY BRITTANI SONNENBERG

Lamma Island

They never tell a single woman to watch out for herself. It's the men you're supposed to keep an eye on, as if you hadn't been doing that your whole life: trying to be irresistible, trying to wriggle away. A tiring game of tag you meant to give up when you moved to Lamma, three months ago, but it hasn't happened yet.

Watch out for yourself, your mother should have said, not mind the length of your skirt or the look behind the look you give a man at a bar or on the street or on a bus. Watch out for yourself.

The men are mere accessories to the crimes, crimes you chose for yourself, as carefully as picking out the fabric for your wedding dress. Getting married—ah, yes. One of your greatest crimes yet, for which you are now serving this sep-arated sentence on Lamma, an exiled penance for another misdemeanor you've never quite managed to regret.

To be plain: an extramarital affair.

To be opaque: the last few years as a long flight of stairs, that you just kept falling down. A bump in the night. A baby bump that never appeared.

Watch out for yourself. Watch out for the self that lies in wait, the one that gave you the initial shove at the top of the landing, or was that God, or your mother, pushing you out? The Fall. The faltering glance.

* * *

Your days now: Wake up in another woman's sublet, her second-floor, one-bedroom flat. Grind her coffee beans. Take the ferry in to Central. Watch the water churn an angry blue. Take the bus to HKU. Teach a creative writing class. Discuss structure, form, plot. Do not explain to your students that you are falling apart. They will want to know more. That's how it works in narrative: the plot as lure, the story as hook, the reader as fish. Or fisherman? Give up on the strained metaphor and go have lunch. Then, at six, a drink with Gillian at Tai Lung Fung. Then the ferry back, the water frothing a darker blue. Close to black now. A spreading bruise.

Watch out for yourself.

Things that surface, sometimes, on your walks around Lamma, walks you take with the relief of a minute hand on the clock, inching around the hour:

1. A beaded clutch hurled at your husband's back, in the Four Seasons hotel lobby, after one of his work events, when he wouldn't listen to how long you'd been looking for him—*Where were you?*—how the contents all spilled out. How you kneeled on the floor, picking up tampons, lipstick, coins, the mother to your toddler having a tantrum, your husband out the revolving door.

2. The front seat of the double-decker bus headed to Repulse Bay, when your thigh touched the thigh of your soon-to-be-lover. Your colleague in the department. A Shakespeare expert. An expert in unraveling you further.

* * *

You consider both husband's and lover's brown eyes, that four-eyed beast, you banish it and them, tell yourself you're safe now, here on Lamma, neatly islanded, just like they did with Napoleon on Elba. You pause your walk at Lion's Rock, watch the surf pound the boulders below, watch a hawk get swallowed by a hill, watch the bougainvillea begin to shiver in the breeze. A clump of mainland tourists clot like thickening blood on the beach. Close your eyes. Watch out for yourself.

You should be safe, but you're not—not yet. Not as long as you pose your biggest threat, a grinning saboteur in lace, a wildly misplaced bet, a clumsy attempt to make yourself feel better, to find some rest, to be able, for once, to relax.

Watch out for yourself. You watch the sky instead. And as it begins to darken, you circle back home, back to not-your-home, back to life as sublet. Life as letting go of everything you thought you should try to get. Life as another evening weakening and passing away on Lamma. Island as hospital bed. From your little balcony in Yung Shue Wan, you watch the sun hang itself over the bay.

Some nights you sleep. Others not at all. On wakeful nights you recall yourself as a child, in the thrall of a crooked alleyway in Shanghai, your mother calling for you to catch up; or in Nepal, wandering from the guided tour, your cheek on cold temple stone, your eyes seeking the dusty mandala inside, before a teacher yells at you to rejoin the group. You wrestle with the sheets. Three o'clock. You see a yard with three magnolias. A drooping muscadine vine. South Carolina. Your mother's childhood home. Locked linen closets. Female rage. Neat folds. Moths. Larvae.

Then morning, gray. The ferry, again.

These nights and mornings: a purgatorial upending following the end.

Tonight the bed is worse than ever. You lie there two hours. Three hours. Four. Then slip on shoes, shorts, a white T-shirt that glows like teeth in the dark. Walk past the photos of intimates unknown to you, close the door that's not your door. Walk to the beach, where silky moonlight soothes the waves—Lamma at night looks much better than Lamma by light. More secretive. Elusive. Not careworn.

You sit in the sand but that's not what you're after. Something else tugs, as insistent as a little kid on your sleeve. You get up, oblige her, ask her where she wants to go. She points to the island hiking trail, ignores your protests of dark and danger, the shadows pooling on the path like blood from a freshly cut throat. You follow her lead, stumble a little over roots, jump at a snapped twig behind you, at the rustle of snakes in the leaves—getting ready to strike or ready to sleep? Bats cartwheel in the air, the jungle groans on either side, insects launching an ancient, endless argument.

The kid presses on, impatient. Then halts abruptly, waits for you to catch up. Lamma's famous Kamikaze Caves. So this is where she had to go. What couldn't wait for dawn. But why? You try to ask her, but you're barely on speaking terms—you've been trying to kill her for most of your life. To your horror, she always revives—survives your strangling, smothering, burying her alive. You could have sworn you saw her draw her last little-girl breath at the altar. But ever since you left your husband, she's begun to come around again. Occasionally with a lopsided grin, like the one she's wearing now.

"You first," you say, and turn on your phone's fluorescent light.

* * *

You came here once, before you and she split, when you were six, trying to keep up with your father and brother on a Sunday hike. They plunged inside the man-made caves but you hesitated . . . because of what your father had said. About why the caves had originally been built. For the Japanese to store their kamikaze boats, during the war.

"What's a kamikaze boat?" you'd asked, and your brother gleefully described the boat's design: "Four forward speeds and no reverse." So the soldiers inside would explode along with whatever they hit, couldn't turn the boats around, even if they tried.

"That's enough," your father interrupted, seeing you go pale. You refused to step in the caves then, nor did you want the two of them plunging in without you, but in they went. You sat feeling sick, in the dirt, the cavern's musty breath on your neck.

You could see the Japanese soldiers' faces, white knuckles on the sides of the boats, clenched jaws, then all of them a burst of red, the unsuspecting British too. Too cruel.

You've passed the caves in the last few months, pacing the island, but never stepped inside. You do it now, turning off your phone's unhelpful shine.

"Why here? Why tonight?" you ask, but the little girl is gone. How long have you been standing in the cave alone? You start to walk out, feeling silly, when something stops you. A twisting in the gut.

A Japanese soldier. Your old friend. You'd imagined him, as a kid, outside the cave that day, to make yourself feel better, even though your brother had laughed and said it was good they blew themselves up. His class had just studied the Japanese occupation. What they'd done to local women.

How they'd massacred an entire village after surrender, in '45—"That's enough," your father said again.

But sitting alone, you couldn't stop seeing one man's face. One kamikaze soldier must have escaped, you decided. When the captain gave orders to go, one soldier would have just slipped out, unnoticed. He wouldn't have stayed to watch the boats explode. He would have watched out for something else, instead. He would have tiptoed farther into the cave, betrayal metallic on his tongue. He would have reached the end, to where they'd chipped through pure rock weeks earlier, and stopped. He would have felt all over, touching spiders, and guano, and God knows what else, for the opening of a tunnel, like a drunk man's wink, built to escape a British attack, but now he would be running from his own side, escaping himself.

You saw his fingers finding that hole, then him scrambling into it, a narrow birth canal. He would have come out somewhere near the quarry, on the other side of the island, and then, for years, lived on berries and whatever he could steal from village gardens and fish farms, growing feral, trying to bury his mother tongue, his myriad loves, his everyone he once was.

Watch out for yourself.

It was the only way you could bear the thought of the Kamikaze Caves back then, by inventing him: the one who survived. And here he is now. Scratched. Bleeding. A ghost. Alive. He takes your hand in his, leads you deeper into the dark. You stop at the back wall. He guides your fingers to the tunnel, smiles proudly in the dark.

"I know," you say. "This is where you went."

He wants you to crawl through it too, for you both to make escapes together, over and over, every night. You stop him from helping you up.

"It's done," you say. "They're dead. Your soldier friends. My husband's wife."

That's when you both sink to the cave's wet floor and cry. For the life you were spared. For the lives you sacrificed. You hold him to you, all rags and bones and guilt and lice, and as his arms encircle you, he melts away, abandons you, like he abandoned his own suicide, leaving only the stench of sweaty relief behind.

You get up to go, but near the entrance of the cave something else has come. Some things. Some ones. Three of them. No, six. Dogs and women. The dogs closer to foxes. The women closer to gods. Goddesses. Not Kuan Yin, Buddhist Goddess of Mercy. Not Mary, Christian Mother of God. Not any of the bitter, martyred saints. The three figures standing before you are older, fiercer than that. The triplicate Greek Hecate, Goddess of the Crossroads, barring your way out. They raise their gray, grave gazes to you. You start to speak, to politely ask them to step, just a little, to the side, so you can pass, when one of them springs upon you like a cat, and the other two follow, light as spiderwebs, strong as rainforest vine, trying to bind your arms behind your back. You flail and kick and scream and fight, the foxes quietly circling the struggle, eyes aglow. You clutch at holy ankles, hair, throats, thighs. And after what feels like hours, just when you think they're finally tiring, you suck in a long ragged breath and that's when the smallest one smites you, when you're not watching, right in the hollow of your hip.

You howl, but don't let her or the other two go, pinned as they are beneath you. Bless me, you growl, and their hounds echo the moan in your throat. The Hecates struggle, you bark in pain but stay strong until the three of them touch your hip again, where you were just hit, and reluctantly, eyes averted, they bless it.

As the last syllable leaves their lips, the first light spreads into the cave, a milky dawn, the rock's strange curves becoming clear, and with the light all the night's nocturnal beings disappear. It's just you, with filthy knees, bleeding palms, a fiercely aching side. You limp back to your sublet, your un-home, spread out on your unmade bed. Unwed. Alone. The light blazes on the curtains fierce as a sacred fire, but for you the dark is finally descending; you close your eyes, you dream of nothing, not even the sun, not even, for the first time in your life, becoming someone else. You simply sleep. Watched over. Watched out for. Yourself.

From the balcony, if you were awake, you might barely glimpse a container ship making scant progress across the bay, asking for another continent.

PART II

OBEDIENCE & RESPECT

YOU DESERVE MORE

BY Tiffany Hawk

Lan Kwai Fong

A t forty-one, I'm probably too old to be elbowing my way through the crowds moving up D'Aguilar Street toward the bars and clubs of Lan Kwai Fong. I'm certainly too married to be sneaking around like this, and God knows I'm far too sweaty and jet-lagged to make the impression I'd hope to when meeting the ex-boyfriend I've spent almost two decades trying to forget.

Sweat rolls down my temples, pools between my breasts and at the back of my knees, yet I breathe in the humid air and car exhaust as if returning to this city can bring me back to life.

I'd forgotten the world could be so vibrant and bright and alive. It's been a long and bitter winter in Fairfax, Virginia. No leaves on the trees, no people on the streets, nothing but dirty snow covering the ground. Even at the best of times, the DC area is a dark and paranoid place, where everyone seems to work for the government and you're never more than ten feet from someone wearing black sunglasses and a coiled-tube earpiece.

My husband Paul fits right in. For him, this trip to Hong Kong is nothing more than a means to an end, a chance to network with potential clients and diversify his computer security business, which is currently too dependent on feast-or-famine government contracts.

I'm just happy for an excuse to be here, on my way to Liang Hai Jun, or Leon as he called himself then, fresh from a year at Oxford.

My mind bounces back and forth—should I sleep with him or shouldn't I? It's a pointless internal dialogue because it's obvious that I shouldn't. It's equally obvious that if given a chance, I will.

I hear the slow ping of the *Don't Walk* signal turn into a fast metallic rattle and watch a tour group of mainlanders follow their red flag–wielding guide across the road. Every last one of them carries shopping bags emblazoned with names like Louis Vuitton or Giorgio Armani. That's something you wouldn't have seen twenty years ago.

It's not quite seven p.m., when the streets will close for cars and begin to fill with tourists and expats from all over the world, laughing and yelling in Cantonese and Mandarin, Korean, Hindi, the occasional Portuguese or Arabic, and of course English accents of every variety.

Right now, the road is still crammed with delivery trucks and boxy red taxis. A double-decker bus whips around the corner onto Wellington Street, nearly slamming into a white van. His is the first honk I've heard all day. Hong Kong may never sleep, but it is no New York. It feels more genteel, more charming, more welcoming. Especially to an obvious outsider like me, the five-foot-nine blonde bobbing awkwardly above the crowd. I feel a twinge of guilt thinking of how the city's character is rooted in colonialism. Not only am I accepted in this neighborhood, I'm expected. I'm part of the history and social fabric of Hong Kong. In fact, despite Leon's pride in China, I know he once saw my fair hair and native English as a status symbol.

* * *

We met at Club 1997 in 1998, an oddly in-between era. The much-anticipated handover from Britain had just taken place, but its effects were yet to be understood. The world eagerly awaited the new millennium, and the idea of "partying like it's 1999" still had some cachet.

I can still clearly see Leon as he was then, a chic Chinese boy who moved easily through the world of boisterous expats. Everyone seemed fully aware that he would become someone they needed to know.

We glanced at each other for the better part of an hour before we spoke.

We discovered that his year at Oxford overlapped with the semester I spent studying abroad at University College London.

"We might have even crossed paths," I said.

"No. I'd remember *you*."

And like an old-fashioned Westerner in the sweltering co-lonial tropics, I swooned.

He ordered us two gin and tonics.

I shook my head. "The last bus back to the hostel leaves at ten thirty." There was no way I was going to hoof it all the way up Mount Davis. He promised to walk me back down to the harbor to catch my bus.

He looked so elegant as he held his drink and cigarette, like something out of a classic movie. He offered me a ciga-rette. Smoking was already passé by then in the States, so I had never touched a cigarette. But I took one. And coughed.

He laughed.

Based on the expensive suits of the crowd he was with, I figured he was someone important, but I didn't ask. He seemed to be enjoying the anonymity of hanging out with someone who didn't know anything about him.

"You're so tall," I said.

"I'm from Beijing," he replied, as if that explained any-thing. Looking back, and knowing what I know about him now, there may have been some snobbery in his tone. Regard-less, he was the most impressive boy I'd ever met.

I missed my bus. Then I stayed for the summer.

Should I have stayed forever?

I quicken my pace up the steep sidewalk and under bamboo scaffolding, looking behind me for God knows what. All day I've been unable to shake the feeling that I'm being followed. I know it's irrational, but it's remarkable what a guilty con-science will do.

I promised Paul I wouldn't contact Leon. We probably both knew it was a lie, but he didn't push the issue. Paul trusts that I'm not the kind of woman who would cheat, definitely not the kind of woman who would risk a scandal with the son of a high-ranking Party officer, one rumored to work with a triad if it means getting what he wants.

I'd like to be that kind of woman.

After years of playing the good wife, I'm desperate for something more, something unpredictable. Part of me even wants to throw caution to the wind and bring Leon back to my hotel room. The thought of such a huge risk is thrilling. And so is the thought of revenge.

Can Paul really blame me?

He must know that I know. Unless he thinks I'm really stupid. He didn't even hide it well, which was almost more insulting than the affair itself. Leaving receipts for Victoria's Secret right out on his desk, acting suspicious while taking late-night texts and calls in the other room, going to a hotel in the middle of the day.

He was practically begging for me to find him out.

It's especially galling because I thought I'd married the safe choice, the glasses-wearing intellectual geek who spends his spare time writing code.

Blissfully chilled air streams from the open front of a 7-Eleven. I stop and stand with my back to the shop, pulling my wet dress away from my sticky back and fanning it in a vain attempt at drying out. I was going for glamorous when I bought this blue silk A-line from Shanghai Tang, its mini-Mandarin collar just Chinese enough to be special without making me look like I'm trying too hard. Between the dress and the impractical four-inch heels that are already pinching my feet, I thought I would be irresistible.

Instead I'm so nervous my stomach hurts. I hope this bar still has Western toilets.

I turn down the alley toward *our garden*, as Leon said in his text. He means Le Jardin, a lush little bar tucked away down an alley behind D'Aguilar Street and above the al fresco restaurants of Wing Wah Lane. Back in the day, we spent many an early morning there after the other bars had closed. I'm not sure if his text was cute or cryptic. Who would he be worried about finding us? Paul? His own wife?

In all the times I've walked this path, I don't believe I've ever seen it in the daylight. Everything looks the same nonetheless— the Chinese graffiti, the back of a high-rise with a hundred spinning air conditioners raining condensation onto the street below. The gray stone wall that Leon pressed me against that first foggy night as we kissed until the sun came up.

At the end of the alley and in front of Le Jardin, I see a man. His back is to me. He is smoking a cigarette.

Perhaps hearing my steps, he turns. It is indeed Liang Hai

Jun in the flesh. He flicks his cigarette onto the ground and snuffs it out with a twist of his foot.

A current of electricity surges through me. It's like seeing a movie star.

Leon smiles at me with a tenderness that catches me off guard. Even from here I can see that he now has pronounced laugh lines and crow's feet, but they only make his smile deeper, seemingly more meaningful. He is looking at me the way you might look at a child who is suddenly all grown up, beautiful and successful. If he only knew the fundamental level at which I have failed.

Paul doesn't even see me anymore. If I wore a skimpy negligee—or hell, a studded leather harness and a ball gag—and got between him and his computer, he would crane his neck to look at the screen.

But Leon, Leon just stands there beaming at me as if I am a world wonder.

"Hi," I say from a little too far away. My voice sounds quieter and more nervous than I want it to.

"Hi," he says as I get closer. He doesn't reach for a hug, and I don't want to initiate. I step back.

I notice his hair starts a little farther back but is still almost entirely black. The sexy but severe angles of his cheekbones and nose have softened just a touch. The top of his shirt is unbuttoned casually, but his jacket and pants have obviously been well-tailored, if not custom-made. He looks every bit the part of CEO and heir to a corporation that owns a monstrous portion of this island's real estate and commerce.

I can practically hear Paul now. "Don't you find it strange that a Communist princeling is running a multibillion-dollar conglomerate out of Hong Kong?" he recently asked. "Where's the money going? What's the end game?"

He's currently obsessed with a theory that instead of relying only on tear gas and kidnappings, mainland China is trying to force Hong Kong into servility by buying up its property and businesses. He predicts that in a few years, Hong Kong will lose even the pretext of voting, will be sequestered by censored Internet and state-owned media, and no one will dare question the boss for fear of losing their job or their home.

Then, he figures, like dominoes, Taiwan will fall right in line.

"I'm glad you could make it," says Leon.

That voice. I cannot speak back.

He offers a sideways grin as if he knows he's rendered me speechless.

I've imagined this moment so many times, and in that version of now, he pulls me to him and we kiss, his soft, full lips against mine, his arms strong around me. I haven't thought past that part, as if we could live in that moment of rapture.

"I'm sorry," I say. "It's just weird to see you." In fact, it is a *shock* to see him, even though I've been planning this for nearly two months. I realize I'm still in a bit of a jet lag fog, and I want this to feel more real, not like a dream. I want to savor his every word and look and movement.

"Weird? I was hoping to make a better impression than that." He looks at me and for a split-second I am certain he regrets ending things when his family didn't approve.

I'd told him nothing mattered more than love.

You're so American, thinking only of yourself, he'd said. He meant it as an insult, but I heard a hint of envy in his voice.

"Shall we?" Leon says, motioning toward the green staircase that leads down to the grotto-like Le Jardin, the site of many of our nights out. It's ostensibly a members club, but only so far as it allows the owners to dodge restaurant fees and regulations. All one has to do to join is sign a paper. Tonight Leon doesn't even bother.

The room is as enchanting as ever, with white twinkle lights and red Chinese lanterns glowing against the ivy-covered walls and lush green plants hanging from every surface. I had forgotten just how mysterious and secluded it feels in here, tucked away from the more touristy bars in this neighborhood.

I follow him to a table in the back next to a red British phone booth, now an antique.

Thanks to the early hour, a waiter is immediately at our side. He's young, with a Samurai ponytail and trendy black glasses with no lenses.

Leon leans back on his chair, crosses one leg over the other, and makes the man wait while he finishes looking at the drinks menu. When he settles on a caipirinha, I wonder if he has spent much time in Brazil.

In the past I probably would have been drinking vodka Red Bull, all the rage at the time. Tonight I order a chardonnay.

"*Becky* Powell," Leon says, as if surprised to see I still exist.

"It's Robbins now."

He gives me a look that acknowledges as much.

"And nobody has called me *Becky* in at least a decade." I don't add that I like him calling me Becky. Becky was adventurous and confident. I want to feel that naively powerful again.

"Okay, Rebecca Robbins. It's good to see you."

I smile. "It's good to see you too."

I'm surprised to recognize a little tiny mole on his neck, not even memorable, not a feature, but I remember it exactly the same.

Our drinks arrive. We talk about my flight over—mostly

pleasant, but no, I didn't sleep much; what I've been up to all day—wandering around town and noticing all of the colonial walkups that have been replaced by shiny new high-rises; where I'm staying—the legendary Mandarin Oriental, where we have staggeringly gorgeous views of Victoria Harbour and the Kowloon skyline. Then we move on to people we both knew and what they're up to these days according to social media. As we skim the surface, I feel desperate to move into something more intimate.

After all these years, he is still entrancing. He doesn't seem anything like the man Paul sees him as—a sinister insider-trading, money-laundering authoritarian who crushes anyone who gets in his way. Of course it's not just Leon that Paul distrusts. His entire view of humanity is pretty grim. I'll call him a pessimist, and like all pessimists, he'll tell me, *No, I'm a realist*, as if his worldview is more real than mine.

"You were always so funny," Leon says, apropos of nothing. I half expect him to ask what happened.

I don't know when I lost my sense of humor. Maybe part of why I'm so drawn to Leon is that he doesn't know about any of my disappointments. I'm grateful he hasn't asked why I never had kids.

Although it's probably too late for me under any circumstances, I wonder if Leon and I might have better luck. I know it's not fair, but it's not the first time I've fantasized about having sex with another man just to get pregnant and prove it was Paul's problem all along. As if we haven't spent enough time blaming each other for the years of unexplained failure.

Leon has obviously had disappointments in his life too. In so many ways, he looks like the same boy I knew, but there is something more complicated behind his eyes. That underlying darkness makes me feel even more tender toward him.

I'm waiting for one of us to venture into flirty banter that leads to an accidental touch that leads to a purposeful touch and so on and so forth.

But infuriatingly, Leon keeps checking his phone, a sleek black titanium-and-leather number that looks all too much like the one I read about in the inflight magazine. It supposedly has military-grade encryption, the world's fastest Wi-Fi technology, access to any world network, and a price tag of more than fifteen thousand US. And he once intimated that his wife is too into status symbols.

Is that who he's texting? I have the urge to say something demeaning about her. I want to say, *Leave her. Be with me.* Doesn't he realize that I loved him before he was a powerful name in China, when he was just Leon?

"Is your wife wondering where you are?"

"No. My wife is understanding."

My wife is understanding? What an odd thing to say. Do they have an arrangement? I think of all the Western women he has as Facebook friends.

"How about your husband?" He mockingly looks around like he's expecting Paul to show up and catch us together. "Where is he right now?"

"He's in meetings down at the ITC. They'll probably be at it most of the night," I say, hoping he'll take the hint.

Paul made it almost too easy on me. I danced around it all morning, but when I finally asked about his schedule, he made it clear that I shouldn't wait up. I took it as fate bringing me to Leon.

"Yes, you mentioned he was a—how did you phrase it—workaholic?"

I nod. Paul is the *DSM-5* definition of a workaholic. Loathing long weekends, never taking vacations, joking about shoveling the entire beltway by hand if it would mean making it to work on a snow day.

"All that for computers?" Leon asks, saying the word *computers* as if pooh-poohing Paul's job, like I married a man who spends his days playing with toys. I momentarily feel defensive and almost say something Paul would—*It's national security, it's world order, and besides, do you have any idea how much IVF costs?* Instead I say, "Ha-ha. That's the way of the world now, right? I'm sure it's the same here."

"You deserve more," he says.

I sigh, flattered but disheartened by the irony. Paul said virtually the same thing years ago when I was brooding over the breakup with Leon. We started dating, and I assured Paul he wasn't just a rebound. Until a few months ago, I didn't think Leon's name would ever come up again.

The thing is, I know it's not all Paul's fault that my life has folded in on itself. I chose to sacrifice my needs for his job, going along with anything and everything to avoid rocking our mundane but comfortable boat.

More banker types flood into the bar. White men in suits. Asian men in suits. White men in suits with young Asian women in Chanel. All of them clearly flush with optimism and cash. As empty beer bottles pile up on a nearby table and the music gets louder, I feel the night slipping away too quickly. I look at my watch. I want to stay out later, to dance with him, to get drunk and hold him, but I know Paul will be back at the hotel in a few hours.

I cringe as Leon glances at his phone again. I notice it's vibrating, and it takes all I have not to complain.

"I'm sorry. I hate to do this," he says, standing up.

Then don't, I think, knowing all too well where this is headed.

"I have to take this call. Can you excuse me?"

I want to yell—*I've waited twenty years for this moment. I was hoping you had too.*

"*Wei*," he says into the phone. Mandarin, not Cantonese. Do he and his wife speak to each other in Mandarin? They must.

As he walks away from me, he puts his finger up like it won't take but a minute. He looks like he feels bad for me, which is the last thing I want.

I watch him walk outside. Through the window, I see him light up a cigarette. His head is tucked low and he seems to be speaking quietly, but he looks agitated.

I can't help but wonder who he's talking to. As my fears metastasize, I realize Paul has gotten into my head. But the thing is, I know it's not totally crazy. I've seen that essay linking Leon to the notorious gangsters Wilson Wan and Tse Kwok-Wing, who—along with your everyday drug trafficking, fraud, and prostitution—supposedly manipulate the region's stock and real estate markets at the behest of the Communist Party. But that paper is as fear-mongering and McCarthyist as Paul. If you believed them, you'd think there is a worldwide Communist cabal twisting their mustaches in unison while hacking and buying and killing their way to world domination.

And so what if Leon is what they say he is? Do I care?

I try my damnedest to appear relaxed and in my element, even though I never go to places like this anymore. Certainly not alone. I pull out my phone. Unfortunately, it's working so slowly I can barely navigate to my browser let alone load any pages.

I give up and am surprised to see an attractive Asian man checking me out. I wouldn't go so far as to say it makes me feel young again, but something like that. I vow to dress up more often, to get out into the world more often.

The Samurai waiter returns. He asks if I'd like another drink.

"No thanks, I'll wait for my friend." I nod toward the door lest he think I'm here alone and trolling for a hookup. I no longer see Leon out there. He must have gone up to the alley where it's quieter.

"Are you here for work?" the waiter asks, as he plucks my empty wineglass off the table.

"No, my husband is."

"Ah." He clearly thinks he knows everything there is to know about me. I'm that woman, the one who tags along with her husband on business trips, nothing worthwhile of her own going on.

It makes me want to take off my wedding ring. Just for fun. Just to see what my hand would look like without it.

"You like Hong Kong?" he asks.

"I love Hong Kong." In fact, I dread going home to the subdivision where my neighbors pull into their garages and disappear without even a wave.

Would I move here if Leon asked me to? Hell yeah. He knows important people. He could get me a new job. A new life.

The waiter leaves and I'm alone again. With no one to see, I slide my wedding ring off my finger and into my purse.

Moments later a man with an Australian accent slides into Leon's seat and places a fresh glass of wine in front of me. I know better than to touch it, but I don't run him off. Not only is the attention a welcome change, but a juvenile part of me hopes it will make Leon jealous.

He introduces himself as Darren, and without even asking my name, he launches into a spiel about his job at HSBC.

I manage not to roll my eyes. Then I feel a text come through on my phone.

L: *Just a bit longer. Wait for me.*

God, he's as abrupt as Paul.

Darren puts a hand on my knee. I stand up so quickly my chair squeaks along the floor. I leave a wad of Hong Kong dollars on the table and nod a curt goodbye.

It's completely dark outside now but still hot as hell. I look left and right but don't see Leon. I poke my head into the alley, but I only find a rat as big as a terrier. I stumble backward and then feel embarrassed by my overreaction.

Why am I still waiting for him anyway? It hits me that I'm in my forties and I'm chasing after a man who isn't that interested. I'm *still* wondering what might have happened if I hadn't been too proud to fly out here and fight for him. It should be obvious. Has anyone who ever had to fly across the world to make someone love them ever been successful?

Leon can call me if or when he's done with whatever he's doing.

The streets of Lan Kwai Fong are now closed to traffic and shoulder to shoulder with drunk foreigners. As I weave my way through the barely penetrable crowd, I envision the stampede that killed twenty people here not that long before my first visit.

By the time I reach the Mandarin Oriental, I am as wet as if I'd showered, only far from fresh. Nevertheless, the doorman in his classic red jacket opens the door and greets me with reverence.

I breeze through the dramatic lobby with walls made of gleaming Black Forest Chinese marble. I stand in front of the elevators, tapping the up button repeatedly. When the doors finally slide open, I almost walk into the people getting off. As I press sixteen, I notice my reflection in the brass—with my frizzy wet hair, red cheeks, and running mascara, I look cartoonishly ugly. For a fleeting second, I fear Leon was fielding a prearranged escape call.

Why should I care if he did? Fuck him.

I finally wind my way to my room, the balls of my feet burning. I slide my key card into the lock, expecting to find respite in the luxurious room, with its Hermès toiletries and pillow-top bed that has probably already been turned down. I throw open the door, and there is Paul.

He should be out for at least another couple of hours. But there he is—working, of course—at the burl-wood desk at the end of the room overlooking the harbor and the iconic circular windows of Jardine House.

Paul glances up from his computer.

My heart starts beating faster.

He looks as surprised to see me as I am him. If I'm not mistaken, a flash of guilt crosses his face. Was he looking at porn? Chatting with *her*?

I stiffen, fearing that he can sense what I've been up to in this expensive dress and fuck-me heels.

"What are you doing here?" he asks.

I expected him to ask me where I've been, not why I'm back. I'm supposed to be here. He's supposed to be at the ITC building.

"What are *you* doing here?" I reply, faking a little smile like it's a good surprise.

We stand there looking at each other. Through the windows behind him I notice the white lights of a Star Ferry making its way across the bay.

I realize that Paul is sitting in front of not one but two computers, and that there is a room service tray on the armchair behind him. He's been here awhile. Since I left?

He glances at his phone, which is hooked up to his laptop. A government-issue smart-card reader hangs on from the other side. Paul starts shuffling things around, acting as if nothing is amiss. Unbelievably, he's just going to get back to work. I should be relieved, but I'm insulted that he doesn't care. Is he seriously not going to wonder what I've been doing? Who I've been with?

I turn to go freshen up and notice the suitcases on the bed, half-packed. We put everything away neatly the moment we arrived. It's what Paul always does.

Paul notices me notice. "We're flying home tomorrow," he says.

I look around the room with its warm wood paneling, fresh flowers, and breathtaking view of the city I don't want to leave. I should be trying to appear calm, but I know the emotion is all over my face. Can I possibly just pack up and go back to that same claustrophobic life?

It occurs to me that I could tell Paul to go home without me. The hotel is booked through the week, my visa is good for three months. I'm not afraid to be the oldest person at the hostel, and finding some kind of English-speaking work wouldn't be impossible. With or without Leon, my time here feels unfinished. There *must* be some way to stay, even on my own.

He laughs. "Haven't got what you came for yet?" Something is off.

"What's going on?"

"I should be asking you."

I don't know what to say.

He starts packing up the electronics on the desk and slowly disconnects his phone. I feel a reflexive good-girl need to explain. I walk past the bed and toward him.

That's when I really look at the phone. It's not Paul's. In fact, it's just like Leon's. But it can't be Leon's. My first instinct is to cover my ass—think of how to explain our texts—but then, wait, why would Leon's phone be here? Was he here? Could he have possibly come looking for me?

It has to be someone else's phone. I try to act normal, but I can't take it and blurt out, "Whose phone is that?"

Paul looks at me like I'm stupid, a look that says, *You know exactly whose phone that is.*

I feel dizzy. This can't be happening.

He rubs the back of his neck.

"What happened to, to . . ." I stutter.

"Your boyfriend?"

I'm taken aback not only at the accusation, but by the amusement in his voice, as if he's been waiting for the day he could catch me in a screw-up. "I don't have a boyfriend."

"Do you think I'm an idiot, *Becky?*"

"I haven't done anything wrong." I don't add the qualifier *yet.* "Besides, what about you?" I ask, ready to finally confront him, let him know how much I hate him for ignoring me, for cheating on me, for pretty much ruining my life.

"What *about* me?"

"Oh please. You don't think I know all about your affair?"

I'm so angry I'm shaking. But Paul is as calm as ever. In fact, he looks like he's enjoying this.

"*I* didn't have an affair."

"Oh, drop the act already. The phone calls, the late nights, the fact that you were at the Omni Shoreham when you said you were at work." I cross my arms over my chest.

"If I was having an affair, I guarantee you would never know about it."

"That's ridiculous. I *know* you were. I *heard* you whispering into the phone. I *saw* the lingerie receipts. I *followed* you to the Omni."

"Trust me." He gives me a patronizing look.

I press my fingers to my temples.

He smiles a creepy smile, like he's pulled one over on me. "I was just giving you permission."

I shake my head to try to clear it. This is making no sense. "Permission? For what? You wanted me to see Leon?"

"Want? No," he says, and if I didn't know better, I would think he was about to cry. But no, he's already icy again. "I would have been pleased if you didn't fall for it, or act on it, but I know how the world works."

Pleased. He would have been pleased if I didn't cheat on him. Even when he thinks I'm sleeping with another man, he can't seem to get worked up about it.

It takes me another beat, but I finally figure it out. "You wanted an excuse to leave me for her." I feel tears behind my eyes and hate that I'm so jealous of this woman when the prize is obviously such a prick. He wasn't always like this, though. Was he? Back before he started drowning his problems with work, back when we bought the four-bedroom house with the big yard and the perfect climbing tree?

He gives me a look of absolute disgust. "You're still not getting it. Let me say it more slowly. There is no *her*. I'm not as fucking needy as you. And it's not all about you, Rebecca. Some things are bigger than you."

And now I'm shouting—"What in the hell are you talking about? Why are you always so patronizing?"

He looks at me like he's considering telling me more. Or maybe that he's already told me too much.

My sense of dread is so strong that I no longer care how I come across. I say firmly, "What happened to Leon?"

"It's about time you know the truth about him. He'd sell out every person on this island to consolidate the Party's power, his family's power." Paul starts to get energized. "You can't expect me to do nothing about it. Or to actually let him fuck my wife."

I close my eyes and try to block out his words.

"Besides, if you could only see how much of a pussy he was."

Was. Past tense.

"Where is he?"

Paul says nothing.

"When did you see him?"

"When you invited him up to your room."

"I didn't."

"Yes," he says. "You did."

"No. I'm telling you I didn't." As if it matters at this point, but I will not be called a liar.

"Yeah, babe. You did." He nods at the computer. At first I think he's implying he read my e-mails or texts, but I really didn't invite Leon up. Did Paul hack my phone? Did *he* invite Leon up? I open my purse to check my texts for I don't know what, but in my nervousness, I fumble and drop my phone.

This isn't possible. I try to remember how I first discovered his affair, when he started whispering and laughing into the phone late at night, turning his screens away from me, lying about his whereabouts. It was about the same time he started nonchalantly asking about my time in Hong Kong, which of course made me think of Leon. As Paul knew it would.

I feel cold. I'm suddenly envisioning masked men throwing a hood over Leon and secreting him away. It seems impossible. Seventeen years together and I've never known Paul to be violent. He may not be in love with me, but he's always been courteous and thoughtful, docile. He's a freaking Eagle Scout, the kind of guy who says *ma'am* and *sir*, and stops to help people push broken-down cars.

He moves toward me. I step back.

"Stop being so dramatic." He gives me a look like, *Come on, I'm not going to hurt you.*

I lunge past him for the phone or computer, to try to figure out what the hell he has on Leon.

He stops me. Pushes me just a little. I push him harder.

I reach for the computer, but he snaps it closed and it pinches my finger.

"Don't take it personally. It's national security."

I can't bear to hear that it's not even about me at all. It's about work. If he killed Leon in a fit of jealous rage, I could almost understand, but this? This is too much.

"Pack your shit," he says, turning and motioning to our suitcases.

While his back is turned, I reach past him and grab his closed laptop, ripping it free of its cords. Before I even realize what I'm doing, I heave it into the air and whack him on the head. The crack is louder than I could have imagined. My fingers are numb from the impact.

He looks at me with surprise; it's almost as if he's proud of me. But only for a second. He reaches for me roughly but misses and stumbles. Then he looks up and stares in my direction, but it's like he doesn't see me.

I feel like I'm going to throw up.

"What the fuck, Rebecca?" His voice sounds funny. He touches his head. Blinks.

What have I done? I should run, but he's between me and the door.

I put my entire body weight behind me this time like I'm

swinging a bat. My right foot wobbles, and I nearly twist my ankle in the process, but I manage to hit him again. When his knees buckle, I whack him yet again. He falls to the ground with a thud.

I drop the computer and squat down next to him. There is blood on the floor, a lot of blood.

I want to panic, to run or scream. I need to think. I check for a pulse, already knowing I won't feel one.

I'm suddenly aware of the quiet in this room far above the chaos of Hong Kong.

I should be focused on the man I've spent almost my entire adult life with, but all that I can think of now is what will happen if I get caught. In the window, imposed over the sparkling skyline of a city where anything can happen, I see the faint reflection of a middle-aged white woman who will spend the rest of her life in a foreign prison. Decidedly not the new life I've been imagining.

I look down at the cracked computer, over to the burlwood desk and Paul's papers, Leon's phone. I stand up in my ridiculous heels and walk around Paul to the desk. I pick up Leon's phone.

His people will know how to make a body disappear.

PHOENIX MOON

BY JAMES TAM

Mong Kok

I watch his penis swallowed by the phlegmatic vortex, leaving behind a faint shade of pink in the stained toilet bowl. Ha, I can picture it cruising down the sewer with other turds from the neighborhood. I close the wooden seat cover and sit down on its worn surface. It feels coolish and slippery against my sweaty skin. I'm exhausted, yet calm and relieved. My head has stopped pounding. The noise is gone. In its place is an uncanny clarity, a detached awareness of the surroundings, of my life, the here and now, and why I'm holding a pair of bloody scissors. I can recall every detail of what happened a moment ago, and fully understand the consequences without the slightest concern. How weird, this inner peace immediately after the horrific crime and the tumultuous reaction of my victim.

I wonder if this is sudden enlightenment. Alice said many Zen masters have attained enlightenment under wacky circumstances such as getting shit on the head by a pigeon or falling into a cesspool. Hey, what if de-sexing Kit has somehow elevated my insight to new heights? I must ask Alice when I have a chance, now that she's given up prostitution to be a Buddhist nun.

I throw the scissors into the bathtub. They make a sharp loud clank, shattering the unusual silence.

It's about nine in the morning, very early for us lot, late

for normal people. The howling wind and gushing rain have quieted down, consolidating into a dense grayish mass. Maybe Hong Kong, like me, is trapped in the eye of a big bad storm?

This section of Portland Street, three stories below, is rarely so quiet. Running between the snazzy facade of Nathan Road, a main artery of Kowloon, and the fatalistic bustle of Shanghai Street where real people live, it's a murky transition in which day and night change shift without color or drama, as if tired and underpaid security guards. In this neighborhood, a ten-minute walk from the heart of Temple Street, is a full spectrum of human activities and commodities at knockdown prices. One block away is a busy wet market. Chickens with gleaming feathers squawk in crowded cages weaved from bamboo strips. The sight of their ex-cage-mates, necks slit in one quick cut, flapping inside a bucket right next to the cage, doesn't seems to bother them. They crane their necks majestically high, gently nudging against each other, like proud aristocrats queuing for the guillotine. Next to the chickens is a long linoleum-lined table covered with ice. On top of the ice bed are skillfully dissected sections of fresh fish. Half their bodies are gone, exposing their air bladders for market assessment, yet they continue to twitch. Sometimes they make me wonder if I'd also grope for life with my last breath, or just let go, if someone cut me into halves.

After the market, toward the center of Temple Street, is a row of *dai pai dong* food stalls. Like the wet market, the ground is always wet there, even during the drought. They serve fragrant coffee sweetened with condensed milk, inch-thick toast with a crispy crust and fluffy heart, a hundred kinds of fried noodles, steamy hot-pot rice, snake soup when in season, and my favorite congee with pig chitterlings and miscellaneous guts. During their busy hours, the apartment gets impregnated with their mixed aroma if I keep the windows open. They occupy half the road, leaving barely enough space for trucks to pass. Trespassing private cars will be inadvertently scratched, guaranteed. Behind their tin-box stalls is the pedestrian pavement, occupied by boxes of goods spilled over from dusty boutiques, hardware and kitchenware stores, Chinese medicine herbal shops, more established eateries, and a few mahjong schools. Nobody will teach you anything about mahjong there. But if you don't play according to their strict gambling rules, you'll be dealt with by the bouncers rather than a mahjong tutor. Pedestrians walk in the middle of the road, or navigate between stalls.

Of course there's sex and entertainment. This is the real world. On the floors above the shops are residential units used for various purposes. Some are occupied by hardworking families with hopeful kids studying to become doctors and engineers. Others have their windows painted permanently black, isolated from the outside, oblivious to the passage of time by design. They display signs of massage parlors, nightclubs, cabarets, personal barbers, intimate private tutors, and movie-screening studios on the outside, giving the neighborhood a unique cultural air. Then there're girls like me. We are the most honest and straightforward, leaving no ambiguity as to what our business is. Yet other apartments are used as urban churches, operated by religious brethren trying to fit in, or dreaming of taking over.

On a normal day, life starts at about four in the morning, as final vestiges of the previous night get reabsorbed by predawn darkness. Garbage and delivery trucks rev idling engines while workers bang buckets and holler friendly abuse to each other, as if to avenge those who can afford to sleep while the mess they have created is being cleaned up. I'm not one of them, though. I would have just finished work, eating my early-morning meal before going to bed. As I climb into bed, the indistinct hubbub of hawkers and vehicles and shoppers and tourists is my lullaby. By the time I wake in the early afternoon, they have usually gathered in full force, energetically sustaining the reputation of our district—Mong Kok, the brisk corner.

Most days I start to receive customers in the late afternoon, mainly warm-ups—good family men needing a quick fix before going home to their good wives and innocent children. Prime time starts after dinner, when customers emerge from the dark, lured by the cheap glow of neon signs, like phantom moths. Neon signs are always red. Ours at the main entrance of the building—*Horny Miu Miu and Sexy School Girl 3D*—costs us fifteen bucks a month. Miu Miu is horny for sure, but I'm no schoolgirl by any stretch of the imagination. My "stage name" has always been kind of academic because I did go to college for nearly a whole year. That's rare in our business. Being the only functional literate in my class, my dumb high school actually offered me a scholarship to attend college. Nice of them, wasn't it? So I did it, went to Teacher's College, out of uncertainty, curiosity, vanity, a wicked sense of irony, and a hidden soft spot for the schoolmaster, Miss Yeung. That old lady sincerely thought she saw a glimmer of hope in me because I could read, bless her virgin soul. I also wanted to spite my mother who was confident that I'd continue the family tradition of whoring. Oh well, I eventually did, though only part-timing at the nightclub at first. The scholarship was barely enough for tuition fees, and I couldn't wait any longer to run away from my mom. Anyways, a stage name's obviously only for marketing. No customer's stupid enough to expect it to match the person who opens the door half-naked.

For most of the night, our flat, 3D, is enlivened by the happy rhythm of beds creaking and theatrical moaning. Miu Miu can drink beer, chew gum, burp, fart, and moan ecstatically at the same time. The night finally nods off when the men disperse. Before long, it's jolted out of a brief snooze by bawling drunks, piercing sirens, or gang warriors threatening each other with their own lives.

The bathroom window, panes translucent with grime, hinges frozen by rust, is half-open. One of these days, a typhoon will take it down, then we'll get a new one. I can hear birds twittering nervously outside. Miu mentioned some time ago that birds had nested behind the leaky pipes barely attached to the building wall, adjacent to our window, but I had not noticed them before. What kind of bird would leave the forest to hang around this slum? Is that fate? Insanity? Stupidity? Birds have small brains. But do they have fate? Another question for Alice.

I wipe my hands on my naked body. Broken streaks of blood trail from breasts to thighs, like a calligrapher's exhausted brushstrokes. My thirty-three-year-old body is well past school age, seriously overused. I still trust it like a cabbie trusts his old taxi. Not perfect all right, but will do the trick at least one more night, then one more night. My sunless flaccidity still looks good in dim light, good enough. Most men like pale skin, and are incapable of noticing its subtle defects once I've got them by the quivering dick. Occasionally, a jerk may make a few smart-ass comments too many. I'll tell him to go fuck his own mother instead. If he freaks out, well, he'll have to talk to Ah Bill or one of his buddies. The girls in this building are protected by the 14K triads. Ah Bill is our resident *da dun* security manager, invisible unless there's trouble.

Ah Miu—once my best friend, roommate, and coworker—taps tentatively on the door, calling my name softly: "Feng Yue. Feng Yue. You okay?"

Her feigned concern gives me the creeps. The two-faced bitch will flee at the slightest hint of me making a move. I heard her opening the front door as soon as she came out of her room. Very wise, Ah Miu—first thing first, get the escape route ready. Ah Bill promptly came over to inquire. I wonder why he was still around this time of the day. Must be the new girl in flat 1A. Anyways, he took off before Miu could finish her incoherent account. He doesn't deal with this kind of shit, especially when a cop is involved. The neighbors are dead quiet. In this building, the first response to a scream for help is to bolt the door and stay put.

Miu then called 999. We never call the police for help. We settle everything our way, without government interference. I suppose this is an extraordinary situation. "Yes, yes. The crazy woman's still in here. She's locked herself in the bathroom. She's got a knife," she said breathlessly, unnecessarily loud. "He's fainting, bleeding a lot. Maybe dying. Hurry, *lah*, Ah Sir!" To support her claim, Kit Zai groaned in the background like a pig in the slaughterhouse.

Well, she was wrong. I don't have a knife. I have a pair of scissors, brand new, German made, top quality, used only once so far to fantastic effect. His dick offered less resistance than blanched pig chitterlings, my favorite bedtime snack. She may be right about me being a lunatic, though. I've been suspecting that for years. But hey, look around, who isn't? Only that I know and they don't. They're crazier!

Miu has stopped pretending to want to talk to me. She's mumbling urgently to Kit Zai, who's gone quiet. I wonder if he's dead. Nobody's supposed to die from a severed cock. He's probably looking for his gun, dripping blood all over. I hid it under the bed before the operation, darling. I may be crazy, but I ain't stupid, huh?

In the past few weeks, since I found out about this treacherous pair, a noise in my head has been helping me plan my revenge, working out details. It's the noise that insisted on investing in a pair of good pinking shears. *That way, the damage will be irreparable.*

They can't repair a cutoff dick anyways! I told myself, or the voice. The woman who was sharing my table at the congee stall kept her head way down and spooned scalding-hot congee into her face at double speed, pretending not to hear anything.

Remember the guy who got his dong sliced off by his girl a few years back? The doctor sewed it back on. One of the girls even saw him use it again a year later!

I find that hard to believe, but you never know these days. Technology seems capable of any voodoo. But good pinking shears are grossly overpriced, so I settled for a pair of strong scissors instead. A good idea had dawned on me at the store: flush it down the toilet. Much cheaper that way.

This morning, the noise issued a simple command: *Now!*

All right! I got out of bed, temples throbbing with excitement. He was snoring like the thunder god.

He had come in around two, unexpectedly. I had switched the neon sign off earlier than usual. Miu was still out, probably singing at a Temple Street cabaret. It had been a quiet night except for the weather. I should have taken the night off as well.

After the condom incident, he had stayed away for a few days but called to say he was busy, missing me. Ah Miu had kept up an outrageously innocent face, more vacuously jolly than usual, assessing me through sideways glances.

Not that easy, bitch. Nothing happened.

Had he disappeared, would I have let go of him and focused on Miu after the episode had dimmed in her tenuous memory? I don't know. The voice assured me he would come back, though.

Oh yes, he will. He thinks you are paralyzed by his charm. He needs to prove that. He needs to nourish his ego with unconditional forgiveness from a vengeful whore. He needs to watch tears well up in your eyes.

The voice was right.

"I thought you were bouncing at the mahjong school tonight," I said.

Kit Zai's a cop, now a victim of the newly established anticorruption agency, ICAC. Unlike its numerous predecessors which would go away after getting paid, the ICAC seems to mean business, and has caused a financial crisis in the force. Many, especially plainclothes detectives like Kit, have started bouncing at nightclubs and gambling dens and whatever to sustain a lifestyle they had long taken for granted. The same mix of cops and thugs are now hanging out at the same dumps under a different symbiotic arrangement. A comedian once suggested solving the triad problem by recruiting more police: *The law of conservation tells us that having one more cop means one less thug on the street.*

"Hardly anyone there so the boss asked everyone to go. The boys went for food and drinks, but I thought I'd come to see you instead. Romantic, huh?"

"I'm touched. Where're the flowers? For your information, Ah Miu's not home yet."

"Come on, be nice!" He appeared more pleased than surprised that I had brought up Miu. "That was only a one-time thing which you have no proof of."

Listen! He confessed! He called it a one-time thing. That means they did it more than once!

I smiled sweetly. I'm a pro in smiling sweetly.

"Lawyers call it allegation, you know, based on circumstantial evidence. It doesn't count. Hong Kong's a lawful place now, Feng baby. Even *we* need evidence before charging anyone. Yesterday, my inspector told us no more forced signatures on blank statements or bathroom beatings until further notice. Otherwise, we're on our own. Imagine. Crime rate's gonna soar." He winked and showed his straight white teeth.

He was technically right. I had come home unexpectedly one afternoon exactly twenty-two days ago. I was supposed to be swimming at Tai Wan Shan, the new modern government pool everyone talks about. It was closed for emergency maintenance so I took the bus back. I suppose it was one of those bad luck cases designed by God to trap multiple victims at the wrong time in the wrong place. I thought I heard a hushed confusion inside as I unlocked the door and the triple-bolted gate. Her room was closed. This early? He was "napping" in mine, a bedcover pulled over his lower body. *Aha.* I yanked it away. He was in his briefs.

"Are you not warm?" I asked. The noisy air con in my room wasn't even on.

"Hmm . . ."

Sure, Kit, you're drowsy all right. I'm a much better detective than you lot.

I noticed a wet spot on his underwear. I quickly yanked them down before he could protest. A condom was semi-attached to his limp little brother. "Why are you wearing a condom?"

"What? Am I?" he said blearily, eyes half-closed. What a stupid response, so unlike him. Pathetic. His mind must have had gone blank, or frozen.

But mine wasn't. I didn't push. I went to the kitchen for a glass of water, to think.

I saw the chopper, but quickly decided against using it. I didn't want to slice him up, partly because he had a gun. What about Ah Miu? I had always known her to be streetwise but brain stupid, but to do this behind my back? With Kit Zai? Right here? Why? What for? A real orgasm? To hurt me? Come to think of it, I shouldn't have bragged to her about Kit. Whatever her reasons, the betrayal is infuriating, yet forgettable if unforgivable. I'll get her, no hurry. Perhaps Bull Dog and his boys will give her a good gang bang, one that she'll never forget. But right that moment, I had to play dumb and pretend nothing had happened.

When I returned to my room, he had put his pants on. I wondered if he was still wearing the condom. He lit a cigarette, and said he'd had a long shift, someone got stabbed a few times, bled to death in the gutter, a 14K Red Staff Warrior, one of Broken Tooth's boys, and . . .

I didn't register the rest of his diabolical bullshit. The blood in my head was roaring, but my mind was still somehow calm and calculating.

Hey, nothing happened.

What other option anyways? It'd be stupid to push him into a corner.

That's right. Nothing happened. Not yet.

He lit another cigarette with the butt before stubbing it in the ashtray. I smiled sweetly.

Everyone in our marginal world has stained teeth, panda eyes, and liver-colored smudges on their lips. They are marks of our lowlifestyle. But Kit's teeth are sparkling white despite two packs of cigarettes a day. His lips are red and plump and fresh-looking, though he does have dark circles around his eyes. I loved kissing them, probably still do if we ever kiss again. You see, I only sell parts of my body, parts that good girls regard as sacred and untouchable. But I never kiss my clients—not the mouth-to-mouth kind with tongues crossing anyways. Kissing is a big deal to most of us working girls. If we kiss someone—trouble. I kissed Kit Zai the third time we slept together, after he had brought me my first bouquet, and given me my first orgasm ever. Look at the trouble we're in.

He was born to break hearts: handsome, tall, strong, boyish, cheerful, and pleasant; savagely scary if pushed. I'd heard about him before, so I can't say I wasn't warned. Let's say he's quite popular with the girls. But in our business, you don't believe everything you hear, not even if it comes from your own mouth. Plus, what do you expect? If all the guys were like him, prostitution would suffer. Many of us would be doing it for free.

Before Kit, a fuck was a fuck to me. There was no such thing as good or bad.

It used to be two hundred bucks plus a cut of takeout fees when I worked the nightclubs. I was young and pretty, highly educated by their standard. My photo was prominently displayed in the reception area: *Sexy School Girl Little Phoenix*. Had I not quit college after the first term and gone on to become a teacher, I would have had to work at least two weeks in my old school to make two hundred bucks. What an educational sludge tank that was, corralling the poor and hopelessly disinterested until the boys were ready for a career with the triads or the Royal Hong Kong Police, and the girls were ripe to join the nightclubs, or enslave themselves to a factory, making happy plastic babies. We were color-coded as soon as we entered subsurface society. The boys became yellow if Royal, black if triad. Girls like me turned red under the light which people saw us in. Those joining the factory class remained colorless, invisible. Same difference, we were all bred from the same pot. In that dump, I was weird. I secretly enjoyed reading. I had read *Dream of the Red Chamber* and the erotica classic *Jin Ping Mei* by ninth grade. Of course, I kept that a secret lest I get teased, even bullied, for being "bookishly antisocial."

Well, good old days.

I'm still quite popular, mind you, and increasingly affordable. Anyways, suffice to say I'm not easily impressed by male performance due to professional exposure. Except Kit . . . I really don't know how, or why. Maybe it's age. Alice might say it's karma. Perhaps I can no longer suppress a hidden desire to have a real man who brings me flowers and makes me come. It's infuriating. It's a cliché that working girls like cops, but, oh well, analyzing the reasons would be too philosophical for right now.

I know your misters Wong and Chan out there think prostitutes are anything but cultured, never mind philosophical. Their ignorant opinions could not be further from the truth. In the old days, when women were mostly illiterate, and their only "skill" with men was limited to blushing with the head down, courtesans could read, write, sing, dance, and play instruments—real and euphemistic ones—in and out of bed in a hundred different positions. Brothels were the only place a gentleman could find a worldly, elegant, irresistible, learned, challenging, understanding, interesting, and amorous woman. Many five-star courtesans became multimillionaires and eventually married distinguished suitors who immortalized their charm and beauty with poems. Household names such as Ma Xiang Lan, Li Xiang Jun, Dong Xiao Wan, and Chen Yuan Yuan still trigger fantasy and admiration centuries later. And how could I leave out Xiao Feng Xian, the love of revolutionary hero General Cai E in the early 1900s? There must have been a dozen movies made about their love story. Her haunting memorial verses, sent to his funeral, are even studied in schools.

Xiao Feng Xian—Little Phoenix Fairy—was a phoenix like me. What a beautifully whorish name I have—Feng Yue—Phoenix Moon. Can't say my mother lacked foresight when she named me. Unfortunately, Xiao Feng Xian was the last celebrity prostitute. This is the 1970s, the modern world. They even made polygamy illegal a few years ago, after so many thousand of years. Can you believe that? What man would be happy with just one wife if they could afford more? Some girls thought it might bring us more business, but we have seen no evidence of that so far. The law has simply driven junior wives underground. They've become secret mistresses—less accepted, less recognized, less protected, children relegated to the shadows. The senior wives are now more suspicious of their men than ever, wondering what their mistresses are like, feeling more insecure. Nobody gains. Stupid.

In any case, we don't have the same good karma as our sisters from the dynasties. *Phoenix* is now a euphemism for *chicken*, which means *hookers* in Cantonese slang. Poets are extinct. We have become just chickens.

That said, I've met some very smart men over the years. Unless you're a pro, you can't imagine the kind of men who come to us. We've seen the most complete cross section of male humans. Most show up with tongue hanging and pants halfway down, as you'd expect. Perhaps less expectedly, some are more desperate to talk than fuck. They need to relieve secrets locked away from their wives, buddies, parents, siblings, doctors, priests, even themselves. Their secrets eventually rot inside, driving them nuts. I bet they have noises in their heads too. With us, they talk freely, for we don't matter. A girl like me who'd been to college for a while is a real find to some men, though they're usually not the type who pay extra, so I don't listen unless he's a regular.

A certain professor used to come and see me every Wednesday afternoon at three fifteen. He wore sunglasses even when it was raining, and a hat pulled way down to his nose. He was gentle but stingy. Academics are always stingy. After spending barely five minutes on my body, he'd talk about a boy he met in church. They had been to a movie, a love story. "It was so sad. He cried," Professor told me, incredulous eyes glittering. And another week, they picnicked at the South Bay Beach. "He made Singapore noodles, absolutely delish!" He licked his lips.

"Sounds like you love him," I finally said.

"Oh, no! We're only friends!" He waved both hands frantically in front of his face, as if his nose were on fire. "I'd be ruined if they knew." He looked like he was about to burst into tears.

"It's okay, you can love him all you want in my house." I hugged him like a friend, then asked him to get going. "I'm expecting someone in a few minutes," I lied.

He apologized profusely for having taken up my time, then paid the exact amount. No tip for listening and counseling, or a momentary display of genuine friendship. Haven't seen him for a while now. Perhaps he has finally given up women.

There was this super-hairy Brit who often looked for me

after a few beers. If I was busy, he'd make an "appointment" and return after thirty minutes rather than giving Miu the business. He had my respect for that. He liked me partly because I could speak some English. One day he told me he was a spy, and showed me his pistol. "Look, cops don't have guns like this!" He put it in my hand to let me feel it, then let out a huge beer burp.

"*Choi!* I don't touch guns! Bad luck!" I gave it back to him right away. He grinned so hard his bushy eyebrows lifted like wings.

I told Ah Bill about the Brit. He checked through his Royal pals and confirmed that this guy was from Special Branch. "They can make anyone disappear. No fucking questions asked. You take care, huh." Unfortunately, I could hardly understand half of the Brit's boasts. He also took up too much time, but I was careful to be diplomatic. "Okay, okay, handsome James Bond. Bond girl need you fuck now!" He loved me calling him James Bond.

While our clients tell us their boring secrets, we girls hide ours.

We all have stories that would make you weep, stories we keep inside until forgotten, or until we die. I can hardly remember my own anymore—don't want to—except that of course my mum was also a hooker, hopefully still is, a toothless wrinkly one working out of some lice-infested cardboard dump in Kowloon Walled City for five bucks a shot. Well, forget her. I haven't thought about her for years.

Anyways, hard-luck tales are like ice water to a hard-on, the centerpiece of our profession. We are here to make life fun. We get into character like actresses do. *Enjoy the sexy miasma of musty sweat! And the oral funk of alcohol and tobacco! Look at my sweet smile!*

Inside every prostitute is an actress, psychologist, and phi-
losopher. Her philosophy is a private interpretation of life to
make it bearable. High-lifers talk about "philosophy" to look
smart, to stroke the ego—something that she sold long ago.
We are just chickens. Chickens are supposed to be dumb, with
feelings only for money. *Yeah! That's right! Money money
money!*

This morning, as the typhoon landed, we "made love."

The term normally makes me cringe. How do you make
love by pushing a sleazy indiscriminate wiener into a KY Jelly
dump? *Just say fuck, for fuck's sake!*

Kit once told me he loved me. I feigned disgust. "What
do you think I am, your teenage darling? You're sickening!" I
bit his nipple playfully, a little too hard. I made him scream—
though not nearly as loud as just now, when I cut off his dick.
I kept swearing, even more foulmouthed than usual, and
laughed hard to cover the tears welling in my eyes. It was
devastating, the happiest moment in my life. I couldn't sleep.
I lay in his arms all morning, dreaming of possibilities, possibilities which I had never believed, and still don't, possibilities so
naive it's too embarrassing to talk about. A whore has nobody
but herself to blame for being *that* stupid with a man.

Five days later, I discovered him napping in my bed with
a wet condom on.

But this morning I wanted to make love, knowing very well
there wasn't any. When we finished, I giggled. When I'm really
sad, I sometimes giggle. It amused him. He finished a cigarette
with a few deep drags, then popped a sleeping pill as usual. I
dozed on and off next to him, suppressing the urge to cry, or
giggle. I heard Miu coming home.

Then the voice woke me: *Now!*

The rest was easy. I hid his gun under the bed, took out the scissors, grabbed his dick, and *snip*. Boy did he scream. I ran into the bathroom, a cock in one hand, scissors the other. I closed the door and pushed the knob with my elbow to lock it.

The cops have arrived. Kit's moaning again, now that there's attention. As far as I'm concerned, he deserves the death penalty. He's a cop. He should know better than to dick around with a whore's heart. You can toy with her body all you want, but underneath the calluses that you rub and squeeze and lick is a heart so tender she doesn't even dare to look herself lest it shatter into a thousand pieces. You, Tsui Man Kit, molested mine for fun, just to show you could steal even a whore's heart, to brag to the boys in the locker room. You asshole. From now on, you're changing with the girls.

"Police! Put down your weapon and come out with your hands up!"

The wind is up again, whistling outside. Action everywhere all of a sudden. How exciting!

Well, I'm waiting right here, officer. Kick down the door if you want me. About time you boys do something manly.

Oh dear, looking down at my feet, I can see that my toenail polish is badly chipped. Better remove the polish before they come to a committee decision on how to apprehend the naked and unarmed woman. I get up to open the cabinet above the washbasin, where my polish remover is kept, and catch myself smiling impishly in the mirror, like a schoolgirl.

ONE MARRIAGE, TWO PEOPLE

BY RHIANNON JENKINS TSANG

Ma On Shan

Lizzie

"Sweet pea, sweet pea, Mummy's sweet pea!" Lily, my baby, our baby, had just woken from her afternoon nap. She was warm and cuddly in my arms, smelling of milk. I rocked her, singing my silly song, kissing the top of her head, drying my tears in her hair. "Let's see! Today's a special day." I drew the living room blinds, putting on a smile and my cheerful Mummy voice. "It's the thirtieth of June, 1997. Today the Crown Colony of Hong Kong is handed back to the People's Republic of China."

Our tiny flat in Ma On Shan had a superb view of the Tolo Harbour. Ma On Shan means *saddle peak*. It was this strange-shaped peak with its enchanting name and the other mountains in the New Territories that had seduced my husband Handel. Born and bred in Shanghai, he had seen his first hill at age eighteen and had been besotted ever since. I stared down at the black swimming pool twenty-seven stories below, cold, unblinking. When the sun was out, it was a beguiling South Sea blue. The window had a little safety catch. It needed fixing. Some days it seemed there was only one thing holding me back: Lily. I loved her so much.

Handover day and the weather was foul, a last defiant stand in the face of the inevitable—the coming of China. The wind whipped the sea into tufts of white, and low clouds gathered over jagged peaks. It looked like the gray-green Scottish highlands on a winter's day painted by a Chinese artist.

"Mummy's sweet pea, Mummy's sweet pea . . ." I was singing again, to mask my fear and desperation, because I didn't know what else to say to my child.

Anxiously, I turned to the bedroom door, taut like an animal anticipating a fight. Handel, too, was taking an afternoon nap. Even I had managed a little snooze. Soon he would wake. He had been difficult ever since Lily was born, worse in the last month.

I changed Lily's diaper, holding her close to my chest, enjoying her soft warmth. The flat was stifling. It smelled of the rotting garbage both of us had forgotten to take out. Handel kept the air-conditioning off as much as possible and absolutely refused to sleep with it on.

"It's for the baby, Little Bourgeois," he would scold in Mandarin. His once affectionate nickname for me had become like a sly pinch from a schoolyard bully. There was no compromise. During the night, mold grew on our clothes in the wardrobe. By day, heat and humidity made us bicker and fight.

"Mummy's sweet pea, Mummy's sweet pea . . ." I smiled through the tears. It had only been six months since Lily was born. Handel and I didn't talk anymore. What was it I fell in love with? I was so tired I couldn't remember. Was it the idea of him? Was it Hong Kong? Was it China?

I went over to the open-plan kitchen at the back of the living room. Balancing Lily on my hip, I mixed up a small portion of rice cereal from a packet and heated up half a cup of milk. Then I settled down to feed her at the little table.

None of this was what I'd signed up for: not Handel, not the baby, not our tiny rented flat in Ma On Shan. But I lie to you now and I lied to myself back then. The responsibility was mine alone. I married him. I had gone into it with my eyes open. I wanted the child and so did he.

It's not that I wasn't warned. They had all tried in their different ways.

"But he's a Big Six," my Hong Kong Chinese colleagues at the newspaper had whispered to me as we stood next to the water cooler. Big Six is the name Hong Kongers have for people from Communist China. It's a Cantonese pun on the word for mainlanders. "They," the emphasis was on the otherness of the *they,* "they have no traditional values, only care about one thing: money." And now that I had no illusions left about Hong Kong, I understood the subtext. As a white English girl, I was marrying beneath myself.

"Best go home. Choose one of your own. The gap is too great." My wise old Mandarin teacher had brought fat American cherries to our lesson and washed them himself. "You'll be waking up every morning, each of you wondering what on earth is going on in the other's head." He was being cruel to be kind.

"You can't do both. People won't accept it." My boss at the paper had a Hong Kong Chinese mother and an English father and had been educated at Harrow. "In the end you'll have to choose. Believe me, I've tried." He meant that in Hong Kong it was difficult if not impossible to function socially in both the Chinese and the expat worlds. But I had ignored all the advice.

"*Sweet pea, Mummy's sweet pea!*" There was so much I wanted to tell Lily, but how could I when I didn't understand it myself? I was trapped, suffocating in this sweltering matchbox apartment away from my own people. The tiny place was home to four of us including the maid. People back home might have thought it quite luxurious with its marble floors and modern conveniences. There was even a swimming pool, a laundry room, and a gym. But the whole apartment was the size of my parents' sitting room in Berkshire.

Handel and I first met in London at an Anglo-Chinese corporate event. I was an aspiring business correspondent angling for the newspaper to post me to Hong Kong or Beijing. He was a young banker with a British bank. I wasn't sure if it was love at first sight, but his face broke into such a gargantuan grin of delight when I addressed him in Mandarin. We ended up having supper in a Chinese restaurant in Soho, and over the weeks and months things went on from there.

Yes, he was handsome, well over six feet tall, with big eyes, high cheekbones, and a cheeky smile. He wore an expensive suit with a green-and-purple jewel-patterned tie. His outfit was topped off with a smart black coat embellished with a yellow cashmere scarf, which reminded me in a cute way of Paddington Bear. The waitresses in the restaurant that night certainly thought him dapper. He sweet-talked them into extra helpings and the softest *doufu hua* dessert. He could charm the hind legs off a donkey!

We chatted in Mandarin and then slipped into English since he spoke it much better than I did Chinese. His mother was a teacher and his father a Party man. He had been separated from them during the Cultural Revolution. His mother had been held in a makeshift Red Guard prison known as the "cattle stall," and his father relegated to cleaning toilets. As for Handel, he was sent down to the countryside for "reeducation" with his classmates. His face had clouded over at this point in the story and he talked about keeping rabbits for food and how he had been the one chosen to wring their necks. Over the following weeks and months I got to know

him better. He had come to the UK in 1990 to study econom-
ics and business, paying his way with a loan and by working in
kitchens in Chinese restaurants. The customers had no idea
their meals were being cooked by gangs of ex–Red Guards
now studying for degrees.

"Poor little white cabbage!" he said when our first meal
together was nearly over, reaching with his chopsticks to fish
up one remaining leaf. "Here, Little Bourgeois, eat up!"

Perhaps that's when I fell in love with him, that night in
the restaurant when he first teasingly called me Little Bourgeois. Perhaps it was when he cooked me sweet soup balls with
sesame filling and we ate them out of one bowl in bed. Perhaps
it was the old photograph: Handel when he first arrived in
London, thin and gaunt in his blue trousers and white shirt
with a bowl haircut. I was proud of him then, proud of his
determination to educate and better himself, excited by his
transformation from Red Guard revolutionary to modern city
boy. I delighted in his success, and enjoyed being in the arms
of such a handsome man. I helped him with his English and he
with my Chinese. The sex was gentle, kind, if unadventurous.
He made me feel good.

Where had it all gone so wrong? People told me that he
was using me. But if that were true, then surely I was equally
guilty of that charge. He was my key to things Chinese, career
advancement in Hong Kong and China. Think of the stories
I could get that others would miss! On my side, my dad was
a Conservative member of Parliament. Had Handel thought I
was his way into the British establishment? He was ambitious
for sure, but then so was I. Yet I had come to understand that
for him it was something more than ambition, rather a kind of
desperate frenzy to make up for the deprivation of the Maoist
years, all at once. Pizza, sex, croissants, French wine, opera,

golf, horse riding, even cricket at Lord's! He was like a child in a candy shop.

The bedroom door opened and Handel shuffled out, his plastic slippers scuffing lazily on the floor.

"Happy handover!" I chirped brightly, determined to start the afternoon positively, for the celebrations would soon begin. I had given the maid a week off over the holiday period and she had gone home to the Philippines. Without her in the flat, I thought the two of us might talk. Handel noisily cleared his throat and spat into the kitchen sink. It was his regular waking-up routine, learned from his mother. He knew I detested it. His eye fell on the empty bottle of milk and the dish that I had fed Lily from.

"You've been giving her that stuff again, Little Bourgeois," he sneered.

I didn't rise to the challenge.

"Congee not good enough for her? It's not done me any harm."

I gritted my teeth and shuddered inside. It was hopeless, day after day, always the same. There was no physical violence, but with constant criticism and verbal assault on everything I did, there might as well have been.

He picked up yesterday's *Ming Pao* newspaper. I stared at him sitting at the table in his wifebeater and boxer shorts. Who was this man I had married? I didn't know him anymore. I busied myself playing with Lily, sitting on the floor making towers with her colored blocks. He watched me out of the corner of his eye. What did he see? I was wearing a yellow-flowered nightdress that I had bought in Mong Kok. It was more suitable for a grandma than a young woman of twenty-eight.

It had started after we moved to Hong Kong, small things at first, so I almost didn't notice. He missed me. He didn't like me going for drinks after work with *gweilo* colleagues. My lipstick was too bright, my skirt too short, my underwear too revealing. I thought it was a joke. I wasn't exactly a socialist virgin. Did he want me to wear my hair in braids under a Mao cap with a little red star?

Pushing aside the newspaper, Handel cleared Lily's empty bottle and dish, clattering them to the sink. The dish detergent was all used up.

"Damn that girl," he said in Shanghainese, thinking I wouldn't understand. He was referring to the maid, but he meant me. I couldn't do anything right.

His eye fell on Lily and his face relaxed into a smile, that wonderful joyous smile that I had first loved. He came over and sat cross-legged on the floor opposite us. Lily laughed and offered him a bright yellow block with her pudgy little hand. Despite myself, I softened and was drawn in. I dared to hope. We played a little, the three of us, silently passing blocks, building towers, knocking them down. Then gently, very gently, I looked him in the eye.

"Handel, we need to talk."

"What about?" His face clammed up, hard, unreadable.

"You know—this, us, everything."

"What's the point? You're not Chinese. You wouldn't understand." He grabbed the remote and switched on the TV.

The British governor of Hong Kong and his family were leaving Government House for the last time. He stood on the podium, holding back the emotion as the band played "God Save the Queen." It began to rain. Onlookers' umbrellas went up. The "Last Post" was sounded and the Union Jack lowered, folded, and presented to the governor on a velvet cushion.

The return of the British Crown Colony of Hong Kong was not very straightforward.

China is a totalitarian Communist state, and despite the "one country, two systems" promise, the people of Hong Kong were being left without any meaningful democratic rights. It was a shameful betrayal. I began to cry, wiping away the tears with the back of my hand.

"Good riddance to bad rubbish," Handel said in Mandarin, and something inside me snapped. It was China that had brought us together and China that was driving us apart. I began to put away the blocks one by one, red, yellow, blue, green, placing them in their box. And when I was done, I picked up Lily and very carefully, walking as if on eggshells, I made my way to the bedroom door.

"You'd better get dressed, Little Bourgeois." The nickname was no longer a joke. His words, all of them, were knives, jabs, stabs, slashes, cutting deep wounds. "*Chi fan*," he taunted.

Chi fan literally means *eat rice*. With Handel it was code for meeting his Chinese friends, not my *gweilo* ones. We were supposed to be going out with a group this afternoon to celebrate the handover.

I didn't reply and locked the bedroom door behind Lily and me. My stomach twisted with the agony of realization. For him, I was like the horse-riding lessons, the opera, the cricket at Lord's. Once experienced, I could be rejected, spat out, nothing more than a half-eaten candy discarded on a marble floor. Coldly, calmly, I dressed Lily in her new pretty red dress, the one I had bought specially to celebrate the day as if it were Chinese New Year. Handover, a new start for Hong Kong, for us?

"*Mummy's sweet pea, Mummy's sweet pea . . .*" She gurgled, kicked her legs, and smiled. I put on my little white summer dress, the pearls my grandma had bequeathed to me, my highest heels, and my most audacious red lipstick. I got our passports, my credit cards, and the cash I had hidden, rolled in a walking sock. I packed a small duffel of essentials: diapers, a few clothes, and the chewed cuddly seal named Sally that Lily couldn't sleep without. At the last moment I removed my wedding ring, placing it on Handel's bedside table. I knew then that there would be no turning back.

I took a deep breath, unlocked the door, and Lily and I went back into the sitting room. Handel lolled on the sofa cutting his toenails with the kitchen scissors and didn't look up. Staring at the top of his head, quietly, steadily, I took an umbrella from the shoe stand by the door and balanced it on top of my duffel. *Snip, snip,* a toenail fell away into the *Ming Pao* newspaper he had placed under his feet.

"Lily and I are going out. " I announced. "*Chi fan?* You'll have to go alone."

Handel

That's not my real name, of course. I've never really had a name, at least not in the way a Westerner would understand. I was born a number: fifty-eight, the year of my birth. During the Cultural Revolution my father gave me the name Wei Lie: Defending Lenin. It was for my own protection, or so he said. And later, in better times, I chose the name Han for myself. Han means China, as in Chinese civilization. Later still, when I was a student in London, Han became Handel. I heard his "Music for the Royal Fireworks" performed in Hyde Park one summer. Such a triumphant piece! So that's the story of my names, if not exactly who I am.

To tell you the truth, when I first saw the way it was going with Lizzie, I just went along with it. I don't believe in love. Marriage is business. I've never told her or anyone else exactly how I got out of China. Westerners will pour out their life story to any stranger in a bar, but we grew up differently. The less people know, the better. It's safer that way. I was involved in the 1989 student protests in Shanghai. In the aftermath, I tricked an official in Shenzhen to let me escape to Macau and then to Hong Kong. All the years I was studying in London, no one back in Shanghai knew where I was, not even my parents.

Looking back, I suppose I thought I would stay in London, and Lizzie was kind. She wasn't very pretty—too thin, a bit scrawny for my taste—but she was a generous soul. Of course, I regret it. But I couldn't seem to help myself—me, her, the baby, and the maid, all of us cooped up in this tiny flat. I never had time to myself.

What's so hard to understand? The world is changing. Europe and America are dying. The twenty-first century will be the Chinese century! The West has been top dog too long. Now it's our turn. You won't believe how much China had changed in the years I was away. There were fortunes to be made back home. Some of my classmates were already multimillionaires and I was late to the game. Lizzie didn't get it, of course. She never understood that I was looking for something, I always have been.

I guess motherhood changed her, made her more English. She couldn't wait to work in Hong Kong, and then she was desperate to go home. There was no satisfying her. She hated being in the New Territories away from her British friends, complained she was lonely. And sex too—she always wanted more. Little Bourgeois! She was always spoiled. They all are, Westerners, too soft.

The baby, you say? Of course, it's sad, but she's mixed blood, better off in the UK.

Do you know that when we lived in London, I used to admire minivans? I set my heart on a sky-blue Peugeot.

"We'll have four children, and then we'll have to buy one of those!" I used to say to Lizzie, heaven knows why. Anyway, the British were leaving Hong Kong at last. It was over. I was going to marry a rich Hong Kong Chinese girl and retire at fifty!

The doorbell rang. It was getting late. Lily and her mother still weren't back. I had just returned from our handover dinner and was desperate to be alone. It was Lao Wang, damn him! I needed to see him; indeed, I had invited him to pop in sometime, but why this night of all nights? He was a clever one, make no mistake. It was the old way of doing things in a new disguise.

"Welcome! Come in! Sit down."

Lao Wang was already making himself at home, slumping proprietarily in the middle of the sofa, his black leather man-bag on the coffee table, ready for business. In his pink Ralph Lauren polo shirt and cream-colored khakis, he was a very modern man, except he wasn't. I had grown up with the system. Designer clothes and hair gel can't fool me. We think when we go abroad we'll be free, but we're not. Wherever there are Chinese, it's there, like a great hydra. Its tentacles stretch into student digs, university lecture halls, Chinese restaurants. All smiles, offering banquets and cash, it slips into foreign institutions. For Chinese there's no escape. It's in the food, in the tea, in the air. You find it in a nod or a whisper, a tap on the arm, a few careless words marked on your file in the Chinese Embassy. The Chinese Communist Party, the most powerful organization the world has ever known. Old stench in new bottles.

Thankfully, the years of eating bitterness are behind us. Let bygones be bygones. But a man has to do what a man has to do. Number one thing, survival, and a man needs money for that, the more the better. Best not be too clean.

I smiled at Lao Wang. "What are we drinking, tea?" I had already drunk far too much beer with dinner.

"As you wish." Lao Wang waved his hand imperiously and my mind whirred. That meant I had to present tea, beer, and possibly whiskey. My precious malt I rationed so carefully.

"Nice place." Lao Wang stretched back, arms behind his head and feet up on the coffee table. "How much?"

"It's just rented." Some of Lizzie's English manners had rubbed off on me after all. Didn't he know it was rude to ask about money?

I put the tray down on the coffee table. Tea, beer, whiskey, nuts, and a few Marks & Spencer chocolates left over from Christmas. Lao Wang took out a packet of cigarettes and carefully chose one, as if somehow it might be special, different from the others. Without asking, he lit up, blowing smoke lazily into the air. My blood boiled, my throat tightened with panic—or was it rage? It was seven years since I left China. Everything had changed, yet everything remained the same. One little gesture said it all.

I had never liked Lao Wang. We all called him Old Wang out of habit, deference, fear, although he was not much older than the rest of us. It's always best to keep your options open, not burn your bridges. We first met when I was a student in London. He sought me out in the student cafeteria one day at lunch. I recognized him immediately from the strutting way he walked with his hips thrust forward, and the pigeon-like turn of his eyes. He was the Party man, there to keep us in line. Freedom, democracy! What a joke!

Lao Wang picked up the remote and flicked on the TV. He helped himself to a whiskey, obliging me to do likewise. The channels were running and rerunning the handover events throughout the day: the arrival of President Jiang Zemin and Premier Li Peng by air from Shenzhen, the farewell speech of the last governor.

"Today is a day of celebration, not sorrow," the governor, Chris Patten, affectionately nicknamed Fat Pang by Hong Kongers, began. He looked exhausted, close to tears.

"Whore of the East." Lao Wang stubbed out a cigarette and poured more whiskey for the both of us.

The scene changed to cover the soldiers of the People's Liberation Army spilling over the border. It teemed with rain and their faces glistened. But they stood tall, three abreast in the back of the green trucks, eyes front, white gloved hands placed at perfect intervals gripping the side rails. The TV played patriotic marches and my heart swelled with pride. *Beijing Blesses You Hong Kong,* said the banners in a shot from Tiananmen Square.

"Where's your old wife?" Lao Wang crushed out yet another cigarette. Damn him! He never beat around the bush.

"She's gone to the yacht club with some friends." I met his eye, steadily poured the tea.

"Hmm. Imagine them all up there, those foreigners, singing "Rule, Britannia!" and firing their silly old canon. Rule bloody Britannia! Long live China!"

"Long live China!" I raised my glass. It was really late now, pitch black outside. Suddenly I felt sick.

The television showed the reception at the convention center, all the Hong Kong great and good, the ladies discreetly adorned with jade and diamonds. It panned to clips from the British farewell parade: "Auld Lang Syne," a lone

Scottish piper in his kilt in the pouring rain. And then it was fire-works from Beijing, exploding stars and rainbow fountains of joy.

Lao Wang yawned, helped himself and me to yet more of my precious malt, and asked if there was any ice and soda. What a peasant. I didn't have any, so he was forced to carry on drinking it neat, and me too, for if I was to press my case, I needed to keep him company.

"Here's to an end to the century of humiliation." Lao Wang raised his glass. "Death to the blood-stinking imperialists!"

"*Gan bei! Gan bei!*"

The toasts went on and on. Lao Wang's face bloated, flushed red then purple. My head swam and I forgot Lizzie and Lily, ignored my anguish and confusion, blanked out my pain.

It was getting on toward midnight, reaching the climax of the day with the formal handover ceremony. On the TV, Prince Charles began his farewell speech on behalf of the Queen. Here was my chance. It was now or never.

"Actually, Lao Wang, there's something I wanted to talk about." It was me speaking but my voice was so gruff and hoarse that I barely recognized it. "I've been offered a job in Shanghai—a good one with an American bank." I didn't need to say more.

The band on the TV played "God Save the Queen," and for the second time that day the Union Jack was lowered.

Lao Wang's face locked down, his jaw tight. He swirled the whiskey in the bottom of his glass, looked at it, and swirled it again. My fate was in his hands. Then he beamed, and roared with laughter, slapping me on the back. "Well done! Welcome home!"

Suddenly it was as if it had all been a big joke: Tiananmen, the years in exile studying in London when I was too terrified to write home.

The handover ceremony was nearly over. The flag of the People's Republic of China with its five stars was being raised, red, red, red, high, higher, higher. Lao Wang stood, unsteady on his feet, blasting out the Chinese national anthem, and I was up too, singing with gusto.

"Arise, all ye who refuse to be slaves. Arise! Arise! Arise!"

Exhausted, inebriated, but elated, we flopped down on the sofa. Lao Wang wiped his brow with his handkerchief and stared at me.

"And your old wife? A journalist like her could be a great friend to China."

He knew I knew, and I knew he knew. That's the way the system works. I thought of Lizzie. Bless her. She tried so hard, but really she had no idea. And then there was her member-of-Parliament father. I remembered him pruning his roses in his country garden. He was always kind to me. It was he who introduced me to the joy of single malt.

But Lao Wang had got his teeth into my weak spot. He gnawed and chewed, relishing it, toying with me.

"Does she know about the job in Shanghai?"

"No."

"Do you think she'll go?"

I shook my head. "Does it matter? It doesn't to me."

Lao Wang shrugged. "Shame. She might have been useful to us."

The whiskey bottle was nearly empty by the time he tottered to the door.

"The Party needs young men like you," he lisped, putting his arm paternally around my shoulders. "Don't worry about a thing! Old Wang will sort you out."

Softy, I closed the door behind me. For a few moments I rested my head on it. I had drunk far too much. I began to worry about Lizzie and Lily. They still weren't home. My head swirled, everything pale green—green, the color of my childhood. Everything was painted that color in those days: offices, schools, hospitals, even our tiny little state-owned apartment. Imagine it, the whole country green. I don't think I knew what color was until I got to London and saw all the girls in their pretty summer dresses: pinks, reds, yellows, oranges, and, goodness me, the gardens and the flowers. My guts churned. The old smells returned—coal and cooking oil, sweat, shit leaking from overflowing latrines. My mouth tasted like iron, a memory, blood. I made it to the sink just in time, vomiting lumps, pale puke green.

I retched until I was utterly spent, then went over to the window. I had to fix the safety catch. For the moment, I threw it open, wide open, raising my head, welcoming it, begging for it, the lashing, slashing rain.

PART III

FAMILY MATTERS

TICKET HOME

by Charles Philipp Martin

Yau Ma Tei

Almost. That could have been Jun's nickname. Since childhood every prize in life lay just out of his reach.

He should have made it into the army like his older brother Wing, who joined after the family paid a fifty thousand–*yuan* bribe. But the sergeant took one look at Jun and said seventy-five. His parents, shopkeepers who scrimped for years and took bribes of their own, could only manage sixty.

Almost.

Had Jun been born a few years earlier, he might have joined the gang that pulled off the robbery at Sun Cheong Gold and Jewelry in Kowloon. That one made the papers even in Swatow. It was a professional operation, run by the Sun Yee On out of Mong Kok. But even that triad, the largest and most resourceful of the city's criminal organizations, preferred mainland talent for the big jobs—good ex-army people who knew weapons, could follow orders, and who needed money. Jun's cousin Mak was twenty-four, the right age for the job. The papers said he whipped his team through the shop in four minutes and snatched a good thirty million dollars in diamonds.

Jun was only fourteen that year.

Almost.

And today he had almost made it into the getaway car,

having been the last man out of Yip Fung Fine Jewelry in Yau Ma Tei. But while backing away from the shattered counters, he tripped over a customer's briefcase. The few seconds lost were enough. By the time he found his footing, a van loaded with cops was screeching to a halt, blocking him from the anonymous Mitsubishi across the street.

The other three on Jun's team had burst from the doorway and scrambled into the van, clutching their Black Star automatics. Lucky Ma, never one for thinking things through, took hasty aim and fired at the police transport. The cops returned fire, and that was that. The team was pinned down, three crew and the driver, forced into a gun battle by the reckless Ma. One of the trapped crew was his brother Wing.

Jun watched uniformed men herd back screaming onlookers. He had to move now. Removing his balaclava and gloves, he ducked sideways out the door and slipped behind a knot of pedestrians gathered on the corner. The cops, pinned down by a gang of thieves taking wild shots, couldn't follow him.

An alley appeared midblock and Jun let it swallow him. Here and there a worker pushing a loaded cart paused to watch him run by, but no one followed, and Jun eventually felt safe slowing down.

The Sun Yee On had chosen to hit a place in Yau Ma Tei for a reason. The district was sandwiched between Tsim Sha Tsui and Mong Kok, both of which presented getaway problems. Tsim Sha Tsui, at the tip of the Kowloon peninsula to the south, had loads of jewelry shops, but was crammed with tourists. That meant lots of police on patrol, and cameras everywhere. Mong Kok, on the other hand, had few tourists, but was the densest place on earth, a black hole of compressed humanity just north of him. A job on wheels was suicide there: they'd list your cause of death as traffic.

So Yau Ma Tei it was—populated enough to give you cover with all its teeming stores and office blocks, but still a place that moved.

Emerging on the other side of the alley, Jun did his best to match the pace of the street's foot traffic and rein in his gasping lungs. No one seemed to be in pursuit; he'd achieved his goal of dissolving into the oblivious throngs on Woosung Street, looking like any other salaryman on a lunch break.

Except he looked nothing like that. As his breath slowed, he eyed the stream of Hong Kongers around him. They seemed to be eyeing him back, these people who looked foreign even though they were Chinese.

Next year, you get yours. The handover was coming, less than a year off, and all this, the tall buildings and the cars and the gold, would be shoved neatly under Beijing's heel. *Next year, I won't be the foreigner here.* But right now that was of no concern.

A man strode by wearing a dark suit with a plush silk tie. His shoes had thin soles, not thick rubber ones like his own. The man gave Jun a once-over, then vanished in the crowd.

He'd never get back home if he were noticed, and his cheap garments seemed to label him a product of mainland China. Blending in was the answer; looking like everyone else would give him time to think.

You don't find good suits hanging on a clothesline, he knew. Jun needed money. Funny how spare cash is the last thing on your mind when you come to Hong Kong to steal diamonds on Jordan Road.

Money had been on his mind for weeks, though. The days of rehearsing the heist, the teeth-shattering ride on a watermelon truck, borrowed papers in his pocket, weapons tucked under the melons in the back—it had all been for money. The boring hours in the Tai Po flat with dim lights, no fan, not even a radio—he'd endured it in the name of a rudimentary financial plan: to head back to Swatow with all the cash he'd ever need. But he'd tripped on that briefcase. The duffel flew from his hand, along with the Black Star that he'd only fired eight times for practice in a field outside the city. The gold was gone, traded in haste for a ticket home.

Would Wing be there when he got back? Lucky Ma might be an idiot, but Wing was clever, and he knew the plan backward and forward. Once the driver got going, Wing would know how to evade the cops. He, at least, would make it home with his share.

Cash. Reflexively he patted his pockets and drew out a souvenir from what seemed like a hundred years ago, back when the plan was working. He had a vision of the shop's customers laid out side by side like bream at a fish market, the showroom eerily quiet, the only sounds his own breathing and the muffled sweep of gloved hands shoveling gems and gold into bags. That was before the clang of the alarm and the shriek of the onlookers and the whine of the police siren and the shouts of the unit leader and the bark of the guns.

Almost.

Back in the showroom, Jun had kicked in the glass on a display of Credit Suisse .999 bars. Nice, fat, twenty-gram ones. While chucking them into the bag, one by one, a box flew open and two of the bars, each about the size of a cigarette lighter, fell out. Jun stuffed them in his pocket for luck and went on loading up the duffel.

He had a plan for the gold bars. This past year, every moment Jun didn't spend thinking about the robbery he'd spent worshipping Su Yin. She was no great beauty, with her unremarkable figure and a mouth that seemed to hold five or ten extra teeth, but her eyes were warm, and she laughed politely that time when Jun tried to make a joke. He'd asked her to a movie once—a nice, safe group of five was going and she'd be the sixth—and she'd accepted.

But at the movie she'd gone rigid, and then inert, when Jun placed his arm around her shoulder. Since then, Su Yin had made it clear she had no interest in being his girlfriend. It made no sense to Jun—she wasn't going out with anyone else, but she rebuffed his advances and made herself scarce when he was around.

The Yau Ma Tei job would have changed that. Back in the Tai Po flat, he rehearsed over and over a scene where, safely back home, he'd greet Su Yin with a casual hello. He'd pull out a diamond necklace—a piece he'd kept from his share for just that purpose—and dangle it like a fisherman's lure in front of her eyes. She'd melt into a passion-laden kiss right there.

There would be no necklace now, but the bars would do. *Every girl loves gold.*

He knew the way home—the top man, a Wo Shing Wo 432, had discussed escape routes should they have to disperse. Like any good businessman, he'd studied the work of his competitors, and he was determined to equal the success of his rivals in the Sun Yee On. Any man who couldn't make it back to the van was to hire a boat to Ling Ding, an island belonging to the People's Republic that lay just a few miles off the Hong Kong coast. It was forbidden to Hong Kongers, of course, but flashing a couple of those big red bills would get an enterprising fisherman to take you over.

Ling Ding lay west. Jun would have to get to the water and look for boat people. Wing couldn't help him now; he needed to stay calm, blend in, and not attract attention. A vision of Wing, beaming in pride at his brother who made it back home the hard way, formed in Jun's head. They'd have some stories to tell each other.

Jun resolved not to speak—the people in the shop had heard his brother shouting orders and would have nailed down his accent. The cops would be looking out for a man from Swatow dressed in black jeans and a black polo shirt.

He'd have to keep quiet. He'd have to get some Hong Kong clothes. And he'd have to eat. There was no telling how long the trip to Ling Ding would take.

In his pocket the lucky gold beat like a heart. There would be no Su Yin without it. But there would be no Su Yin if he couldn't get back to Swatow. He resigned himself to another failure, another *almost*, and walked with a new purpose in mind.

The pawnshop took less than ten minutes to find. A friend had said they were all over, because on Friday everyone needs money for mahjong, and then on Monday everyone needs money to eat.

The red swinging doors kept no one in or out; they were ceremonial, a way of sorting the down-and-out and desperate from the legions who were at peace with their striving. The doors opened into a dim, high-ceilinged room where a bald middle-aged man sat at a desk raised a half foot above Jun's head. Hong Kong pawnshops were considerate in that regard; having a pawnbroker perched high meant you could submit your goods while concealing your shamed face. Needing money was as humiliating as it got in this city.

Not showing his face worked fine for Jun. He held up the Credit Suisse bars and stared at the dingy tiled walls.

The man above him made no greeting and did not smile. He took the objects that Jun handed him and scanned them with an unsentimental eye. "Forty grams total—3,630."

Jun nodded. A sign on the counter showed the day's spread—the buying and selling prices for gold—but Jun couldn't make the calculations; the price was in taels, and the Swiss bars were in grams.

In the background a radio burbled news: a robbery in Yau Ma Tei, four men dead, no police hurt, one bystander in the hospital. Money recovered. One man still at large.

Jun closed his eyes and turned away from the pawnbroker. *Not Wing!* But Wing was surely dead, along with his two army friends and some kid they picked up as a driver.

At that moment he realized that his brother had really been his whole family. Jun's father paid little attention to him. His mother, he thought, wished Jun were someone else, someone who brought in more money, who got compliments from teachers and employers. It was *Mama* who had disciplined him, who tried to make him into a man like his brother, one slap at a time.

Wing was dead, and for some reason Jun's hand went to his cheek to feel heat that wasn't there. Instead he felt the familiar warmth of a tear, the one that always shamed him worse than the blow from *Mama* that brought it on.

But *Mama* and *Baba* had only him now. If Jun didn't make it back, no one would care for them in their old age. That's what the money was for. Some of it, anyway. That, and a place for him and Su Yin to raise children.

In a stealthy move, he wiped the tear and turned back to see the pawnbroker put down the gold and point to a sign that Jun had missed until now: *ID NUMBER REQUIRED FOR ALL TRANSACTIONS.*

Jun froze. "I forgot it," he said, almost a whisper, as if that would keep his accent from escaping. He grabbed the bars. "Later."

By the time he got outside, panic had once again overtaken him. There was no place to go; every step seemed to be in the wrong direction. He had assumed Wing was making his escape through the New Territories, guiding and reassuring the others, using his wits to evade the cops. But Wing wouldn't be rooting for him, wouldn't be waiting at the flat in Swatow to slap Jun on the back and welcome him home; no one would.

Jun stared into the window of the bakery next door, pretending to look over the cakes but thinking of Swatow, two hundred miles northeast of Yau Ma Tei. His brother was dead and he was trapped in Hong Kong like a fly in a bottle—the police after him and his gold useless. His breath began to quicken again.

Inside of a minute, a man, younger than the pawnbroker and with a more animated face, emerged from the pawnshop and approached him. Jun hadn't seen him in the shop; he must have been in the back.

"Looking to sell something?" the man said. He was in his late twenties, with short hair with a splash of gel at the front. Like Jun he wore black, but the jeans seemed sleek and expensive, and the shirt, buttoned to the top, was silk.

He didn't act like a cop, but what did Jun know about Hong Kong police? The guy ran his eyes over Jun from top to bottom, lingering at his feet. *Got to get rid of these shoes.*

The man continued: "I know it's a pain to have to go all the way home to get your ID card. I'll give you 2,500 for the bars now."

Jun started to say that they were worth more, then remembered his Swatow accent.

The man seemed to understand anyway. His eyes narrowed but his unfading smile did the talking. *You know, I know, that you'll take it. No one forgets his ID card at home.* He put his hand in his pocket, waiting for the signal.

Jun nodded.

In a doorway beyond the bakery, the man drew out a wad of cash the size of a mango and peeled off five brown bills.

Jun nodded again in thanks. The cash was enough to disguise him and get him back to Swatow.

"Good luck, Ah Tsan," said the man as he headed back to the pawnshop.

Ah Tsan. Everyone's favorite bumpkin from China. Hong Kongers loved to make fun of that ignorant TV character, with his unquenchable lust for money. So the man—and the pawnbroker too, probably—had taken him for a mainlander right off. He had to get out of these clothes now. He was dressed for a robbery, one that was all over the news.

Jun snaked through streets and alleys, never moving more than a block in a single direction, searching for clothes. He felt too conspicuous to enter a small trendy place in the window of which stood a cardboard man dressed in a tank top and sport coat; a big store was needed, one where he'd be just another faceless shopper.

Somehow his wandering took him back to Jordan Road, a few blocks east of where he'd left millions in gold and diamonds, bundled for easy transport, on the floor of a jewelry shop. He started back, petrified at the thought of being so close to where his brother was killed. But the entrance to the Emporium, a department store stocked with goods from the mainland, came into view, and he headed there instead. Upstairs in the men's department he grabbed the first suit he saw, a slate-gray two-piece. Then he picked up a shirt and a pair of shoes, and left about nine hundred dollars lighter. His own socks and underwear would last till he made it home to Swatow.

Clutching the bag to his side, he walked north on Nathan Road, then west on Pak Hoi Street, a warren of grimy concrete heaps covered with hanging signs dense enough to blot out the sun. A fast-food outlet turned up. Nothing but a shabby storefront lined with yellow plastic walls, it was a good enough place to get something to eat and finally become, for a few hours, a Hong Konger.

A girl in a yellow shift accepted Jun's grunted order. Changing outfits now would attract attention, so he ate at the rearmost table in his old clothes while a Sammi Cheng hit crackled through hidden speakers.

The restaurant's cramped bathroom made it difficult to strip off his black jeans and polo shirt, but with contortions he managed to don the suit and tie his shoes. Not until he'd shoved the Emporium bag with his old clothes into a street bin did he begin to feel lighter and freer. But he was still far from home.

Ling Ding. He had to get there. Once he made it onto the island and was officially in the PRC, a boatman would take five hundred to ferry him back to the China coast. But he didn't know where to start, and the people who brought him here, the only ones he knew this far south, were on a table in some police morgue.

For a half mile or so he kept away from any street where he might feel conspicuous, though he didn't even know what that meant now that he was dressed in a suit. Was his haircut wrong? His posture? Was he still Ah Tsan to everyone he passed?

Suit or not, he felt their eyes on him. Were they stealing glances at his feet? The shoes were good: an exact replica, as far as he could tell, of the shiny ones on the feet of men he passed. It couldn't be the shoes.

A reflection in a real estate broker's window assured him that he looked good. If only Su Yin could see him now.

Farther on, Jun found his way blocked by barriers hastily erected in front of a construction site. A sign proclaimed the birth of a new commercial building, and under it was a man in a yellow hard hat and dusty blue coveralls, squatting against a wall and eating a late lunch of *char siu fan*, roast pork and rice. He spoke to his mate in a dialect Jun recognized from a city near his own. Jieyang dialect, a little different from Swatow, a little clumsier-sounding to his ears, but as clear and familiar as a letter from home.

The man in the hard hat would know Jun's life, would see Hong Kong the way Jun did, and might remember when he too first arrived in this roiling stewpot, confused and scared.

Up to now Jun had uttered maybe five words out loud. He'd worked to escape everyone's notice. That would change if he spoke to the hard hat. Trusting a stranger—one from a city near Swatow, but a stranger nonetheless—could cost him everything.

He was not raised to rely on strangers, much less ones in a hostile city. But the men he trusted were dead, and strangers were the only people who knew the way home. He'd have to take the risk.

When the second man walked away, Jun approached. "Friend," he said, "could you help me with directions?"

"Mmm."

"Where are the boats to the islands?"

"Which one? Lantau? Cheung Chau? Go to Central."

Did he know those islands? Maybe from a movie. "Heard there's one with cheap beer . . ."

The man nodded. Bright sun and concrete dust had pummeled his complexion for years, making him look older than

Jun, but he sounded young. "Ling Ding. Tough to get there."

"Just curious. I heard you can pay a sampan driver."

"Too far for a sampan. You'll need something bigger, a *walla-walla.*"

"Know where I can find one?"

"Sure. But you don't want to advertise this, right?" The construction worker thought a second. "Wait here." He got up and ambled to a shed on the far side of the site. Jun watched a crane until he returned.

"Eight o'clock," the man said. "There's a *dai pai dong* near the night market, Saigon Street, the first food stall west of Shanghai Street. Wait there. My guy will get you to the boat. But it'll be a hundred up front."

Under the spell of the familiar speech pattern of his home and thoughts of Swatow, Jun dug into his pocket and placed a bill in the man's creased brown hand.

To kill time, Jun ducked into a movie. Entertainment was the last thing on his mind, and staying in one place would be torture, but theaters were dark and he needed a place to think. He paid and watched the film from the second-to-last row. Or rather, he sat with his eyes open, chained to his dread, while a Stephen Chow comedy paraded irrelevantly on the screen.

Wing was dead. As far back as he could remember, just seeing his brother's face had been enough to keep out the cold. Now there would be nothing left of him save a few photos Jun had collected in a drawer. He remembered his favorite, one that a stranger took of them both on a boat in Guilin— Jun looking stiff under the camera's eye, Wing as serene and eternal as the limestone peaks behind them.

Then there was Su Yin, who would never be his. He was returning to Swatow with nothing to give her.

The money was gone, along with the life it would have bought him. Once he'd dreamed of a wife and a car and a large flat. Now all that mattered was that he make it home to have nothing and be nothing. And to get that, he must follow the orders of a construction worker he didn't know and maybe shouldn't trust.

Every few minutes a sound or movement would draw Jun's attention to the comedy, but he never picked up the plot, and didn't care. By the time he left the theater, his skin clammy from the air-conditioning, dusk had fallen and Temple Street was aflame with a hundred thousand lightbulbs. The night market's hawkers had turned the streets into an outdoor bazaar.

Jun began to feel invisible among the people milling through the market. He had no more interest in shopping than he had in the movie. Nevertheless, he threaded through displays of toys, jade, watches, and artwork, occasionally fingering a wallet or Buddha statue to look casual. Again he felt eyes on his feet for some reason. Twice he compared his shoes with other passersby. They were fine.

It occurred to him to buy a gift for Su Yin. By then time was short, but he found a shiny compact with a mirror and the inscription I ♥ HK laid over an illustration of the city's skyline. Not much, but he needed to conserve his cash. The movie and the compact had left him with about fourteen hundred.

At a few minutes to eight he sat down at Mak's Dumplings on Saigon Street. A waiter placed a glass of *ching cha* in front of him and took his order. Jun's stomach was tight, but everyone else was eating, and now was not the time to stick out or act strange.

He watched the hawkers across the street while turning the small compact over and over in his hands.

A man approached his table at ten after eight. Slowly, almost meekly, he took a seat alongside Jun, not facing him. Older than Jun, older than the construction worker, he wasn't one of your fashionable men, not any kind of gangster that Jun could see. He wore a tweed sport coat that covered a barrel chest, plain shirt, no tie. A serious expression, tight, determined lips.

His eyes, like Jun's, were looking everywhere, sweeping the landscape and most likely catching everything: the man across the street hawking bags of dried pork intestine, the woman pushing a cart full of duck eggs, the sign advertising foot massages, the tea shop, the store selling embroidery from China, the compact in Jun's hand.

The one thing the man's eyes didn't take in was Jun. Instead he accepted his *ching cha*, took a small sip of the plain tea, and placed it back on the table with an extra degree of care that mesmerized Jun.

"So, Ling Ding, is it?"

Jun said nothing.

"Not much of a place, if you ask me. Nice rocks and trees, I suppose. You a nature lover?" The man took another sip of tea, still looking everywhere but at Jun. "You can play cards there, mahjong. Girls too. You going for the mainland girls? A handsome guy like you, needing to pay for it?"

Again Jun didn't speak.

"Didn't think so. No, Ling Ding is just a stopover, right?"

Jun stood up. This felt wrong.

"Sit down, Zhang Jun."

Hearing his name weakened his knees. He plopped back into his seat.

"Listen carefully. Your team is dead. We know their names—three were ex-PLA, and their fingerprints are on file.

The Public Security Bureau in Guangzhou worked with us on this. I've got friends there, and they can move fast when they want to. They sent out officers to speak with the families, and it turns out one of them had a younger brother they couldn't locate. Does this look familiar, Jun?"

The man slipped a piece of paper from his jacket pocket and unfolded it to reveal a younger version of Jun: his graduation picture from Swatow No. 1 High School. Photocopied, enlarged, faxed, but clear enough.

"That construction site where you found your friend? It's across the line, in 14K territory. Everyone knew the robbery was Wo Shing Wo, and your 14K friend was happy to stick his thumb in the eye of a rival triad and earn some cash in the process. The big guys aren't getting along too well since that knifing last month. If you'd spend time reading the papers instead of planning heists, you'd know that. But we were already onto you. The pawnshop owner's son heard about the robbery on the radio and put two and two together when you walked in and sold a bona fide gold bar for less than it's worth. Only a crook does that."

Jun shifted in his seat.

"Think you're the only one who likes cash, Jun? Reward money is irresistible. And it's a lot easier than the kind you went after. Just pick up the phone. And those Credit Suisse bars? They're numbered, you know.

"So we had your picture. And thanks to the phone call from the pawnshop, we knew you were still in Yau Ma Tei. When your 14K construction worker buddy from Swatow called us and said a mainlander was trying to get to Ling Ding, we were ready."

Jun placed his hands on the table, braced himself for a run.

"You're not ex-army, are you, Jun? Not like your late brother. That's why you can't run backward. A good skill— the army teaches that for a reason. But you tripped, I'm told. That's why you're still alive."

Jun scanned the street, planning his route, finding places where the market stalls would make it hard to follow him.

The man read his mind: "Don't think of running, Zhang Jun. Look around." He nodded toward the street.

What Jun had taken for passersby were men in their late twenties, feet planted firmly, jackets open, eyes on him as if their careers depended on it. And now the sage-colored shirts of the uniformed policemen appeared, two officers at each end of the *dai pai dong*, four across the street flanking the plainclothes men.

"My name is Detective Inspector Herman Lok, Royal Hong Kong Police, Yau Tsim Division. You know what Yau Tsim is, Jun? That's my beat. If you screw up anywhere in Yau Ma Tei or Tsim Sha Tsui, I get the call." He stood up. "I'm arresting you for attempted armed robbery." Lok drew handcuffs from his side pocket and in two swift moves bound Jun's wrists; the compact dropped to the ground and shattered.

Another officer threw a hood over Jun's head and adjusted the eyeholes. The city around him darkened. In shame he lowered his gaze until all he saw was pavement and the feet of the men surrounding him, shod in black leather over black socks.

Jun's socks were white; framed in the eyeholes, they stood out like a dove among crows. Now that he thought of it, no Hong Kong man wore the white socks that were so common in China. Not even the construction worker.

Arms from unseen bodies ushered Jun to the waiting van.

A VIEW TO DIE FOR

BY CHRISTINA LIANG

Repulse Bay

I t was the end of a long day and Serena Chen was especially in need of a drink. Thank God Heather had just
popped in for one of their weekly wine-and-gossip ses-
sions. They sat on the sofa on Serena's balcony, sipping sauvignon blanc, taking in the unobstructed view of Repulse Bay
on Hong Kong Island's south side.

Heather was always one to lend a sympathetic ear. Serena
was complaining about a work lunch where she was forced to
welcome yet another newbie couple to town, a husband and
his trailing spouse. "Can you believe the wife referred to Hong
Kong as a hardship posting? What kind of hardship is it living
in one of the safest cities in the world? Is it a hardship to have
a helper cook, clean, and nanny for you? A driver to take you
around town?"

"Do me a favor," Heather said.

"What?"

"Do *not* introduce me to her."

Serena laughed and gazed out at the sea. She had a view
to die for at Bamboo Towers, the luxury compound at the foot
of the Repulse Bay inlet. Despite its not-so-glamorous name,
said to be derived from a time when British troops *repulsed*
the pirates living along the shore, Repulse Bay was one of the
more posh areas of Hong Kong. On either side of the bay were
verdant hills, with luxury villas and apartment blocks built on

their steep slopes. On weekdays, Repulse Bay Beach filled up with nonstop tour groups, usually mainland Chinese taking pictures of each other with their iPads. On weekends, families would gather under rented beach umbrellas seeking shelter from the scorching sun, while groups of young expats would cool off with the help of copious amounts of alcohol.

But on a Friday evening like this, in the distance lay nothing but the horizon and the occasional passing cargo ship. The sights and sounds of the big city were gone and replaced by the tranquility of a tropical resort.

Serena never tired of looking at the ocean. She'd earned this view with her own hard work, sweat, and tears. Hell, it had even cost her her marriage. She would damn well spend as much time on her balcony as possible. She'd even had a fancy wall garden installed, and she tended to her plants and flowers, especially her camellias, with great care. These were the constants of her home life, along with Heather Wong, her best friend, who lived upstairs.

Although the buildings of Bamboo Towers were numbered one through eight, there were only seven, as there was no unlucky number four (the word for *four* sounding like the word for *death* in Chinese). The complex had its back to the mountain and face to the sea, and one of the towers was fitted with a big square hole in the middle, a "dragon gate" that enabled the dragon a clear path from the mountain to the sea. "Good feng shui," her relocation agent had said. At the base of the towers were the remnants of a colonial-era hotel, said to have been frequented by playwrights, actors, and some European royals, where you could have traditional afternoon tea and imagine yourself in 1950s grandeur.

Bamboo Towers was a pretty straightforward choice for Serena when she moved to Hong Kong from New York. Her employer, Silverman Brothers Bank (SBB), held corporate leases throughout the complex, so even analysts had their rents subsidized. But Serena wasn't an analyst. She had made partner, and in her years in Hong Kong, she had managed to up-tower from Tower 1 all the way up to Tower 8. There really wasn't a rational reason for Tower 8 to be more aspirational, other than the luck thought to be associated with the number. But people in Hong Kong believed in luck and its role in creating and maintaining wealth.

Adding to the prestige was the fact that the Wong family of Wong Luck Holdings lived in Tower 8. The Wongs owned the entire complex, were majority shareholders in SBB, and owned the office building housing the bank in Central. But expats, even C-suite expats, rarely moved in these Chinese moneyed circles. The sphere of money, power, and influence of the Chinese tycoons made expat careers in Hong Kong seem rather quaint. At best, they could console themselves with a big paycheck, a debenture to an international school, and membership to the American Club.

Despite living in Hong Kong for over a decade, Serena still felt like an expat, even though she was Chinese. This allowed her to live a comfortable distance from the fiery politics back home in the US, which she was especially thankful for these days. It also allowed her to view local politics from afar and not get anxious as Beijing tightened its grip on the city. But as comfortable as she was, she also felt like she was cheating a little, never being fully invested in either place. Though there were definite upsides to being an expat. Serena and Heather would joke that as "long-term" expats, they lived in the Venn-diagram intersection of the "new" expats and the local Chinese, giving them license to gossip and gripe about both sides.

Hong Kong was full of *hua qiao*, overseas Chinese like herself—ABCs, CBCs, BBCs, Eurasians—and Serena found that they occupied the same cozy sphere: Western education and values but brought up in an Asian household. Now she could commiserate with her peers about her tiger mother— something she could only previously do with her cousins. Cole, her ex-husband, tried to understand the notion of a tiger parent, but never really got it. He didn't get lots of things. Her mother was always upset about something Serena did, or rather, never satisfied. Nothing was ever good enough. Not her Stanford education ("Your cousins are at Yale and Harvard. Why can't you go to one of those?"), which she chose explicitly because it was across the country from her mother and her aunties. Nor her choice of husband.

"You are really going to marry Cole?" asked her mother.

"Yes, Ma. We're in love," said Serena.

"Isn't there a nice Taiwanese boy at business school?"

"None that I want to marry."

"Well, at least he is white."

"Ma! You can't say things like that!"

"Don't be so serious. I'm just joking."

When she told her mother that she and Cole were moving to Hong Kong, her mother was aghast. "Why would you want to move to Hong Kong?" she had asked. "Hong Kong people like to gamble and they sound like they're always arguing."

Serena had to admit that Cantonese didn't have the same musical lilt as Mandarin or Taiwanese, but she learned enough to get by day to day. Cole, on the other hand, had no interest in learning Chinese, not that you had to speak any to get by in Hong Kong. "The language of business is English. Who needs Chinese?" he would ask.

Funny that he had no interest in the Chinese language,

since he certainly had an interest in Chinese women. Serena used to tease him about his yellow fever—his girlfriend before her was also ABC. But over their time in Hong Kong, Cole seemed to lose interest in her. At first she thought it was because he was distracted by the overwhelming number of pretty, size-zero (or 000 at the Gap), Hello Kitty–collecting girls in the office. Then she realized it was something more disturbing. She was smarter and better at her job than he was and he just couldn't take it. When she made MD before him, he left SBB for a competing bank. He said he was tired of being referred to as "Serena Chen's husband," or worse, "the boss's husband." After a while, they found themselves home together only for brief periods between their respective work trips.

Near the end of the road, they decided to try for a baby. Serena was already forty at that time, and although many of her friends were having babies at this age, she and Cole were not getting any traction. But Serena refused to have IVF. She told Cole that if it were meant to be, she would get pregnant naturally. Looking back, Serena knew that this was just an excuse. She wasn't opposed to having a baby, but she thought that if she were to bring one into this world, she should be more excited about the prospect. Was her hesitation because she wasn't sure she wanted a baby or was it that she wasn't sure she wanted a baby with Cole? She knew deep down that her marriage was falling apart and this clichéd last-ditch effort to save their marriage with a baby would probably end in tears.

The day she came home and announced that she had made partner at SBB, Cole announced that he wanted a divorce.

"I can't pretend anymore. We're both not happy," he said.

"You could have been happy. If you didn't flinch every

time I did well at work, we could have been very happy."

"You put more time and effort into your job than our marriage," said Cole.

"Maybe it was easier to avoid you altogether than try and walk around on eggshells to protect your fragile ego."

He had met someone at work. She was a junior associate at his bank, a local Chinese, educated in the UK.

"You're such an asshole, Cole. Are you that pathetic that you need a twenty-five-year-old to make you feel like a real man?"

"I'm sorry. It just happened. And she's almost thirty, by the way."

"But she probably still lives with her parents!"

"That's normal here, you know that."

And that was the end. Cole moved out that weekend into a renovated walkup in Kennedy Town with his new girlfriend, but not before Serena had dumped his whiskey collection down the toilet and his cigars into the garbage.

Back on the balcony with Heather, Serena was in awe how Heather could always look so effortlessly put-together, even in an old McGill T-shirt and denim cutoffs, her blond hair in a loose braid. On paper, Heather seemed like she and Serena wouldn't have much in common.

Heather was a mom of four kids, married straight out of university, and had never had a job. But she and Serena had hit it off after meeting at a book club years ago; they discovered they had a mutual passion for new world wines and philosophical discussions on the state of pop culture. Heather wasn't like the other ladies in the complex at Bamboo Towers with their constant nattering about school admissions, ah-ma drama, absent banker husbands, and shopping trips across the border for fakes. Heather was intelligent, confident, and didn't care for the social climbing that went on around her. Serena thought it was funny to see everyone want to get close to Heather because she was a Wong and her husband worked at Wong Luck Holdings, even though they were what Heather called "poor, distant relations." Serena also thought the fact that Heather was a white girl married to a Chinese guy gave her a little extra cool factor.

"Why do they all hate me?" asked Serena, in mock self-deprecation, referring to their expat neighbors.

"Because you make them feel bad about themselves," said Heather, lounging across Serena's outdoor sofa. "All these trailing spouses, they're highly educated women who left their jobs, their careers, to follow their husbands here. They see what you have achieved and they don't want to be reminded of what they could have had."

"It seems to me they have it pretty good. A big flat, an ocean view, domestic help, constant holidays . . ." Serena waved her hand dismissively.

"A gilded cage," said Heather. "Don't underestimate us."

Serena's face turned serious, "*She* had the baby." She pulled out her phone and went onto Cole's Facebook page. "Just look at these photos. He finally got the happy family he always wanted." She continued scrolling through the photos and winced when she saw some of her friends holding the baby. "Jerks. I can't believe they chose *them*." Serena threw her phone across the sofa. "They say it's nothing against me, they just do things in couples and it's easier to invite them than me. I might as well wear a sign that says *Single Loser*."

"Forget about them," said Heather.

"Maybe I made a mistake in letting him go without a fight."

"No, it's better to be alone than with someone you're not sure about."

Serena gave Heather a knowing look. Heather was alone now, but due to a combination of family dynamics, finances, and Chinese face-saving, she remained legally married to Victor, who lived in the flat two floors above her. Neither of them wanted to move from their piece of paradise by the sea. He had a rotation of young girlfriends, but on the condition that they were never to meet the boys. Heather's sons were her reason to live and she didn't want another woman figure in their lives, "especially not some transient gold digger." Victor kept her in her current luxurious lifestyle on the condition that she didn't openly date.

"Is it worth it?" Serena had asked her once.

"I could never go back home to that small town. Firstly, divorced with four Eurasian boys? My mother would revel in her victory of being right about him. She's afflicted with a fear of the yellow peril. Besides, life here is easy. I have two live-in helpers, a driver, and the beach at my doorstep. We have it good."

Suddenly, there was a loud bang behind them. Serena turned and saw that a section of the wall garden had fallen and some of her beloved flowers were now splattered on the floor. "Damn, this thing is falling apart," she said, trying to fix a piece of rotten wood back onto the wall. "My poor camellias. This wood can't handle the humidity. Can you give me the number for your handyman?"

"Don't worry, I'm sure Jack will happily sort it. He'll be keen to use his tools. He knows he owes you big after you helped him with his Stanford essay. I still can't believe he got in."

"He's a good, smart kid. He got in on his own merit," said

Serena. "How is he doing? I haven't seem him in months."

"He's really good. Super excited to be leaving home. I'll send him down tomorrow to try and fix the wall. I still have your spare keys."

The next weekend, Serena attended a corporate charity gala in one of the big hotels. She sat down at her seat and scanned the name cards around her, as her immediate neighbors would determine whether this would be a fun evening or one that was extremely dull. The card on her left was for someone she didn't know that well. The card on her right was for Victor Wong. *I wonder if this is Heather's Victor? What am I going to talk to him about all night?* Although she had been close friends with Heather for years, she hadn't spent much time with Victor one on one. She went back out to the lobby to have another glass of champagne before they rang the dinner bell.

Victor approached Serena and they greeted each other in the lobby with a double kiss on the cheeks.

"So, it looks like we're sitting together tonight," said Serena.

"Great! Then we're in for a fun night. You look stunning, by the way," said Victor.

"Um, I think you've already been hitting the wine too hard," Serena replied, laughing.

"Stop being so Chinese and just accept the compliment!"

When Victor turned to talk to someone else, Serena looked him up and down. *Nice, smartly cut tux, looking a bit like a young Andy Lau. I never knew he could look so good.*

As they sat down at the table, he said, "I know you're not a big fan of mine."

"We all have to do what's best for us. No judgment here," Serena said.

Victor appeared to relax a bit and they went on to discuss the wine, the charity, and mutual acquaintances at the gala.

"Did Heather tell you that Jack fixed my wall garden? He did a great job."

"Yes, he was really keen to thank you for all your help with the university essay."

"It was my first time seeing him in months. He has grown and filled out so much. He's not a boy anymore."

"I hear you. I think he weighs more than me now!"

After a few more drinks, the conversation turned to the gossip at Bamboo Towers.

"The Cartwrights are splitting up," said Victor.

"Cheating?"

"Yes, but it was her."

"Really?" gasped Serena. She was always surprised when it happened this way. She thought cheating to be the domain of men.

"I guess women can misbehave as much as men," Victor said with a cheeky grin. Serena wasn't sure why, but she blushed. "Fancy some Veuve?" he asked.

"Why not?"

They finished the bottle between them.

After dinner they shared an Uber home together. "My driver gets off at eight p.m.," he explained.

"Problems of the 1 percent," she laughed.

"Lucky we got one before the typhoon hits. It's already a T3."

"They're expecting the observatory to raise the T8 flag overnight."

The mundane weather talk quickly turned into drunken flirting.

"For the record, I think Cole is a complete loser," said

Victor. "What was he thinking letting someone as smart and gorgeous as you get away?"

"I guess he isn't very good at thinking," said Serena with a giggle.

"He wasn't man enough to appreciate what he had."

"And you think *you* would be?"

"Definitely."

She didn't do anything to actively discourage Victor. It had been awhile since a man had so conspicuously found her attractive. They got out of the car and walked arm in arm to the lift. When it stopped at Serena's floor, he grabbed her hand and said, "Nightcap?"

She considered it for a second, but then shook her head. "Heather," she responded.

"No one needs to know," said Victor.

"It's very tempting, but I can't. *We* can't."

"Message received," said Victor with a smile.

"Thanks for a wonderful evening." She kissed him on the cheek before he continued up in the elevator.

Serena felt like she was on a high. She hadn't felt that way in such a long time, and it was Victor Wong of all people who made her feel desirable again. She had never really thought about him in that way before, but there was no denying that he was attractive. She decided to forego her everyday Marks & Spencer sensible pajamas and put on her red silk slip from Agent Provocateur. It used to be her Saturday-night go-to outfit when she and Cole had their standing appointment for sex. But it had been sitting in the back of her top drawer for too long. She checked herself out in the mirror. *Not bad for forty-three,* she thought. From the fridge, she pulled a half-empty bottle of wine and headed out to the balcony. *A nightcap is not a bad idea after all.* She relaxed on the outdoor sofa watching the imminent storm roll in across the ocean.

There was a light knocking at the door. *Victor, I can't believe you have the cheek to come back*, she thought as she walked toward the door. She opened it and was startled to see not Victor, but Jack.

"I forgot my pocketknife outside and I need it in the morning for my hike," he said. "I came by earlier but no one was home."

"Of course, come on in. Thanks again for everything."

They went onto the balcony and he found his knife next to the wall garden.

"Doesn't look like you'll have decent weather for a hike tomorrow," said Serena.

Jack eyed the wine bottle. "Is there enough for me?" he asked. "I was just at a beach party, but we had to pack it in early because of the storm."

Serena laughed. The beach was a favorite drinking hangout for underaged international schoolkids, who partied literally right under the noses of their parents.

She poured him a glass of wine and they drank in silence, both leaning on the railing, holding it tightly so they wouldn't get blown away by the wind.

"You have a really nice view," said Jack.

"You have the exact same view, just from higher up," she said.

"The roaring sea looks beautiful. You look beautiful."

She ignored him and continued to look out at the horizon.

"The typhoon is about to land." The brewing storm, the thrashing wind, the champagne, the nightcap—it all contributed to her relaxed state. He looked at her, eyes moving down her silk slip, resting hungrily on her erect nipples visible from underneath. She felt a slight degree of satisfaction that he was turned on by her. *He looks so much like Victor now, maybe even better.*

"You are very sexy in red." He touched the small of her back gently.

She was surprised at his confidence. But she didn't pull back or flinch. He moved his hand lower and caressed her bottom. *Oh my God, this is so wrong.*

"Wait," she said as he kissed her neck.

"Wait for what?" he asked, slowly lifting her slip. He kissed her with his soft full lips and she couldn't bring herself to say more. He gingerly moved his fingers between her legs before gliding them into her. First one, then more. She was surprised that she was so hot, so wet, so inviting. She didn't want him to stop. She sucked her breath in and tried to muffle her moans. They moved to the sofa, legs intertwined, and he lifted her slip further and revealed her breasts. He caressed them and gently bit her nipples. He kissed her stomach and then slid down between her legs, moving his tongue in ways that delivered concentrated bursts of pleasure, before finally plunging himself into her. As he moved in and out, her pulse raced and all her senses were heightened. Her cries of delight were masked by the storm to all but him.

After they lay on the couch in silence for a few moments, Serena got up. "You should go home," she said.

He gave her a gentle kiss on the cheek and left. Serena promptly ran to the bathroom and threw up.

From that night onward, Serena avoided Heather out of shame and guilt, making up excuse after excuse.

"You're missing book club?" asked Heather one afternoon over the phone.

"Sorry, work call. New York this time."

"Okay, but are we still on for Friday night?"

"About that, I have to take a rain check. Big client in town and I have to take her out." One side of her head told her that it was no big deal, he was eighteen and about to leave home for good. The other side reminded her that she had betrayed her best friend.

Serena couldn't sleep and started seeing things that weren't there. Jack on the balcony, in the window reflections, in her dreams. Sometimes she would dream that they were having hot and heavy sex, other times that he was crying into his mother's lap. Serena went to her special pharmacy where everything was available without a prescription and stocked up on sleeping pills. She started taking the maximum dose before bed every night.

Based on her recent messages of concern—*Where are you? Don't work too hard!*—Serena guessed that Heather had no idea what had happened. She imagined that Jack would post about their encounter or that he had discretely taken some photos of her in her red slip. But even though she checked it every day, there was nothing on his Facebook or Instagram. *What if he uses Snapchat?* she thought. She needed to get away for a bit. If she could avoid bumping into Jack for the next few weeks, he would be off working at a camp in the US for the entire summer and from there straight to university. She checked out Cole's page. More baby photos. More happy-family photos. This firmed up her resolve to get out of town. Serena engineered a four-week trip to work out of the London office, telling her colleagues that she needed to oversee the details of a hostile takeover in person.

Time away in London turned out to be just what Serena needed. She felt like her misstep was just that, and now she was back on solid footing. Maybe she needed to travel more with work, be on-site more. That would get her away from

Cole, his wife, and their new baby. She deleted her Facebook account one night so she wouldn't see their tagged photos of weekend junk boats, group hikes, and free-flow brunches, all things they used to enjoy doing together. She also resolved to find new hobbies and new friends. Maybe she'd download that dating app where she could swipe right. At work, there was a deal brewing in Shanghai and a road show through Southeast Asia that she could supervise. That would keep her out of Hong Kong for most of the summer.

Decision made, Serena finally fell asleep. It was the first time in weeks that she slept without the aid of any pills.

Serena arrived home rested and relaxed. Four weeks had done wonders. Only now had her head cleared enough for her to realize it had been six weeks since her last period. She grabbed a taxi to a pharmacy in Aberdeen, where she was sure she wouldn't bump into anyone she knew. She got home, ripped the cellophane off the box, and peed on the stick. Sheer terror filled her as the double pink lines appeared.

That evening, Heather came into the flat with a bottle of Veuve. "Time to celebrate! Jack left last night for California. And we haven't had a drink together in weeks!" As much as she tried, Serena could not stop her body from shaking and tears from welling. "Oh my God, what's wrong?" asked Heather as Serena sobbed on her shoulder.

"I'm pregnant." She made up some story about a drunken one-night stand with someone in London. Serena continued to sob and blubber, while Heather stroked her head. "I didn't think I really wanted kids, but now I'm not sure . . . Maybe I do . . . I'm forty-three . . . This might be my only chance."

Heather asked Serena again about the father.

"There is no father . . . I don't even know his name."

Heather took her by the shoulders and looked her in the eyes. "You can raise it by yourself. You have the financial means, and you would have help. It's not a bad place to be a single mom. Plus, you have loads of friends who would support you."

Serena was comforted by Heather's faith that she would be a good mother. But guilt made bile rise to her mouth. She would never tell anyone who the father was. Ever.

Serena started spending her evenings reading up on what to expect in the next few months, searching Pinterest for nursery décor ideas, and cooing over the cute array of baby clothes available.

On Thursday evening of the following week, Serena heard loud banging at her front door. *What the hell is going on?* She looked through her peephole. Heather was disheveled and mascara was smeared down her face. Serena opened the door to let her in. "Are you okay?"

"Am I okay? No, I'm not fucking okay!" snapped Heather. "You selfish bitch! You slut! What did you do to my poor Jack?"

Serena stood there mouth agape. "What are you talking about?"

"You lying bitch. Don't you pretend you don't know what I'm talking about. I just spoke with Jack. He asked me how you were and I let it slip that you're pregnant."

A wave of panic filled Serena from head to toe.

"Then he started crying, asking if it's his. You fucked my son?! What were you thinking? You are ruining my family. This is my life that you are destroying!"

Serena tried to deflect the truth. "It's not his . . ." she started.

"Don't even go there. You're a shitty liar."

"It was an accident. I'll raise it on my own. Jack never needs to know who the father is," pleaded Serena.

"But I will know! You're ruining everything I have ever worked for! How dare you take advantage of him?" She pointed her finger accusingly in Serena's face.

"I did not take advantage of him. He was the one who came over to my flat."

"You're the freaking adult in this equation. You seduced him and took his innocence away!" yelled Heather, as spit gathered at the corners of her mouth.

"Wake up, Heather, he was no virgin!" yelled Serena.

Heather picked up Serena's favorite Aalto vase, filled with fresh-cut camellias, and threw it at her head. Serena jumped aside and the vase hit the wall, shattering into hundreds of razor-sharp shards of glass.

Serena started taking pills again to sleep. Herbal pills, so as not to hurt the baby, but sleeping pills nonetheless. Again, she started seeing things, things that weren't there. But this time she didn't see Jack. She saw Heather. Heather screaming expletives at her. Heather pouring her a glass of champagne, then tossing it in her face. Heather on the balcony ripping out her flowers.

A week or so later, Serena was in her drugged sleep when she awoke to a loud bang coming from the balcony. Was she dreaming? No, the noise seemed all too real. She got out of bed, put on her robe, and went to the living room. She opened the door to the balcony and saw that the wall garden had fully collapsed. Plants and dirt were strewn everywhere, her camellias beyond saving.

A piece of paper fluttering in the wind, tucked into one of the hanging planters, caught her eye. She tried to grab it, but it was too high. It was a letter and she could read part of it. *Dear Heather, I cannot face the world anymore . . .* She could not make out the rest.

She grabbed a stool to reach for it, but suddenly felt a heavy hand on her back, a violent push from behind. She looked back and saw Heather on her balcony. As she fell, she glimpsed Repulse Bay—the beautiful view that had cost her so much—for a split-second before it all went dark.

EXPENSIVE TISSUE PAPER

BY FENG CHI-SHUN

Diamond Hill

D iamond Hill—what a glorious name for a place. No one outside of Hong Kong would have guessed it was the moniker of a squatter village in Kowloon East. In the fifties and sixties, it was a ghetto with its share of grime and crime, and sleaze oozing from brothels, opium dens, and underground gambling houses. There and then, you found no diamonds but plenty of poor people residing on its muddy slopes. Most refugees from mainland China settled in dumps like this because the rent was dirt cheap.

Hong Kong began prospering in the seventies and eighties, and its population exploded, partly due to the continued influx of refugees. Large-scale urbanization and infrastructure development moved at breakneck speed. There was no longer any room for squatter villages or shantytowns. By the late eighties, Diamond Hill was chopped into pieces and demolished bit by bit with the construction of the six-lane Lung Cheung Road in its north, the Tate's Cairn Tunnel in its northwest, and its namesake subway station in its south. Only its southern tip had survived. More than two hundred families and businesses crammed together in this remnant of Diamond Hill, where the old village's flavor lingered. Its buildings remained a mishmash of shoddy low-rise brick houses and bungalows, shanties, tin huts, and illegal shelters made of planks and tar paper occupying every nook and cranny. There was not a single thoroughfare wide enough for cars. The only access was by foot using narrow lanes flanked by gutters. The lanes branched out and merged, twisted and turned, and dead-ended at tall fences built to separate the village from the outside world. The village was like a maze.

The last of Diamond Hill's residents were on borrowed time and borrowed land. They had already received eviction notices from the Hong Kong government, and all had made plans for the future. The government promised to compensate longtime residents for vacating the land, but not the new arrivals.

The most recent arrival to the village was a young girl named Ling. She was trouble. She soon wreaked hell and havoc on one neighboring family.

Ling had recently come from China to be reunited with her mother, Mrs. Cheuk, who had been living in Diamond Hill for about five years, short of the seven years of residence required to qualify for government compensation.

Mrs. Cheuk was a Hong Kong native. She had gone to her ancestral village in Hunan province to marry her cousin a few years after the Cultural Revolution. Ling was her only child. When Ling was thirteen years old, her father died, and livelihood issues forced Mrs. Cheuk to return to Hong Kong. She found a dishwashing job in a Mong Kok restaurant. Her pay was commensurate with a Diamond Hill abode.

Before leaving Hunan, Mrs. Cheuk had entrusted her brother to care for her young daughter, and that was a big mistake. Her brother was a sexual predator.

Ling's maternal uncle, whom she called Uncle Xia, worked in a machine factory. Lifting heavy equipment had conditioned him into a rugged man, with big calloused hands, broad shoulders, and bulging biceps. He made good use of his muscles at home too, to discipline his wife.

Xia's wife was a weak and simple woman. She was terrified of him because he was brutal with her. Whenever he was displeased with anything in the household, a fist to her ribs or a kick to her side would make her see things his way.

Xia belonged to a breed of mainland men obsessed with pornography. He watched it openly and frequently, as if it were a normal hobby. He and his pals would gather in the evening in the living room for a long session of skin-flick viewing while drinking and snacking, like American men getting together for Monday Night Football. His wife prepared the snacks and drinks, but made sure her son and Ling were not around for the show. They were told to stay in their rooms whenever Xia's friends showed up with videotapes.

Uncle Xia was strict with Ling, but that was only until she turned fifteen and her breasts had a growth spurt. He started looking at her funny sometimes and made her blush furiously.

As you can guess, Xia sent his wife and son on a long trip one Sunday, and made Ling stay home with him. First, he drank some rice wine and ordered Ling to have some too. She took a sip, and complained that it burned her throat. Uncle Xia said sternly, "I have already poured you a glass. Don't make me angry by wasting the wine."

She drank some more. Her face turned red, her head became light, but the rice wine did go down easier after a few more gulps. Then he put on some porn for them to watch together. Ling didn't know what was going on with all those naked people moaning and groaning. All she wanted was to go back to her room and sleep. Uncle Xia pulled her onto his lap and put an arm around her waist while explaining all the actions on the screen. In his warped mind, he justified his behavior by Ling's need for some sex education.

The booze went to Ling's head fast, and she collapsed on

her uncle's lap. He groped her, and seeing no resistance, he carried her to her room.

She was in and out of consciousness for the rest of the evening. She felt a rough hand running over her naked body. She complained, but the stroking and poking didn't stop. Her breasts were kneaded and squeezed. Then came a sharp pain in her private parts, and she heard heavy breathing next to her ear.

Uncle Xia treated her much nicer after deflowering her. More pocket money, snacks, and kind words. After a porn night with his buddies, he routinely sneaked into her room and reenacted all he had learned from the Japanese blue movies. She was still afraid of him, but she played her hand the best she could. She knew what would make him happy—making the right kind of noises when he was in her, and uttering lame complaints about his size and virility. When she needed a new dress or handbag, she would ask him for it while he was taking a breather next to her after sex. She got by as long as she put out.

That was her early lesson in life—sex pays.

The incestuous relationship lasted two years.

One day, police came to their house and arrested Xia. He was soon brought to court and convicted of embezzlement—a grave crime because he was working for a state-owned enterprise. He was summarily sentenced and locked up.

Xia's wife threw Ling out of her house the same day Xia was jailed. "Don't think I don't know what's going on with you and my husband. Get out, you no-good whore," she seethed.

From Hunan, Ling took a bus to Shenzhen. She was then seventeen years old, but was still baby-faced, with large smoky eyes, pouting lips and pointy nose, a creamy complexion, and a natural blush on her dimpled cheeks. She was still petite, no more than five feet two and a hundred pounds, but her body had filled out, except for her twenty-inch waist.

She found a job as a waitress at a Hunan restaurant in Shenzhen. It wasn't a great job, but her one-year tenure there prepared her well for better things in the future.

Most of the restaurant patrons were men from Hong Kong who thought every mainland woman was an easy lay. Ling learned to speak Cantonese from them. She also learned how not to give anything away without offending any of them. In that respect, the restaurant owner, a woman of forty, was her good teacher.

The owner was also from Hunan. She was a woman with a past, having worked in a Shenzhen sauna for twenty years before she saved enough money to open a restaurant. A sauna in China was where men could pay for a massage, as well as, if so desired, a hand job, a blow job, or the whole shebang. Her "stage name" was Jenny and she kept it after she retired from the business. Jenny had in-depth knowledge of the sex trade. She was also well-informed, shrewd, and worldly. She took a shine to Ling, who looked up to her as an older and wiser sister. The girl confided in Jenny what her nasty uncle had done to her. Jenny said she wasn't surprised, because men were pigs and they liked young girls, the younger the better. She told Ling that her uncle had robbed her of something extremely valuable. Had she been in old Japan, she could have auctioned off the right to her first night as geishas did, and she would have earned millions.

Jenny had been to Hong Kong, and she convinced Ling the city across the border was paved with gold. Sometimes they watched TV programs from Hong Kong together, and Ling was mesmerized by the glitz and glamour. Ling contacted her mother and asked her to bring her to Hong Kong. Mrs.

Cheuk told her that Hong Kong was heaven if you had lots of money, but hell if you had none; and they had none.

Ling begged repeatedly. Mrs. Cheuk finally relented and went to the immigration department to inquire, but was told by the officials that by the time all the papers were processed, her daughter would be an adult nearly twenty years old, not a child dependent, and the chance of government approval would be close to zero.

Jenny came to the rescue. She knew someone back in Hunan who could issue Ling a birth certificate with any date of birth she wanted. All it took was a bribe, and she could bankroll it.

Ling's new birth certificate arrived in ten days, and just liked that she was three years younger. Not a problem with credibility either, because Ling did look like a fifteen-year-old.

Mrs. Cheuk submitted the paperwork to the immigration department. All they had to do was wait for the corresponding government department in China to do its part. Jenny also knew someone in Hunan who handled this kind of stuff, and there was nothing one could not buy in China. All the papers were ready in two months.

"I owe you so much, how can I ever repay you?" Ling asked Jenny.

"Come into my office. I am going to teach you how to make money in Hong Kong, now that you are fifteen once again. I want to make sure you don't give it away for free this time."

Ling settled with her mom in Diamond Hill. First thing first, she applied for and obtained her Hong Kong ID card.

"Who are the richest people in Diamond Hill?" she asked her mom.

It had to be the owners of the Chiu Chow restaurant, the biggest business remaining, and a landmark of Diamond Hill for decades. With a big payout from the government for re-location, they had already bought a place in Mong Kok for a new restaurant. They must have also stashed away loads of money from years of profitable business.

The restaurant was started by Old Man Cheng, who had died a few years back and left it for his oldest son to run. Everyone in the village called the new owner Uncle Cheng; his son looked just like him but fifty pounds heavier. Chubby, the son, worked as one of the cooks, while Uncle Cheng was the manager and cashier.

Ling called Jenny, and they mapped out a plan.

Ling went to the restaurant for meals. The old restaurant needed major repair work, but the owner could be forgiven for the neglect because its lifespan was no more than a few months. The toilets in the back were unusable because construction of the underground railway the year before had clogged up the sewage system. Uncle Cheng had to rent a small tin hut fifty yards away for its toilet facility. Customers had to walk that far to answer the call of nature, but it was Diamond Hill on its deathbed; people understood.

When Ling went to use the toilet, she noticed a neat little room next to the toilet, furnished with a desk and a cot—probably used as a makeshift office and rest area for the boss.

Ling and Jenny talked again.

Getting to know Chubby was easy. He liked playing video games after work in the rustic arcade down the lane from the restaurant.

Ling sidled up to him, smelling good and looking cute.

Chubby turned his head from his game and stared at the

pretty young thing. After a minute or two, he gathered his courage and broke the ice: "Can I help you?"

"How do you play this game?" Ling asked with a coy smile.

Chubby showed off his video game skills. He asked how old she was.

"Eighteen." Her real age.

"You look younger. I'm twenty-five," Chubby said.

Ling commented that he, too, looked young. And handsome.

Two youngsters getting acquainted fast—nothing extraordinary there. It was Chubby's day off the next day. They agreed to go to the movies together.

In the air-conditioned cinema, Ling complained that her hands were freezing, and would it be too forward for her to put her hands on Chubby's thigh to keep warm? She said she felt secure with a big guy like Chubby. She then put Chubby's hand on her bare thigh, and said they were now even. Chubby had never had a girlfriend, and this was heaven on earth. He began to caress her smooth thigh.

Ling rose to visit the bathroom. On her way back, she tried putting her hands back on his thigh, but in the dark she fumbled and "accidentally" brushed his crotch. Ling had proof he was highly aroused.

She cut to the chase, whispering, "I am as aroused as you are. Take me somewhere, now!"

Chubby was too overwhelmed to think straight. Ling took control and suggested they go to the tin hut with the toilet. The restaurant had closed, no one would be using it, and he had the key.

Chubby had experience with sex, but only with hookers. He only knew the wham-bam-thank-you-ma'am kind of sex. Ling pretended she was a virgin. She lay down on the cot naked with her eyes half-closed, hoping he knew what he was doing.

Foreplay was a concept alien to Chubby. He tried to mount her right away, but he wasn't the suave and graceful sort. In his eagerness, he overshot her body and almost fell to the other side of the cot. Ling had to grab his arm to steady him.

He managed to get himself into position, and immediately started to move frantically atop Ling. She could hardly breathe. Good thing it was quick.

As soon as he was done, she pushed him off her. She pulled a tissue from her purse and cleaned herself with it, then dropped it back in her purse. Seeing Chubby's puzzled look, she said, "We don't want anyone to find the tissue in here, do we?"

When they were leaving, Chubby asked, "When can I see you again?"

Ling waved and said, "Yeah."

One down; one to go.

Ling had already talked to Uncle Cheng a few times in the restaurant. He always looked her over, and his eyes lingered at the two swellings on her chest way too long.

He had a wife, but catching him alone wasn't difficult because he was the one who locked up the joint every night.

She showed up around closing time.

"We're closed," Uncle Cheng said. "I can make you something myself, but it will cost you." He was flirting with her.

She looked at him innocently, batting her eyes. "But how much?"

"A million dollars, ha-ha-ha."

"I am not like you—you are rich, I am poor. But I'm young."

"How young are you?" Uncle Cheng couldn't help himself.

"Eighteen."

"You look younger."

Jenny had said, *The younger the better.*

"Okay, just this once, I won't charge you anything."

"Can I go in the kitchen so I can see you cook?" Ling asked.

While he was making the noodles, Ling watched him admiringly. She complimented him on his physique, making it plain she liked men with muscles and not fat. Uncle Cheng, at the age of fifty-three, had a paunch and a receding hairline, and was not exactly a specimen for GQ, but compared to his son, he was a hunk. Besides, what men wouldn't like compliments from a cute girl?

Uncle Cheng was more of a schemer than his young son. He told Ling to carry the bowl of noodles to the tin hut to eat there, because he had to close the shop.

Ling was about done with the noodles when he entered the hut with a bottle of rice wine. He plonked down two glasses and said, "Have a drink with me to celebrate the opening of my new restaurant."

"How much does it cost you to open your new restaurant?" Ling asked.

"I've already bought the shop, and it's going to cost me another million dollars to renovate it, but it'll be perfect," he boasted.

"Waaah. So much money!" Ling stuck out her tongue. "I'll celebrate with you, but I get drunk easily." She batted her eyes at him again.

"All right then, I'll give you a handicap. You take half a glass; I'll have a full one."

"That's still not fair; you are ten times bigger than I am."

Ling put her small hand around his biceps and barely covered half its girth. "Waaah," she said, rolling her eyes.

Uncle Cheng laughed heartily. He felt big.

Ling took a gulp of the wine, then another. Her cheeks soon turned red, and she looked prettier than ever in the dim light. They were sitting side by side on the cot when she leaned over and rested her head on his chest. She didn't have to do much after that. Uncle Cheng pulled her into his lap, kissed her, and undressed her.

It took him awhile to get done. He was older and more ex-perienced, and the alcohol numbed him somewhat. She had to make noises she'd learned from watching porn with Uncle Xia to finish him off more quickly.

Every man who had violated her carried a distinct odor. Uncle Xia smelled like engine oil, Chubby smelled like fried chicken, Uncle Cheng smelled like sweat and tobacco.

Jenny was spot on: *Men are pigs.*

Uncle Cheng was vain. While they were putting their clothes back on, he said, "That felt good, didn't it? You can't get any better than that."

Ling spoke with Jenny again on the phone, and together they planned the coup de grâce. Ling called Chubby to meet.

"I have something for you to show your parents," Ling greeted him, handing him a photocopy of her ID card.

Chubby examined it closely, and after noticing the date of birth, he got the message. "You are not yet sixteen, oh my God."

"You are going to jail, loverboy."

"But you said you were eighteen."

"Tell that to the judge."

"What do you want?"

"Your family is rich, we are poor; you got compensated for being evacuated, but my mother gets nothing. How about you pay us a million dollars to buy a flat to live in?"

"I'll deny everything." Chubby was almost in tears.

"You are fat and stupid. Remember how I cleaned myself with a tissue? It has your semen on it, and a test can confirm it's yours. You can't deny it in court. Talk to your lawyer, loverboy."

"My parents won't pay."

"Then you go to jail. I'll give you seven days."

She left it at that.

For the following two days, Chubby struggled with the thought of killing Ling, or himself, or both. On the third day, he went to his mother and told her the kind of trouble he was in. She flipped out, screaming bloody murder. She rushed toward the door, threatening to go to the police station in her pajamas and flip-flops. Chubby blocked her exit.

"Going to the police is what she is threatening to do, Mom."

She returned to the living room, still in hysterics. "The moment I laid eyes on her, I knew she was wicked!" she yelled. "Such an evil slut, a mainland prostitute, a no-good scum of the earth, cheaper than dog turd, filthier than kitchen tiles!" When she got tired of cursing, she turned to her son. She put a finger to Chubby's temple and savagely pushed it. Chubby stumbled but managed to keep his balance. He kept his head bowed.

"How can you be so stupid?" she spat. "We'll wait for your father to come home. Maybe he can think of something."

"I wish you wouldn't tell him," Chubby mumbled.

"We don't have a choice, do we? I can't get hold of such a large sum of money without him."

"He'll go berserk, Mom. He'll say no, and he'll throw me out of the house."

Mom finally calmed down. She ordered her son to go take a shower.

"You smell like fried chicken. And go to your room after the shower. Let me talk to your father alone. "

She made herself a cup of tea, and began to mull over how to talk to her husband about this mess.

Uncle Cheng arrived home in a good mood that night. Business was good. The bag of money he was carrying was bursting at its seams.

"You are going to the bank to deposit the cash tomorrow, right?" she asked casually. "How much money do we have in savings, anyway?"

"More than a million," he said. "More than enough to renovate and equip our new restaurant."

She began to weep. Uncle Cheng chided her for always spoiling a pleasant evening. He lit up a cigarette, and poured himself a small dram of double-distilled rice wine. He sat next to her on the settee and asked, "What now?"

"It's your son. He is in loads of trouble," she said. "Remember that mainland girl who went to the movies with him last Tuesday? They had sex that night, in the tin hut we're renting for its toilet."

"So?" said Uncle Cheng, who blushed, though his wife didn't notice. She was busy wiping tears.

"Three days ago, she came to him with a copy of her Hong Kong ID card, asking for a million dollars."

Uncle Cheng sat straight up, eyes wide, mouth agape.

"She is under sixteen, and she is threatening to go to the police."

Uncle Cheng turned ashen. He took a big swig of the

firewater, and sucked furiously on his cigarette. "How do we know her ID card is genuine?"

"Chubby saw the original, it's real."

"How can she even prove they had sex? "

"This is where you can help me understand. She wiped herself with a tissue after the sex, and she kept the tissue. She told your son it could be tested for something called DNA to confirm it was his semen. Have you ever heard of something like that?"

Uncle Cheng slumped back onto the settee. He closed his eyes because he was afraid they would betray him. Even with his eyes closed, he could recall the young girl using a tissue to wipe herself, right after he pulled out of her. He had joked, "Keeping it as a souvenir?" while pinching her nipple playfully.

He rose to pour himself a full glass of double-distilled. He took a few quick quaffs.

"Basically, she is extorting him for a million dollars in exchange for that lousy filthy piece of tissue," the wife said.

Two pieces, Uncle Cheng thought.

She started to cry again. "We need the money to open our new restaurant. The government is going to raze the rest of Diamond Hill, and our restaurant will go within months. What are we going to do? Maybe we'll just let Chubby go to jail—serves him right."

Uncle Cheng poured himself one more full glass of double-distilled and sat there quietly for a long while before he spoke. "I think we can manage to open our new restaurant without the money in the bank. We can borrow from my sister and some of our loyal employees, giving them shares of the new company," he said in a monotone, like a robot announcing a death sentence. "We cannot let our son go to jail. It'll ruin his whole life." *And mine*, he thought. "We'll go to the bank tomorrow and withdraw a million dollars in cash."

He swallowed the rest of the glass in a big gulp, then staggered out of the room.

Ling called Jenny. "I've wired you your 30 percent. By the way, how were you so sure they'd pay up?"

"Because no one in the family could object to paying," Jenny said. "The son doesn't want to go to jail; the mother will do anything to save her son; and the father has the most to lose—the publicity alone would ruin his marriage and business. Tell me again: how many more months before you turn sixteen?"

"Four."

"Okay, I want you to move to somewhere more upmarket, right away. I've heard the Mid-Levels on Hong Kong Island is where rich people live. We've got work to do, to make real money. It's time to say goodbye to Diamond Hill."

PART IV

Death & Thereafter

BLOOD ON THE STEPS

BY SHANNON YOUNG

The Pottinger Steps

The old man assembled the skeleton on the steps. Ribs laid out, one by one. Joints clicking and clacking as the pieces fell into place. The skull sat a few feet down, perched on the same worn step where the old man squatted. He focused on his task, switching around the mismatched ribs as if solving a jigsaw puzzle, occasionally reaching for another bone from the pile beside him.

The other vendors paid little attention. The old man had kept his stall along the Pottinger Steps for the past fourteen years. Bones and bloodied limbs and ghastly masks always hung from his racks. The rest of the macabre wares were covered for the night now, hidden away beneath a plastic tarp as the October sun slipped behind the tower blocks.

The old man chewed on his lower lip, mumbling curses befitting his grisly task.

A long shadow stretched across the skeleton as it neared completion. The click-clack of the bones ceased.

"You have come again," the old man said.

The shadow did not respond.

"Will you speak to me this time?"

Again, no answer.

The woman who sold paper lanterns across the steps glanced at the hunched figure squatting above the skeleton. Her customers, backpackers, were whispering to each other about whether or not her pretty painted lanterns would survive their journey. They fell silent, catching sight of the man mumbling to no one over the bones.

"What is the price?" the old man said. "I know there must be a price."

The woman gave an overloud laugh and dangled another lantern before her customers, drawing their eyes to the red-and-gold shimmer. It wouldn't be the first time the old man had scared away her business with his mutterings. His own shop had done uncommonly well in recent years, but his mannerisms had become increasingly unsettling.

"I cannot pay unless I know the price."

The spectral presence seemed to laugh, though there was no sound but the grumble of the city. Then it was gone, taking any chance of absolution with it.

The old man sighed and bent lower to begin wiring the skeleton back together. This one would hang from his stall come morning, ready to draw the eye of the crowds that shuffled up and down the steps each day, playing at bartering, giggling at his grotesquery. The crowds had flocked to his stall these past few years. For his masks and costume limbs. Blood paint. Bones.

Plastic clattered in his shaky fingers as he secured the final rib in place. Just another bag of cheaply made bones. The skeleton would sell, as always, for far more than it was worth. But that came at a different kind of price. There was always a price. The question was when he would have to pay.

His task complete, the old man reached for the skull.

Amanda Choi hurried along Queen's Road Central, dodging shopping bags and skirting around charity peddlers. She was going to be late, even though she'd left the instant she'd recieved the text. She was always just a little too late.

She charged up the Pottinger Steps, taking the uneven slabs two at a time. The steps were at their steepest where they met Queen's Road and climbed past the old Pottinger Hotel, which had recently been renovated to welcome yet another luxury shop. The crisp windows winked at her as she ducked around a wedding photo shoot, passed the juice stand smelling of mango, and reached the first crossing.

A large lorry blocked her view of the second section of the historic steps, which climbed another two lengths through Central to Hollywood Road. The Saturday-morning bustle surrounded her, as more tourists climbed the first row of steps and waited for the lorry to pass. The blare of taxi horns to her right announced trouble brewing between the drivers, but Amanda didn't bother to investigate. She finally had a real story to cover.

The lorry lurched out of her way, revealing the crowd gathered behind a double row of yellow tape blocking off the rest of the steps. Above them, the market stalls lining both sides of the steep lane rose in multicolored layers. Flags, lanterns, and decorations hung from the stalls like banyan vines. Costumes of all shapes and varieties—extra stock in preparation for the holidays—spilled from plastic tubs and swayed from racks on the walls. As Amanda crossed the street, a stiff breeze tore down the steps, making the colorful wares flutter like tropical birds.

Amanda squeezed through the crowd, grateful for her slight stature for once, and ducked under the yellow tape.

Her new boss, Hugh, was waiting for her.

"You're late."

She wasn't. "Yes sir. Sorry."

Hugh gave a wet, throat-clearing harrumph and gestured toward the steps with sweaty hands.

"What do you make of this?"

Amanda was already wheezing from charging up the slope, so she hoped he didn't notice her gasp at the sight of the blood pooling on the steps. No, it didn't pool—it flooded. Crimson spread from step to step in grim rivulets. Blood threaded outward through hairline crevices, some already turning brown. At the bottom, the tide turned into a culvert beside the road, where the evidence drip-dropped into the sewer.

"It's a lot of blood."

Hugh snorted, and Amanda tried to gather her thoughts, to say something intelligent. But the question that sprang to her lips hardly seemed any better. "But . . . where's the body?"

The great flood of blood splattered over half a dozen steps to the left side of the lane, but there wasn't a corpse in sight.

"No body."

"At all?" Amanda struggled to keep the disappointment from her voice. "The text said it was a murder."

"This is enough blood for two murders."

"But there's no body?"

Her boss gave another sticky cough.

Great impression you're making, Amanda.

"So we're here to report on a murder without a body? Were there any witnesses? Any idea who the victim might have been?"

"No word yet on if it's even human."

A uniformed police officer bustled over to shoo them back behind the caution tape before Amanda could respond, but she dismissed that suggestion at once. It couldn't be animal blood. That would be no story at all.

She stood her ground at the front of the crowd, jotting down any information she could glean from the bystanders. No one had seen anything unusual. The pool of blood had been reported by the first vendor to arrive at the steps that morning, a paper lantern maker whose stall was about ten steps up from the crime scene.

"I thought it was red paint," the woman said when Amanda approached her for a quote. "But then I noticed the smell. Blood doesn't stink like paint."

"There were no people around at the time?"

"None."

"Who owns this shop?" Amanda looked up at the stall nearest to the blood splatter; it seemed to specialize in feather boas, animal masks, and sequined hats.

"Mr. and Mrs. Cheung have run that shop for forty years, but they're in Guangzhou now. Their boy is around here somewhere. Probably slunk off to grab a cigarette."

"We'll want to check on the Cheungs," Amanda said. "And make sure all the other shopkeepers are accounted for."

She hoped the victim wasn't one of the old shopkeepers. That wouldn't make nearly enough of a story. A few things were required to make a murder into a real story. Sex. Money. Foreigners—preferably young, wealthy ones.

Amanda caught her boss giving her a flint-eyed look, and she struggled to keep the calculations from her face. She suspected Hugh knew a little too much about her history. This was her first big shot since she came back to Hong Kong, and she wasn't going to waste it. She would have to tread lightly if this murder was going to make her name.

The blood splatter drew her gaze again. The puddle was almost square due to the way it spread and seeped down the steps. The edges smudged here and there, but there wasn't so much as a footprint leading away. Even if the person who had bled so much wasn't dead, she didn't see how they could possibly have walked away—or been carried—without leaving a trail.

She glanced up. No overhanging balconies or scaffolds from which the blood could have dripped. It was as if the victim had bled out on the steps and then vanished.

Pictures of the crime scene exploded onto front pages everywhere. The puddle of blood had appeared in one of the most famous tourist sites in the city. Lined with uneven stone slabs, the precarious street had once divided the neighborhoods where European and Chinese residents lived. Now people from all over the world ascended from the expensive glass world of Central to peruse the ramshackle stalls for costumes, holiday decorations, and stationery. The former East-West divide now funneled people together, a microcosm of what Hong Kong had declared itself to be: Asia's World City, a commercial center for a globalized world.

Amanda played up the iconic locale in her initial article. The Pottinger Steps, as seen in hundreds of postcards and thousands of vacation photos, now marred with a gory mystery. She relayed the facts of the case but emphasized the horror of the bystanders upon learning of a bloody murder in the center of one of the safest cities on the planet.

Hugh gave an approving nod when he read the piece and told her to write another.

She had her angle, but there was still no body. The surrounding buildings, alleys, and construction sites were searched thoroughly over the following week. The Cheungs were indeed alive and well in Guangzhou, and none of the other vendors were missing. In fact, no one had been reported missing in the entire city since that Friday, leaving the police—and the reporters—without a single lead.

Amanda figured it was better this way. The sheer quantity

of blood virtually guaranteed a murder had taken place, but the trail ended at the bottom of the steps. Without a suspect or a known victim, the case was a blank canvas.

So Amanda spun her tale. She wrote a new article as sensational as any tabloid screed. She drew from stories of other famous murders. Poisoned milkshakes and bodies wrapped in Persian carpets. Dismembered heads stuffed in Hello Kitty dolls. Drug-fueled escapades. Sex games gone wrong. She didn't shy away from the most lurid theories and the most unlikely of scenarios.

She posted the article to the paper's blog in the small hours of the following Friday morning, so that by the time her boss noticed it had already been shared thousands of times overseas.

Hugh cornered her at her desk before noon. "What is this shit?" Sweaty fingers held the phone screen in front of her face. "Who are your sources?"

"It's an ongoing story."

"What's that supposed to mean?"

"They're theories." Amanda had prepared for this. "I don't actually *say* any of those things happened."

"This says the victim is a tourist *possibly from a Western country.*"

"It says the victim *could* be a tourist," Amanda corrected, "possibly even a tourist from a Western country who hasn't been reported missing yet."

Suggesting the victim was a tourist would get almost as many clicks and shares as hinting sex workers were involved. She was saving that for the next article. In the meantime, she was already getting messages from readers with theories about who the victim could have been. Missing person cases from all over the globe were pouring into her inbox, accompanied by wild explanations for how the individuals could have ended up on a historic lane in Hong Kong on a Friday night.

Her boss wasn't finished. "Do you know how this looks?"

"There's nothing libelous," Amanda said. "I checked."

"This isn't that kind of paper."

Amanda made soothing noises as she checked her phone under the desk. A Chinese news site had put together an animation showing murder methods that could release that much blood. The local news always used the most graphic imagery. She texted a friend to see if she could get a similar video, with the iconic Pottinger Steps as the backdrop.

A sticky cough. "Amanda."

"People are reading it, Hugh," she said. "You're selling ads off the clicks. Isn't that why you hired me?"

Hugh's phone buzzed, and he fumbled at it with his clammy fingers. "I won't have any more of that stuff here. This isn't like your last job."

Amanda shrugged. Of course it was. Every news job was alike these days. She got the clicks, and that was all that mattered.

Others soon took notice of those clicks. Amanda suspected most news outlets had been about to let the story go. With no leads and no body, it might not even be a murder. But then they saw the kind of traffic Amanda's article was getting, and they wanted in. Then there were think pieces. Hot takes. Specials. Photos of flowers and stuffed toys left on the steps in memory of the unknown victim.

When the police issued a statement reiterating that no body had been found, reputable sites used *Breaking News* banners and flashy graphics to cover it. Amanda's story was already too big to kill.

It didn't matter that no one had been confirmed dead. That's what Amanda understood. People were still clicking, still swapping theories. Reporters all over the globe interviewed the families of missing persons, trying to find a Hong Kong connection, however tenuous, to link their stories. Tourists wandered up and down the Pottinger Steps, taking pictures of the lurid costumes hanging above the now blood-free stones. History buffs dined out on the tale of the World War II air-raid shelter that had been built beneath the steps and later filled in. Bloggers wrote exaggerated accounts of harrowing experiences in the area—rare though they were—and tagged Amanda in their posts. Everyone wanted a piece of the action.

Amanda's work got more and more attention. No one was talking Pulitzer not for this kind of thing, but they were hanging on her every blood-tinged word.

She became addicted to the commentary, the feedback. She'd had a hint of this before at her old job. It hadn't worked out then. The wrong angle turned into a sticky mess that ended with her being packed off to the Hong Kong office. She'd probably taken that last theory too far. But this time was different. She could feel it.

Other reporters wrote balanced meditations on what led people to disappear in this shiny metropolis. They mused on inequality, lack of accountability, economic desperation. Some came up with thoughtful analyses of what made it possible to be so anonymous you could be murdered without being missed in Hong Kong.

Hugh suggested, none too gently, that Amanda should write something like that.

But Amanda didn't care about the balanced takes. She got the clicks, and that was all that mattered.

At least for a little while.

* * *

As the weeks passed without a break in the case, much less an actual victim, new stories began to take precedence. The news cycled. Protests and politicians recaptured the attention of the public. A new food craze overtook social media.

There was still no body, no verified victim, but Amanda couldn't bear to move on to another story. A few readers still followed her, still sent her messages asking for the latest. When they did, she assured them a breakthrough was imminent. She offered up tantalizing details, hints of sex and drugs and dripping blood.

Hugh told her to work on other things, never repeating that single approving nod, never acknowledging the ad dollars she had brought in or the name she had begun to sketch out for herself. She had been so close. She had inhaled the intoxicating vapors of a truly sensational lead. Yet the big break eluded her.

And the news cycled.

"Enough," her boss said one afternoon. "You can't string this one out anymore. Go write about the election."

Amanda took to stalking the Pottinger Steps early in the morning, on her lunch break, late into the night. She needed another clue to what had happened that night, a new development to keep the story ticking.

The vendors quickly learned to avoid her questions, designed to tease out salacious quotes. They just wanted to sell wigs to rugby spectators and knickknacks to backpackers in peace. One day the woman who sold paper lanterns told Amanda she was bad for business, making the steps out to be an illicit corridor of sex and violence. "Go home," she said. "That is not Hong Kong."

The old man who worked at the stall across the way looked up. His rheumy eyes cleared as he met Amanda's gaze. Then he returned to rearranging the masks hanging from his stall. A row of limbs hung below them, painted blood dripping down rubber skin.

"There is always a price," he muttered to a plastic demon head. "Success can be bought, but the price is never up to you."

That Friday night, Amanda didn't leave after the vendors had packed away their stalls and shuffled down toward the bus stop. She was desperate now. She needed an angle that would bring the eyes of the world back to this spot. She sat on a broad step, her phone on one knee and a notepad and pen on the other, listening to the murmurs of the evening.

It was never fully dark or fully quiet in Central. City lights blotted out the stars. Taxis and lorries kept the silence at bay. Voices and laughter drifted over from Lan Kwai Fong, the nightlife district located a block away. Someone was always walking by, always looking on from the towers overhead.

Midnight came and went. Amanda clicked her pen. Click-clack beneath her thumb. A rat skittered over the old paving stones. A cat burst from the shadows, its tail flicking against her arm as it passed.

It must have happened on a night just like this, but it was too busy here, too bright and noisy. Someone should have seen. Someone should have heard. No one could get away with murder here.

Amanda's pen clicked. *What if it was just blood?* Click. *What if there had never been a murder at all?* Click-click-click.

No. She couldn't accept that. Anything but that. She needed some way to renew the cycle, to bring back the eyes and the clicks. She needed another hit.

A long shadow stretched across her back. A muttered phrase came back to her: *Success can be bought, but the price is never up to you.*

A young man stumbled down the steps toward her, weaving slightly. He wore a button-down shirt that had probably been crisp at the start of the night. He had a good-looking face, white, with designer glasses. His shoes hinted at money. They were the kind of shoes that would squeak across the floor of a bank or a law firm. The kind of shoes that held feet that people would miss. And that face would look great on the front page.

The click-click of the pen stopped. Amanda stood, grasping it tight.

The old man shuffled up the Pottinger Steps. Something felt different this morning. Different, but familiar. An extra smell mixed with the mango scent of the juice stand and the early-morning truck exhaust.

The old man's back creaked as he bent to undo the lock on his stall. It was already open. He knew then that the shadow had come again. The cycle continued, as the presence had promised the first time its shadow appeared over his shoulder.

He pulled back the door, revealing the rack holding his wares. Extra limbs hung from the stall, paint-red blood dripping onto the steps. The old man reached out to touch the rubber that wasn't rubber, the bright-white bones.

Four years earlier, desperate for success, he had promised the shadow a blood-price in exchange for a few good years. His mistake was that he never specified whose blood, or when it would be extracted. The shadow had haunted his successful years, reminding him that one day blood would spill, his or another's. The price was not up to him.

He pictured a pair of tourists buying lanterns, their bodies vanishing into shadow. And so much blood.

The shadow had proved crafty. It had used his debt to renew the cycle, to snare a new victim.

The morning crowds were beginning to climb the steps, already thronging toward this fresh spectacle. The old man turned to face them as sunlight cut straight through the long shadow behind him. The presence was gone. A price had been paid today. But not by him. Not this time.

The story was sensational. *Dismembered tourist hangs from vendor's stall alongside costume body parts after night of debauchery.* He had a handsome face. Expensive shoes. An Anglo-Saxon name. He'd been seen with a woman just after midnight, faceless, probably a sex worker. The backdrop was recognizable. Iconic. The body was real, every chopped-up piece of it.

It was the perfect story.

KAM TIN RED

BY SHEN JIAN
Kam Tin

The swine glistened in red, its limbs splayed out on a wooden board, having been carved straight down its front side. Uncle Number Two raised the cleaver high above his head, so that for a moment it reflected the noon sun and made me squint, then swung it down with swift swipes, each chop slicing through the crackling skin, the melting fat, and the juiced flesh, before hitting the board with a thump of finality.

We drew lots for the best pieces, and my father asked Uncle Number Two to chop our chunk of the right thigh into bite-sized pieces. They filled three Styrofoam boxes, one of which I took and opened as I walked through the rusted gates of our family cemetery.

I came here with my family each winter for Chinese New Year, when I would at least receive red envelopes, and each spring for Ching Ming, the tomb-sweeping festival I enjoyed only for the roast pork. This Ching Ming, I bit into another piece with each grave I passed, first the largest, my great-grandfather's, its mound as tall as me, the tombstone marked with euphemisms for anarchy. Here lay a general, not a warlord; a hero, not a fugitive.

Next were each of the general's nine wives. The tombstone of my own great-grandmother, Wife Number Three, was weathered but in a dignified way, as evidence of sturdiness and in contrast, my father always noted, to the grave of Wife Number Nine, which was still marked by only a plaque, and which on rainy days that softened the soil appeared almost fresh.

A few steps beyond Wife Number Nine's plaque was an unusually small banyan tree, and a few steps beyond the tree, a grave unlike the rest, for a relative from a contemporary generation, one of my father's distant cousins. There were no words of glory, not even expressions of piety or accomplishment. Just a man's name, Lee Koon Sang; his occupation, police constable; the year of his birth, 1946; and of his death, 1967.

December 9, 1967, was a Saturday. My father began that day, as he did all school days, by bowing in front of the smoky image of his grandfather, the general, hung too high to be dusted, over the altar at the center of the ancestral hall. The ancestral hall was the fulcrum of the family compound, a small walled village with ten interconnected houses, one for the general and one for each of his wives and their children. The village, run-down since the day it was built, slouched among the pastures of Kam Tin, in many ways the oldest part of Hong Kong, where families like the Tangs and the Mans had settled hundreds of years before the British had even heard of tea, let alone opium. They had fought the British occupation and lost, badly. As a consolation prize, they were as "indigenous" families given certain privileges under British rule, including political heft that they threw around Kam Tin and the wider Yuen Long area. My family is not indigenous; the general absconded to Hong Kong only *after* the British occupation, and his was a constant, fruitless struggle to wield anything close to the kind of influence he once did on the mainland.

He started by building the village, and on the road through Yuen Long between Kowloon and Shenzhen there was a brief incline from which, at least during my father's childhood, you could just make out the eaves of the ancestral hall. Under those eaves, beneath narrow murals depicting the general's military victories and the cobwebs that straddled them, my father lit three joss sticks and lowered them three times in the direction of the general's portrait. It was to thank the general, and receive his blessing, for the education my father received, for the blood the general shed so that his descendants could compete in schools instead of battlefields, for jobs instead of arms. My father was fifteen in 1967; he had been performing the ritual for ten years.

Every child of the village did the same. Brother Sang, as my father called him, did it until the day he was admitted to the police academy. My father wasn't close to Brother Sang—there were nearly a hundred cousins in their generation, some who couldn't recognize others—but he remembers the day of Brother Sang's police academy admission, because it was occasion for such a celebration that a pig was roasted in the courtyard, like on Ching Ming. It was also the last time my father saw Brother Sang's grandmother, Wife Number Nine.

There was a pig every time a child of the village found a way out, to the police academy or teacher's college or, more rarely, university, which was my father's goal and why, despite not believing the general's ghost could do anything for him, despite the sacrament seeming absurdly incongruous in a time of jetliners and the Beatles, he still went to the altar every morning, just in case.

That was what my father really loved: airplanes and rock and roll. When I was in primary school, on some Sunday afternoons—the only time of the week my father took off—

my father and I would take the bus down to Kowloon Tsai Park and sit on the sidelines of the soccer pitch underneath the checkerboard-painted cliff wall, a navigational aide for pilots making their final approach to Kai Tak Airport. My father would take out his portable radio and stretch out the antenna, and he always found at least one station playing a Fab Four hit. He would turn "Here Comes the Sun" or "In My Life" all the way up, so we could hear it over the Rolls-Royce turbofan engines as we watched 747s nearly skim the tops of the Walled City outcroppings before making the checkerboard turn. Sitting beside him, I used to think that was my father at his happiest, but knowing what I know now, I wonder if it was a cruel kind of joy, the covetous kind, if what he really wanted was to be flying those planes or singing those songs, and instead, after all the joss sticks he stuck day after day in the altar pit, he could only watch and listen.

On the morning of December 9, 1967, my father was thinking of Brother Sang as he dug into the sand of the altar pit with his joss sticks. It had been six months since the pig had been roasted in Brother Sang's honor, and having completed basic training, Brother Sang had returned to Kam Tin the day before to take up his first post walking a beat in Chi Tong, an adjacent, larger village where my father took English lessons for which he paid by cooking on weekends at the local diner. As my father bicycled to school that morning, he wondered if he would see Brother Sang in the evening, while going to or from his lesson.

He did.

The first time I saw the grave beyond the banyan tree and asked whose it was, my father pretended he was distracted and just walked away. It was only recently that I found the trial transcripts in the law library and read that my father thought it was maroon paint at first, staining Brother Sang's uniform, because my father had never seen so much blood on one person. My father's English lesson that evening had covered words that are the same in both noun and verb form, and he had so recently stepped out of his lesson that he remembered thinking, or even saying, *surprise* in English before the Chinese word came to mind.

It was almost dark, but my father, about half a soccer pitch away, could see Brother Sang staggering, lifting himself into one step every few seconds toward the police post, a standalone concrete box the size of a small truck. He was nearly horizontal, his right hand using his too-short nightstick as a crutch, while his left hand clenched at his stomach.

"Brother Sang!" my father called out, and he was surprised again by the strength of his own voice, amplified by its desperation but also its isolation; no one else was out on the street. As he ran toward Brother Sang, my father looked back for a moment at his English teacher's second-floor window and saw the light go out, along with several others next to it in succession. It was a detail he only remembered later, on the witness stand.

My father caught up to Brother Sang a few paces short of the police post, and Brother Sang could not stand any longer. He collapsed on the steps of the post, sucking air so violently that each breath seemed to push more of his innards out. My father didn't know what to do or say. He watched Brother Sang's face fade, his eyes lose focus.

Sang was not nervous. Already his second day in Chi Tong felt more comfortable than his first, the village familiar to him and the villagers welcoming of a local boy walking their beat. His partner, Chung, was a few years older and not from the area, but it was his second year on the beat, and all the shopkeepers called out to Chung by name when they walked past. It was Chung who retold, in court, the story of what had happened.

The first day had been uneventful, apart from a domestic disturbance at one of the Tang homes, a young couple already riven with suspicions. The man was actually one of Sang's distant cousins.

"That's the most excitement we'll see all week," Chung said later, over lunch at the Chi Tong diner. In between scoops of roast pork and rice, he introduced Sang to the minutiae of the beat, the long stretches of nothing, the dangers of boredom. "Either you lose alertness and respond to nothing," Chung said, "or you get jumpy, trigger happy, at the first sign of action."

They went to the diner for lunch again on Sang's second day, after their morning patrol of the village perimeter with Chung dispensing more advice, more than it felt like he should have had at his age. The only other patrons were five men sitting on red plastic stools around a round green plastic table at the opposite corner of the diner. Their faded shirts were sweated through, even on this cool autumn day.

"These laborers," Chung said, as he extracted a bone from his mouth, "they always seem to find trouble these days."

Sang brought his bowl to his face, shoveling rice into his mouth to avoid what he thought would be a conspicuous silence, too nothing of a response. Ten police officers had been killed in recent months in a series of leftist riots that had spread throughout the city. It was the worst violence since the Second World War, and was threatening to unbuckle police unity. Even at the police academy, Sang had overheard Chinese constables in his dormitory whispering their doubts about the force's actions against the rioters. The kids in the streets were brainwashed, sure, waving their little red books in a frenzy, yelling nonsense slogans. But part of what they were railing against was colonialism, the end of Chinese servitude to Western masters. British officers, in the name of the rule of law, countered by sending Chinese constables to suppress the most virulent protests, those most likely to explode. Some did, and now ten officers were dead. *Chinese on Chinese*, the constables in Sang's dormitory muttered. *Divide and conquer.*

Chung did not indulge these misgivings, though he heard them too. He was concerned mainly with safety; the village's, but also his own.

"They get tempted, you know," he said. "They haul bricks for next to nothing. They couldn't give a fuck about communism, but they love having those smart-ass university kids shine their shoes. All their lives, they've been taking orders: *Move this shit here, throw away someone else's junk.* Now these kids tell them, *Workers should lead the revolution!* What a joke. It's like banging a whore: it's not real, but it feels good, and makes you do crazy . . ."

Chung abandoned his sentence, anticipating the clatter of the laborers getting up from their stools. They filed past Chung and Sang's table as they exited the diner, none making eye contact except the last, a slim but toned man, not more than twenty-five—Sang thought he resembled the actor Bruce Lee, from that American television show—who looked back at Sang with eyes not of curiosity but recognition, like he knew him. Sang caught the man's gaze then quickly looked away. Too quickly, Sang thought, upset with himself not for being a rookie, but for looking like one. *Project confidence*, they were told at the academy, from the first day to the last.

"Makes you do crazy shit," Chung continued. "Watch out

for those guys. They get in a mood and gather a couple dozen of the other construction workers in Kam Tin and we're sitting ducks. No real police station for three kilometers; backup will take at least ten minutes. They put a number on us anywhere in this village and our guts will be spilling out before we can make it back to our little shithole of a post."

"You seem to have managed," Sang said.

"Complete luck." Chung dug into more roast pork. "Even money, one of us isn't here for lunch tomorrow."

By the time the backup arrived, Sang had been dead for six minutes, by my father's count. As they loaded the body into the back of their police van, one of the constables noticed a small red triangle poking out the front pocket of my father's satchel.

"What's that in your bag, son?"

My father appeared confused and then, once again, surprised, when he looked down at his satchel and saw what the constable was eyeing. He pulled out the little red book and handed it to the constable.

"It's not mine, sir."

"You put other people's things in your bag?"

"I didn't put it there. Someone else must have." My father looked back at his English teacher's window. The light was still out.

"Get in the van," the constable said.

My father didn't move. "It's not mine, I swear."

"Get in the van."

"He's my cousin, sir."

"Don't make me ask you again." The constable put his right hand on his nightstick.

"I'm not a leftist."

The constable took one backhanded sweep, so quickly that my father didn't see the nightstick make contact before feeling his knees give out, then a crunching pain searing through his legs and up his spine. He fell almost right into the arms of the constable, who dragged him into the van.

"Tell that to the judge."

The Crown prosecutor's case against my father was entirely circumstantial. He was the only person determined to be within walking distance at the scene. He had made no effort to save Sang; there was not a drop of blood on my father's clothes or hands. His recent essays in school were laden with anticolonial sentiment, a characterization my father found particularly unjust, given that it came from Mrs. Yick, his history teacher whose every lesson seemed to be on the wrongs of empire. And the possession of that little red book, which my father had continuously denied was his.

Then there were my father's supposed motives, in addition to his allegedly leftist agitation against the colonial police—an intense envy of Sang, whose admission to the police force was in contrast to my father's failing grades and what the prosecutor called *delusions of grandeur* that he would ever make it into a university; the long-running rivalry between my father's grandmother, Wife Number Three, and Sang's grandmother, Wife Number Nine, who were the general's favored concubines—he placed their houses in the village next to his and each other's—competing for the general's affections during his life and for his estate in his death. Finally, there was the prosecutor's coup de grâce: the revelation that the domestic disturbance Sang reported on his first day was between the student leader of a local leftist group—a young woman three years ahead of my father at his school—and my father's older brother, Uncle Number Two, who was newly wed, but to another woman.

"You had a lot of people to protect, Mr. Lee," the prosecutor said in court. He addressed my father at all times as *Mr. Lee*, to make him seem older than he was, I assumed. I remember feeling uneasy when my criminal law professor, himself a former prosecutor, told us he used that tactic against minors.

"The reputation of your dear brother," the prosecutor said to my father, "whose extramarital cavorting with a Communist would not only cause great shame to your family, but could potentially exclude your direct family members from the family inheritance." Police had uncovered a clause in the general's will excluding from his estate any descendants *who bring grave disrepute to the family name*.

"And the reputation of Ms. Tang," the prosecutor said, referring to the leftist student leader. "That she was literally in bed with someone from the old landed gentry, an entitled landowner, a vestige of feudalism the type of which she spends her waking hours denouncing; surely this would bring its own disrepute, toppling the local leftist movement from its moral high horse."

The prosecutor shifted his gaze from my father to the jury. "A movement of which you, Mr. Lee, have become such a devoted adherent, as we have seen from your essays and possessions. A movement which has wreaked havoc on our streets this year. A movement openly challenging the rule of law. A movement that has killed ten brave police officers already this year—and now one more by the hands, the evidence suggests, of the accused Mr. Lee."

My father had remained stoic throughout the trial, but now he wept.

"I didn't kill Brother Sang," he said, the words muffled through his sobs. "I didn't do anything."

* * *

My father was acquitted. His youth alone probably gave the jury reasonable enough doubt that he could have executed such a well-thought-out plan to kill his own cousin. The murder weapon was never found, nor any other suspects, at least not by the police. But what was revealed during the trial shook our family into a frenzy of recriminations, including lingering suspicions of my father's guilt, and the unshakable impression that he was indeed a Communist. Even today, I hear some of his cousins address him as *Comrade*. I had always thought it was in jest, an inside joke, until that day in the law library.

I hadn't been looking for the trial transcripts. I'd barely thought of the grave beyond the banyan tree after my father didn't bother to answer me. I was simply procrastinating. I was studying for my first law school exam—property—and sealed myself off from the outside world, including the Internet, for three whole days. I could no longer stay awake reviewing the many easements attaching to Blackacre, so I unlocked the Wi-Fi on my laptop and in an aimless Internet fix googled myself and each of my family members. My father's name yielded two pages of results, mostly related to his tenure on the board of his vocational institute.

But there were a couple entries that came up in the sidebar showing results from the law library's own database. The transcripts were not online, but the court digests in which they were reported were not hard to find in the library stacks, down an aisle with sliding shelves. I sat in that aisle for the next three hours, reading every word spoken during the trial, every document presented as evidence. At one point I thought about photocopying the transcripts, but somehow felt it would be a betrayal of my father to reprint this part of his past, to bring it back to life on fresh pieces of A4 paper.

I didn't make copies, and I didn't ask my father about it, either. I didn't ask him because as I read about the cold-blooded murder of Lee Koon Sang, police constable 3810, who died at twenty-one, the same age I am now, I remembered there was one Chinese New Year when I was seven or eight, when we came home from the family village with our share of roast pork and my father reached into the breast pocket of his jacket and pulled out all the red envelopes I had collected during the day.

"Big haul today," he said, as he handed me the envelopes. "Go to the study and put these with the others you've collected this week. We'll add them all up after dinner."

I smiled and carried my fresh batch of red envelopes into the study. We performed this ritual every Chinese New Year: My father sat behind his desk and I sat opposite, like a client. The radio would be on, softly, more Beatles. My father would hand me a red envelope, on which he had written the bearer's name, and I would open it and extract the crisp bills. I would announce the amount, and he would write it down on a line in a green ledger book half the size of the desk. "One hundred dollars from Uncle Number Two," he would say, and I would hand the money over. Once I had emptied all the envelopes, my father would add up each line on his solar-powered Casio pocket calculator and declare the grand total. He would use half to buy stock in my name, he said, and the other half was the amount I could spend on G.I. Joes and Transformers at Wing Wah, my local toy heaven.

As my father heated up the roast pork and I heard the hiss of washed *choi sum* falling into the wok, I went to the study and opened what I thought was the drawer where my father kept all my red envelopes. I saw a bright red corner peeking out from under a pile of manila envelopes, then reached under to pull out my red envelope stash. But the red rectangle now in my hand was not that. It was a small book bound with a bright red vinyl cover, on which the year of publication—1967—and five characters were embossed in gold print.

Quotations from Chairman Mao, the characters read. I put it back in the drawer.

FOURTEEN
BY CARMEN SUEN
Wah Fu

The elevator door opened on the fourteenth floor. Siu Wan shuffled out and headed toward her apartment, number 1424, where her family had been living since she was a baby. When they first moved in, Wah Ming House was the newest building in Wah Fu Estate. It was a hopeful time.

But today had not been a good day for Siu Wan, and it had nothing to do with the number fourteen, as one might suspect. Fourteen, *sup sei*, is not the most auspicious number in Cantonese culture, especially in Hong Kong. It sounds like *sut sei*—must die. Some developers would skip the fourteenth floor on their buildings, choosing instead to have the fifteenth floor immediately above the thirteenth. Not the case for government housing like Wah Fu Estate. The government most certainly didn't give a damn whether residents in housing projects lived or died based on superstitious beliefs.

For Siu Wan, fourteen or not did not make any difference. It was the same tiny apartment with no privacy no matter the number. Every unit in the building was the same 300-square-foot cube with a kitchen, a bathroom, a balcony, and an open space in the middle with barely enough room for a dresser, a double bed, a bunk bed—or two, depending on how many kids and in-laws lived there—and the all-important round folding table that served as a dining table–cum–homework desk. In most cases, the table had to be folded up when not in use, so as to make room for TV viewing. To save space, some families would forgo chairs and sat on their beds when they were eating or working at the table. The only separation between the living space and the "bedroom," if you could call it that, would be some curtains hanging from the ceilings to block one or two sides of the beds to create some sort of private space. That is, if the parents cared about privacy at all. Privacy was a luxury not everyone in Hong Kong understood, especially when one was poor.

It could have been much worse for the poor. The government did try to improve social welfare after the 1967 leftist riots and Wah Fu was an ambitious attempt to improve the standards of public housing in the territory. It was the first to have a kitchen and a bathroom in each unit. Dubbed "New Town," Wah Fu was also the first public housing estate to have its own wet market, shopping mall, schools, public library, parking garage, and bus terminal. It was no exaggeration to call it a town. When the eighteen buildings were completed in 1978, about fifty thousand people moved into the development.

If that wasn't enough to tout Wah Fu as one of the best public housing estates in Hong Kong, there was also the million-dollar location. There's a reason why Wah Fu Estate was called the "poor men's mansions." It was the only public housing development in Hong Kong that had full ocean views. A couple of miles away was Victoria Road, where some of the wealthiest in the city lived. Of course, it would be naive to think the government chose that location for Wah Fu because they believed the poor had the right to live well. The truth was, no other developer would build anywhere near Waterfall Bay or Book Bo Wan. There had always been rumors that the ocean was haunted. The nearby Kellet Bay was allegedly a dumping ground for dead bodies during the Japanese occupation. Despite Wah Fu's good feng shui—having the sea on one side and the hills on the other—there was too much to risk developing a high-end residential project there.

Obviously, none of these were any of Siu Wan's concerns. In fact, like most other kids in Wah Fu, she quite enjoyed all the ghost stories that were circulating around. If only she had friends she could share these stories with.

To Siu Wan, ghost stories were just that—stories. If she were to believe in every superstition in Chinese culture, she might as well not do anything, which, on this particular day, was not such a bad idea. Sure, the elevator smelled like urine and was covered in graffiti of every curse word you could imagine, and she was drenched in sweat after walking home from school in the sweltering heat. But that was nothing un-usual. What made it such a dreadful day was that it was Siu Wan's last day of school as a primary school student. She was going to start middle school after the summer ended.

Siu Wan did not look forward to the summer or to middle school. Although she was somewhat relieved there would be no school in the coming months, it meant having to spend more time at home with her older brother Chi Wan. Not that Siu Wan disliked her brother, but it wasn't exactly a twelve-year-old girl's dream to hang out with her fifteen-year-old brother all summer long.

Other kids went to the park and did fun things with their families when school was out. That would have made summer much more bearable. Unfortunately for Siu Wan, that was not an option. She hadn't seen her dad in years, and her mom, Mrs. Wong, worked two jobs just to make enough money to pay the rent and not much else. Mrs. Wong had neither the time nor the extra cash to spend on fun things. Fun was as much a luxury as privacy. When you're poor, you learn to live without both.

Like most girls her age, Siu Wan liked to wear nice clothes and feel pretty. She didn't mind hand-me-downs from relatives and neighbors. She knew she couldn't afford new clothes, and she was fine with that. The problem was that her clothes always looked dingy. Mrs. Wong could never find time to do the laundry, and so Chi Wan, being the older sibling, had to do it. No matter how hard he tried to clean them, there always seemed to be a grayish tint on the clothes. Kids at school didn't like to play with Siu Wan because they thought she was dirty. Neither did any other kids in the neighborhood. Except for Ah Yan.

Ah Yan was a seven-year-old girl who lived in Wah Hing House, just a couple of blocks from Siu Wan's building. Siu Wan had met Ah Yan for the first time a month earlier when the younger girl was playing alone on the beach by Book Bo Wan, just a short walk from where they lived. Maybe it was getting dark. Maybe Ah Yan didn't pay attention to Siu Wan's clothes. Ah Yan did not think for a second that Siu Wan looked dirty. Much like Siu Wan, she only wanted to have a playmate.

What puzzled Siu Wan was why no one wanted to play with Ah Yan. At seven, Ah Yan was every bit as adorable as any other girl her age. She remembered that Ah Yan was actually popular at school before she got sick. She had been hospitalized and things changed for the worse after she got back from the hospital. No one was playing with Ah Yan anymore. She looked so lonely when Siu Wan saw her sitting on a big rock on the beach the day they became friends.

Siu Wan enjoyed the company of her new friend. It was nice to take a break from Chi Wan and hang out with a girl.

Sometimes she would help Ah Yan braid her silky black hair. Other times they would paint each other's nails with nail polish that Siu Wan took from one of Mrs. Wong's drawers.

The two new friends would meet on the beach where they first met. It might have been a bit of a stretch to call Book Bo Wan a beach. It was more of a landing along the shoreline at the end of its namesake waterfall. Because it was small and quite rocky, there were usually not many visitors around, especially late in the evening. In the early 1970s, Book Bo Wan was a popular spot for the two local TV stations to film their martial arts dramas. The film crews stopped going there after the waterfall started to dry up. Once in a while, you would find someone fishing near the bottom of the waterfall or swimming in the bay. For the most part, it was quiet.

Siu Wan thought Ah Yan would be at the beach earlier in the day, as she didn't expect her to have any homework on the last day of school. But she didn't see her until sunset.

"Sorry *ar*, Siu Wan! I'm so late," Ah Yan apologized when she finally showed up.

"It's okay. But don't tell me you had homework today!"

"No, my mom said it was too hot outside and wouldn't let me out until the sun went down. Parents can be so *ma fan*."

"Well, at least your mom cares enough to be a pain in the butt! Mine is too busy working and who knows what else she's doing. She's never home."

"Okay, okay, enough about the parents. Let's do something fun! Hey, have you heard Leslie's new song 'Monica'?"

"Of course I have. I love it! I just saw his music video. Let me show you his dance moves."

The girls started dancing and singing to the tunes of the Cantopop. *Thanks! Thanks! Thanks! Thanks! Monica! Who can ever replace you?* At the chorus, Siu Wan waved her right arm up in the air, her left hand holding onto her waist as she swung her hips from side to side. Ah Yan, dancing right beside her friend, was trying hard to keep up. They bumped into each other at the hips and the girls could not help but burst into laughter.

"That was so much fun," said Ah Yan. "Thanks, Siu Wan."

"Yeah, it was fun!" Siu Wan replied as she affectionately patted Ah Yan's head. "It's getting late. I'd better get home before my mom does. She's been in a bad mood lately. I don't want to get in trouble."

"I should probably go home too," said Ah Yan. "Will I see you tomorrow?"

"Sure! See you tomorrow!"

The two waved goodbye and headed home in opposite directions.

Sharpen scissors! Sharpen knives! Sharpen scissors! Sharpen knives!

Siu Wan woke up to the roving whetter's holler for business. Around ten every morning, the old man would walk from floor to floor, carrying his tool bag on his bent back, advertising his trade with his booming call. Housewives who needed their knives or scissors sharpened would stop him and ask for his service.

"Aargh!" said Siu Wan from the lower bunk bed. "Why does he have to be so early and so loud? People are still sleeping!"

"You should probably get up anyway," said Chi Wan. "It's ten already. I've made some congee for breakfast. You should eat it before it gets cold. I'm going downstairs to play ping-pong with the boys. See you later!" He grabbed his paddle and dashed out of the apartment.

Siu Wan let out a big yawn and got up to get some congee.

She turned on the TV and started watching a rerun of an old black-and-white movie starring Chan Po Chu. She had watched the same movie several times over the last few years.

"This is so boring!" Siu Wan let out another yawn.

She could hear kids running up and down the hallway, playing hide-and-seek. But it was no ordinary hide-and-seek. Those who grew up in public housing in the seventies and eighties would know this version of the game. Sometimes more than twenty kids from different households in the same building would join in. Wah Ming House was designed in the slab style, which meant there was a long, narrow corridor in the middle of two rows of apartments. On both ends of the building, there were staircases. There was also an enclosed stairwell behind the elevator chute in the center of the building. There were not many good hiding spots, but in a way, it was almost like a maze, only vertical. Kids got a thrill from zipping through different floors, trying to dodge the seeker.

Siu Wan thought about joining them, but quickly decided against it, as she did not want to be rejected again.

She turned the TV off and got up to wash the dishes. *Ah Yan won't be able to come out until late in the afternoon*, she thought. *I need to find something to do.*

After freshening up, Siu Wan went downstairs to join Chi Wan and his friends. She was not a big fan of ping-pong, but she just wanted some company.

It was the first day of the summer break for most kids in the neighborhood. All four ping-pong tables on the ground floor of Wah Ming House were occupied by different groups of kids from age six or so to the late teens. Because not every building in Wah Fu Estate had ping-pong tables, Wah Ming House became a popular destination for kids. It also helped that Wah Ming was located by the water. The area where the ping-pong tables were had an open design. A breeze could flow freely through. When the kids were getting too hot from playing too hard, the sea breeze felt better than any air-conditioning.

At the ping-pong tables, Siu Wan was one of the few female players or spectators. Chi Wan was playing with his usual gang of fifteen-year-olds, all classmates of his. Siu Wan noticed a boy she did not recognize. He looked a little older than the rest of the group. He was sitting on the side, not chanting and laughing like Chi Wan's other friends. He was smoking a cigarette and looked like he was deep in thought. At that moment he looked in Siu Wan's direction. She quickly turned away, pretending to tie her shoelaces and hoping he didn't catch her staring.

"Hi," a coarse voice said.

Siu Wan looked up and there he was, sitting right next to her.

"Hi." Her voice quivered a little.

"I haven't seen you here before—and you should know I never forget a pretty face. What's your name?"

"Er . . . my name is Siu Wan." She wanted to say something clever, and could feel her face turning red.

"Hi, Siu Wan. I'm Tony," said the boy. "Do you play ping-pong or do you just watch?"

"I don't usually play—the boys don't like to play with me because I'm a girl. I just come here to watch my brother. How about you? You don't look like you're here to play ping-pong either."

"Ha! Why do you think I don't play? I'm actually pretty good," said Tony with a smirk. "But today I'm here to watch my little bro. He's playing with that kid in the white tank top."

"Really? Sai B is your brother? The one playing against

my brother?" laughed Siu Wan. "How come you're so tall and he's so small?"

"He's my half brother—we have different dads." Tony exhaled a long puff.

There's a certain sadness in his eyes, Siu Wan thought. She regretted immediately that she'd made that joke. She thought about her own divorced parents and knew firsthand how difficult it was to grow up in a single-parent household. But with a stepparent and a half brother? That must be so much more complicated. She wanted to say something witty to make Tony laugh, but couldn't come up with anything remotely funny. All she could do was watch him smoke and imagine the hardship he'd been through.

Out of nowhere, laughter and cheers erupted from the crowd below and brought Siu Wan out of her thoughts. Chi Wan had beaten Sai B in a close game and the crowd was in a frenzy. Paddles were flying left and right. Everyone was cheering around Chi Wan. Siu Wan saw the excitement in her brother's face. She could not remember the last time he'd been this ecstatic. She wanted to feel happy for him but all she could think about was how she could make Tony smile.

"This is too loud!" Tony said. "Do you want to go get some red bean ice with me?"

"Sure!" Siu Wan shouted out with joy. She could almost taste the crushed ice, red beans, and sweet evaporated milk. But then she hesitated. "Oh, wait . . ."

"What's the matter?" asked Tony.

"Well . . . er . . . I . . . er . . . don't have any money." Siu Wan could feel the heat on her cheeks. She didn't know what to do so she kept her face down. It was too embarrassing to look him in the eye now. She wished she had brought the five dollars her grandmother had given her on her birthday last month. That would have been more than enough to pay for her own drink and maybe even get a *daan taat*.

Tony lifted her chin up and said, "Don't worry, it's on me!"

Did he just wink at me? Siu Wan couldn't stop thinking about it while walking with Tony to the neighborhood *bing sut*.

When the pair finally sat down at the café, Tony ordered two red bean ices and two *daan taats*.

"Thank you for this. It's so nice of you," Siu Wan said.

"It's nothing." Tony lit up another cigarette. "I have a part-time job. It pays pretty well and I can afford to treat my friends."

"Really? What's your job?"

"I help a friend sell stuff. I'll tell you more about it later. And hey, don't be so nosy. Boys don't like girls who ask too many questions. Ha-ha."

"I'm not being nosy," Siu Wan protested. "You brought it up yourself!"

"I'm just joking," Tony chuckled. "Don't leave the *daan taat* sitting there. It tastes better while it's still warm."

He handed her the egg tart and she took a small bite. She had had *daan taats* hundreds of times before. She'd even had some from this same café. But it tasted different this time. The pastry was still warm and she could smell the fragrance of the buttery crust and its soft custard. The yellow filling was just the right amount of sweetness and the crust was so flaky that the crumbs stuck to her lips when she bit into it. Siu Wan grabbed a napkin to wipe her mouth. The last thing she wanted was for Tony to think she was unsophisticated.

Hanging out with Tony soon became the best part of Siu Wan's day. Every morning, except for Sundays when Mrs. Wong was home, she would meet him by the ping-pong tables or the playground by the wet market. Tony would take her to the *bing sut* and always treated. Siu Wan tried to pay him back with her own pocket money, but he wouldn't let her.

"I have a job, you don't," he would say. "And we're friends. Friends help each other. You would help me too, when I'm in need, wouldn't you?"

"Of course I would," said Siu Wan.

Tony introduced her to his friends. Within the first week of summer break, she had made more friends than she ever had in her entire life. But she hadn't forgotten about Ah Yan, still her first and best friend.

"Is he handsome? Are you his girlfriend?" asked Ah Yan when Siu Wan told her about Tony.

"Don't be silly! He's just my friend!"

"But would you be his girlfriend if he asked you?" Ah Yan wouldn't stop teasing her.

"I don't know. It's none of your business anyway. I'm going to punish you for asking too many questions!"

Siu Wan chased after Ah Yan. But Book Bo Wan was a small beach and it wasn't difficult for Siu Wan to catch up with the smaller girl. When she finally grabbed her, Siu Wan started tickling Ah Yan, who tickled back. Both girls couldn't stop giggling. When they were both exhausted from the struggle, they lay down on the sand, panting.

"Siu Wan, I'm so happy you're my friend," said Ah Yan, looking into the orange sky. "Please promise you'll never leave me."

Siu Wan turned her head to Ah Yan and gently brushed the bangs on the girl's forehead. "Of course I'll never leave you. Even if I had a million friends, or a million dollars, you would still be my best friend forever."

* * *

Just as Siu Wan thought things were finally looking up, her home life started to unravel. Mrs. Wong was spending less and less time at home. When she was there, she would start drinking and screaming at her children.

"I can't see the TV with your big head in front of me!"

"What do you mean you don't have money for food? I gave you ten dollars last week! You're fifteen, old enough to get a job. Stop asking me for money!

"Your skirt is too short. And stop using my makeup. You look like a prostitute!"

Siu Wan understood that her mother was exhausted and needed the alcohol to relax. What she did not understand was why she would always drink past the point of relaxation and get dead drunk. Chi Wan and Siu Wan learned quickly that it was best to keep their mouths shut when their mom was around.

It had been about a month since the beginning of summer vacation. Siu Wan was not sure if this was her best summer or her worst. In a lot of ways, it had been really great: she'd met Tony, made a ton of friends through him, hung out with teenagers who treated her like she was their peer. And she had a best friend who simply adored her. But her mom's drinking problem had made her life miserable.

Ah Yan said Siu Wan could go home with her if she liked. "My mom would be thrilled to meet you. I've been talking about you for the last month!"

"Thank you, but I don't think that would help. My mom would kill me if I don't come home for the night."

She told Tony about the situation when they were at the *bing sut* one afternoon, hoping he could offer her some words of advice, both as a mature teenager and as someone who was also from a broken family.

"I'm sorry to hear that, Siu Wan. You know, if you're really unhappy, I do have something that could help," said Tony.

"Really? What is it?"

"Remember I told you about my part-time job?"

"Yeah?"

"Well, I'm helping my friend sell medicine. There's this one pill that can make sad people happy in a snap," Tony said in a whisper.

"Are you talking about drugs? My teachers at school told us drugs are really bad for you."

"Your teachers are wrong about this one. You see, if you take too much of anything, it'll be bad for you. But this pill is safe—if you only take a little at a time. My friends and I have been taking it for a while. Nothing's gone wrong. I actually feel much better! Can't you tell I'm always calm and relaxed?"

Siu Wan looked intently at Tony. He seemed so genuine, and he'd been good to her since the day they met. Surely he wouldn't do anything to hurt her, would he?

"I don't want to force you to do anything. As your friend, I thought this might help you. It has worked great for me." After a short pause, Tony added, "Why don't you just keep this? If you don't want to take it, that's fine. But when you're feeling really sad, just give it a try."

"Thank you," Siu Wan said hesitantly, as she carefully put the pill in her shirt pocket.

"Don't be so sad. Let me buy you another *daan taat* to cheer you up." Tony gestured to the waiter and ordered two more of her favorite dessert.

When Siu Wan went home at five o'clock that afternoon, she was planning to get some food from the kitchen before going out to meet Ah Yan at their regular hangout. Much to her surprise, Mrs. Wong was already home, and looking pretty drunk.

"Where have you been? Why weren't you home? Who do you think you are, coming in and out of the house whenever you want? This is not a hotel!"

Siu Wan knew better than to say anything that might anger her mom. Chi Wan was not home yet. She would have no backup if Mrs. Wong started getting out of control. "I was just hanging out in the playground with some friends," she said as calmly as she could.

"Friends? What friends? And where is your brother? You're both ungrateful children! I should have left you guys when your dad split!"

Siu Wan did not want to hear any more of this. She knew this was not her real mother talking. As soon as she fell asleep, everything would be fine. Maybe some food might help.

"Would you like noodles? I can make some for us," Siu Wan said timidly, then tiptoed across the room to the kitchen.

Mrs. Wong sat at the folding table watching TV while Siu Wan started cooking.

Clang! A loud noise from the kitchen woke Mrs. Wong from her zombie-like state. She jumped from her chair and rushed to the kitchen to see what had happened.

"I'm sorry, Mom. I dropped the lid. It was too hot," Siu Wan said. "I'll take care of it and I'll make you some noodles." As she bent to pick up the lid from the floor, she felt a rush through her left cheek. Before she could made sense of what was going on, she saw a tiny drop of blood on the floor and felt the cut on her lips.

"Forget about the noodles. I'm not hungry anymore. You can't even make noodles without causing trouble! You're worthless!"

Siu Wan could not quite comprehend what had just happened. All she was sure about was that she did not want to stay in the same room as her mom. She needed some fresh air. She needed to get away from this misery.

As she was stepping out of the kitchen, she saw a tiny blue disc on the grayish mosaic floor. It was the pill Tony had given her a couple of days ago. She picked it up, turned around, and poured herself a glass of warm water from the kettle sitting on the stove. If there was a time she needed a happy pill, this would be it. She took a deep breath and downed the pill with a big gulp of water.

Siu Wan felt a peacefulness she had not experienced in a long time. She remembered her mom screaming behind her when she was running down the corridor outside their apartment. She saw the shock and scrutiny in her neighbors' faces when they peeked through the silver metal gates separating their homes from the corridor. But none of that mattered now. She was enjoying the sea breeze on a big rock while waiting for her best friend to come.

There was a weird vibe on the beach tonight. More people wandered about, and a small group was taking a late-evening swim. Yet with all the unusual traffic, the beach seemed quieter than ever. Siu Wan thought it might just be the effect of the pill that made her feel so serene. It really was a happy pill.

"Hey, Siu Wan! Over here!"

She turned around and saw Ah Yan waving at her from the water.

"When did you get here? I didn't see you," said Siu Wan.

"My mom and I were swimming off the coast. I started swimming back to shore when I saw you sitting there."

"Why are so many people swimming here tonight?"

"I don't know. I guess because it's really hot today. You should join us!"

"No thanks," said Siu Wan. "I don't have my swimsuit with me."

"Don't worry, we brought big towels. You can dry yourself after the swim. It's really fun!" pleaded Ah Yan. "Plus, my mom is right there. She'd like to meet you."

Siu Wan didn't want to disappoint Ah Yan. She had asked Siu Wan to go swimming with her a couple of times, but she kept saying no. Maybe the water would help her clear her head. She wanted to forget about what had happened at home. "Okay, I'll join you!" she chirped as she jumped into the water.

Siu Wan woke up the next day feeling a little light-headed. It was three o'clock in the afternoon. She couldn't believe she had slept that much. She also couldn't quite remember what had happened after the swim with Ah Yan the night before. Her last memory was feeling cold water seep through her clothes. She sensed a calmness settling in that she hadn't felt for a long time and assumed it must be a side effect of the happy pill. She got up from her bunk bed and went to the bathroom to freshen up.

The air was thick and humid. The forecast said a typhoon was heading toward Hong Kong. Siu Wan turned on the TV to watch the news. If the typhoon was coming, she should probably just stay home for the day.

"*Typhoon Emma is on track to pass through Hong Kong. The Hong Kong Observatory is warning citizens to make appropriate precautions to protect their homes and be prepared for the typhoon to upgrade to a number eight by tomorrow morning.*"

"*A twelve-year-old girl drowned in Book Bo Wan in Wah Fu Estate last night. Traces of methaqualone were found in her body during an autopsy. No foul play is suspected. This is the second drowning incident at the beach this year."*

Siu Wan was shocked to see her picture on TV. What were they talking about? She felt very confused.

"In May of this year, a seven-year-old girl drowned in the same location. Residents in the area are very concerned about the safety of the beach. We talked to one mother who lived in the area."

Siu Wan's eyes were glued to the TV, trying to comprehend what this all meant. Then she saw a familiar face. It was Mrs. Chan. She lived just one floor below her, in apartment 1324.

"As a parent, I'm really concerned about all these accidents. You know they always say that Book Bo Wan is haunted. I tried not to give in to superstitious beliefs, but yesterday was the Ghost Festival and another girl drowned. It's too much of a coincidence."

Are they saying I'm dead? If I'm dead, why am I still here? Siu Wan decided to go back to the beach to find out.

On the beach, she was surprised to see Mrs. Wong and Chi Wan already there.

"Hey, Mom! Chi Wan! What's going on?"

They didn't answer. They were weeping as they threw paper treasures into a large tin can blackened by the fire burning inside of it. A trail of heavy smoke rose from the tin and merged with the dark clouds hanging low in the sky.

Siu Wan ran toward her mom and her brother. She needed to talk to them. Before she could reach them, however, someone tugged her hand and stopped her in her tracks. She turned around and saw Ah Yan looking up at her.

"Don't get mad at me, Siu Wan. You said we'd be best friends forever. It's going to be okay. We're together now. I won't ever leave you."

BIG HOTEL

BY YSABELLE CHEUNG

North Point

We are born as from a quiet sleep,
We die to a calm awakening.

—Chuang Tze

Six o'clock; Tam Oi Lin is pinning long curls of paper to a wooden board at the entrance of her shop. It is September, and the sun will rise in just a few minutes. When Oi Lin looks down the street, she sees less than a handful of shops beaming rectangles of harsh light into the otherwise still blackness of the night. The funeral flower business is as it has always been: a necessity. Oi Lin moves slowly in the still and silent ink of the day's prologue, awaiting the first break of dawn, when a cool lavender mist will signal the start of a ritual.

Inside the shop, Oi Lin's mother is counting orders. There are thirty-seven today, the majority to be placed at the funeral of a detective who recently passed after a difficult, protracted battle with brain cancer. Oi Lin and her mother switch places; the girl sits at the table and goes over the arrangements, while the senior begins to paint, with a black-inked brush, characters of condolences and names on the papers hung by the edge of the store. A radio is on in the background, tuned to a local news station; after a while, Oi Lin switches it off and inserts a cassette. Songs from the past are lifted from the silky ribbons of film. The two women work side by side, fastidiously, pausing for a drink or a brief interlude about an order or a flower that darkened at the edges overnight. The work is unforgiving. Hours of preparation must go into these displays, but the shelf life of a cut flower, already dead, is brief. At the funeral, these delicate organisms must appear alive, white and crisp, right up until the end, after which they are customarily dumped on the ground around the back of the site.

A few hours later, their work is done for the day. Oi Lin helps deliver the last of the batch to the funeral home down the road and then goes to sit in a loud *cha chaan teng* with a cream soda and a slab of toast drowned in condensed milk. It is her twenty-fifth birthday, and as each year before, it has passed so far as an event of unmonumental proportions. She is a quiet person. Some might even call her slow because of her dreaminess, her inability to snap to focus when she is lost in thought.

As she eats and drinks, she thinks of the dream she had the night before. In it, a man was walking beside her in a park somewhere in Europe, and he was looking at the trees, the ground, and birds that swooped past, their silvery bodies like fat bullets. They neared a bench. He sat down and she hovered close to him; they hadn't spoken. The man then began to write in stretched cursive script, filling the pages of a notebook he drew from his inside jacket pocket. Rain started to fall in solemn, oily drops; he continued to write.

That was where the dream ended. Although he hadn't told Oi Lin his name, she knew instantly who he was. The morning before, she had seen his body in a funeral, laid in a coffin with black velvet padding. She often has these dreams, of corpses she sees at the funeral home. In them, mundane scenarios occur in random, familiar yet also unrecognizable places; a woman might be riding a green-top minibus, or a man might be watching a daytime soap opera and eating airplane olives, leaving purple-black, briny pits on the sofa. Once, a little girl got on a bicycle printed with daisies and pedaled all the way to the shoreline of a beach where the water was gently tugging the white sand. Oi Lin never interacts with these spirits; there are no conversations. She is merely there in the background, watching as if she's the ghost and they are the ones who are living.

"Can I join you?"

She looks up and there is Hao, one of the juniors at the funeral home. He's around her age; similar in mind-set with the capacity of a million years for the minutiae, and not a second for anything else outside their realm of funereal monotony. He orders a hot tea with lemon, which arrives with a crown of wet tea leaves. Hao berates the owner, who takes it away with a glare. Oi Lin is embarrassed; she feels so acutely the crudeness of human interaction.

"You could have just taken it out yourself," she says.

"I don't see why I have to sit with their mistake," he replies, helping himself to a sip of her cream soda. "Anyway, it takes them two seconds to make another one."

They talk awhile about the detective's funeral that is taking place at that moment.

"Aren't you supposed to be there?" Oi Lin asks.

He shakes his head. "They only really needed me to help set up chairs for this one. There's a lot of staff in today."

"Brain cancer . . . I can't imagine."

"I heard his relatives talking about it when they delivered the body. Apparently, he couldn't even talk or move in the last few months of his life. Just lay in the hospital bed staring at the ceiling, knowing he was about to die, but not remembering enough of anything to reflect on his life."

Hao finishes Oi Lin's drink and stands up. "They never brought me another tea . . . I'm going back now. My dad probably wants to talk to me about the events tomorrow."

The pair walk out together. As they part ways—he toward the funeral home, she the flower shop—she sees a woman smoking by the side of the road. A car passes by; its window beams a reflected ray of light onto the woman, covering her in a bright, white-hot aura that appears spectral. Oi Lin realizes she is staring and notices the woman—the detective's wife—looking back at her. A relative pulls the woman away and gestures toward the hearse that is parked by the curb. Oi Lin watches as a procession of four people climb into the car—their spines crooked and stiff, their hair the same unwashed fog of charcoal—then walks toward the industrial entrance of her shop, her feet scuffing against the broken stems and ragged strips of torn flowers all the way to the mouth of the parking lot.

Oi Lin wonders: why is it that she feels things so sharply in dreams, much more than in her waking hours? A pocket of cold wind, a vinegary aroma—all these things stay with her for days, sometimes confusing her mind with what happened and what didn't; what is real and what is not.

She is dreaming. She is in an apartment somewhere, with walnut-wood furnishings and a low dusk light that enters in horizontal slices through the window shutters. There is music playing, a current of drowsy, twangy saxophone riffs. Oi Lin guesses this must be the apartment of the detective, or perhaps the home of someone he knew well. She senses there is someone else nearby; she walks across the room, where there is a door, and pushes it open; the music grows louder. The door leads to the living room, and there's a record player next to a person who is crouching with their back turned. A grinding hum from a dishwasher or washing machine nearby rumbles through the room, and the hint of a half-eaten meal—notes of sesame oil and the glutinous waft of instant noodles—betrays the life of a lonely soul. The music stops and a woman turns and stands up. She is looking directly at Oi Lin, wearing owlish tortoiseshell glasses and a thin cardigan over a shapeless white nightgown that nips at her ankles.

"Who are you?"

Oi Lin is speechless. She feels as if a wall has eroded, one that had been imperceptible up until the very moment it dissolved, and its nothingness reveals what was hidden before.

"Answer me," the woman says in a short, austere tone. "Who are you?" As she steps closer, Oi Lin recognizes the same wan pallor marred by telltale twitches of anxiety that she had seen a few hours earlier. A dark block of hair falls from behind the woman's ear and over her face. Dumbfounded, Oi Lin realizes that this is the detective's widow.

She wakes with the *ding-ding-ding* of her alarm clock, her head clouded and throat dry and gingery. Her mother is already slipping into her jacket when she walks into the front room. "Hurry," she says, her gaze calmly assessing Oi Lin's pajamas and somnambulant daze—she is used to her daughter's nightly visitations and their disorienting aftereffects. "Busy day today."

At the flower shop, forty-five orders await. Mother and daughter begin their morning ritual: cleaning, sprucing, weaving, painting, filing, cutting, trimming, buffing, spritzing. The radio is on; the night sky is fading, in variegated streaks, to dawn. As with most mornings, Oi Lin enters a mechanical, cyclic mode of working as she tries to grasp the events that occurred in her dreams. It is the first time she has dreamed of someone who has not yet died—presumably. Was it a dream or a premonition? The widow's face comes to her again: colorless, aged features drawn in a vacuous arrangement by the weight of grief.

Later that evening, as she is lying in her bed in that half-conscious state where thoughts froth and fall apart like streaks of cirrus in the sky, Oi Lin returns again and again to the conversation in the dream. She considers the strangers in her life; the dead that return to ritual in her dreams, who go through the motions one last time before passing over. In those eclipsing moments in the shadow lands, she feels bound to these people, viewing life as it was for them, through their eyes. Every morning, she writes in her journal about these encounters, these embodiments, and the way the ink flows from the pen is indication that there is so much to say; every detail, every sigh, every heartbeat is another clue to understanding their stories. Are they really strangers if she meets them, walks with them, in another realm?

When Oi Lin sleeps, she dreams again. She is sitting on tall grass by a silver-mirrored lake and the ground is peaty and cold. There are several small plums around her feet. Inexplicably, some are crushed, their wet, golden pulp mingling with the soil, while others are intact, perfect, purple. There are spindly, tall evergreen trees surrounding the lake, obscuring half the sky.

"You again?"

The widow is sitting across from her. She's changed; instead of a white nightgown, she's wearing a simple, sleeveless blue-and-white-checkered dress. Her hair is washed, flaxen, and stirs with the light wind. Without glasses, she looks younger.

"I always dreamed of having a picnic here," she says. She picks up a plum and bites into it; clear juice runs out in rivers. When the widow giggles, Oi Lin notices with horror that her teeth are stained black.

"You're quite clever, you know," she continues, smiling. "Think about it. All these years, you've been fabricating these stories in your head, convincing yourself that you're walking with the dead. Have you ever thought that you've just been talking to your subconscious this whole time? If I were you, I'd be worried."

"Then who am I talking to now?" Oi Lin asks urgently, terrified.

The woman stops smiling. "Don't you remember?"

It is five o'clock again; the alarm rings. Oi Lin wakes, her eyes damp with frustration. She takes out a journal—there are dozens, stacked vertically in boxes under the bed—and writes the details of her dream. With each word she feels a knot dissolving in her gut, as if the act of transposing is causing the event to become a distant memory, or a fiction. She finishes the entry, dates it, and then moves to close the book—but instead pulls it open again, scanning earlier pages for clues, the dreams returning in her mind, but inverted, like negatives in a film reel.

September 1: A teenage girl who died in a car accident. In our dream, she goes to an industrial block in Chai Wan to see an underground metal band play in an abandoned factory. She dances to the music . . .

August 19: An old man who died of old age. We go to a Chiu Chow restaurant in Kowloon and he orders two plates of cold braised goose with tofu and eggs. The owner comes over and congratulates the old man on retiring . . .

June 3: A middle-aged lady who died of breast cancer. She is picking up her daughter from school and has brought her a snack box of apples slices and orange juice. She drives home and listens to the BBC . . .

March 28: A businessman who died of a heart attack. He's watching something pornographic on his laptop; I don't want to see so I just look at his saltwater aquarium, which he has kept in prime condition. There are clown fish, lionfish, John Dory . . .

January 2: A little girl who died in her sleep. Her grand-mother has given her some money to buy candy from the corner store; she runs down the street and buys a packet of ginger gummies . . .

December 23 . . .

"Oi Lin!" Her mother is calling. "Are you coming?"

She looks at the clock; it is almost six.

Work: cleaning, sprucing, weaving, painting, filing, cutting, trimming, buffing, spritzing. Oi Lin finishes her tasks and then sits by the front of the store on a plastic stool, taking out several journals from her bag. She begins to read again, absorbed by the dry, detailed accounts written in her own childish hand. She reads through the last year, and the year before, and the year before that, but nothing stands out. All of the people in her dreams had died and she had seen their bodies in coffins, being prepared with perfumed oils and powders by the mortuary makeup artist or being rolled into white halls. Oi Lin closes her eyes. Was the widow right? Has she been reworking her own memories in her dreams, tooling them into fictionalized accounts of others' lives as a way to come to terms with the monotony of life, the monotony of death? And if so, then isn't the widow also just another creation of her mind—or perhaps some part of herself, reaching out and requesting a wake-up call?

Oi Lin is drifting; she tries to assemble the pieces in her head, but the pieces themselves are amorphous, shape-changing. She struggles to stay focused on the day's proceedings, helping her mother with the weekly cleaning of the store and balancing the cash register. Her calculations keep coming up short, and the more she tries, the more she feels herself slipping further and further from the numbers, the connections between them, and reality.

The day falls away, dragging her along with it. When evening arrives, she is somewhat relieved that it is over, though also fearful that yet another cycle of self-doubt might begin.

"Can you eat something?" her mother scolds Oi Lin at the dinner table at home, pointing with her chopsticks to the untouched scoops of rice and minced beef on her plate. "Focus."

A few more hours pass at home. Oi Lin is lost in thought. She lies on her bed and listens to Chochukmo on repeat. Around ten p.m., she receives an urgent text from Hao: *I'm alone and it looks like someone has broken into the funeral home. Please come. Hurry.*

She runs over; her apartment is a few short blocks away. The September evening is pale and on the cusp of turning, the thick, salty breeze bringing in warm blankets of humidity from the sea. Hao is waiting by the front doors, whose gold edges, under the dim streetlights, appear dull and tacky.

"What happened? And why didn't you call the police?" she whispers. The large building is dark, looming.

"Are you serious? My dad left me here to lock up," Hao says. "If he finds out that someone might have broken in, he's going to murder me. Anyway, I don't think the person stayed. I checked and nothing was taken. Probably got freaked out and left."

Oi Lin shakes her head. "So why am I here? I ran all the way over. My mother thinks I went out to buy tampons."

"I need to lock up, okay?" Hao gestures for her to come inside. He nervously peers upward. "Someone else should be here just in case, and you live the closest."

They start on the ground floor and work their way up to the top. Each room has its own lock and within each room are vitrines for the coffins, also with locks. The rooms on the ground floor are the largest; there are two main halls with closets for storage. The second floor comprises seven smaller rooms, the silk stall, and a broad public area with a few armchairs and a hanging Georgia O'Keeffe print. In it, stone-shaped clouds of opaque white fill a sky that is a soft blue unlike any Oi Lin has ever seen.

It takes them no more than twenty minutes to complete the lockup, by which point Hao has shed his earlier, nervous self and has begun to rant about his dissatisfaction with the funeral home.

"My father wants me to become a director one day, but I really don't see it," he says. They are sitting on the front steps of the building, the gleaming structure firmly locked behind them. Hao is smoking; every so often Oi Lin tastes the peppery, watery fumes in her nostrils. She has always liked the smell of cigarette smoke—her father used to light one after the other, leaving a trail of ashed surfaces and burn-scented clothing behind him. It is one of the only memories she has of him: a smell that resurfaces on streets, in clandestine bars and *cha chaan tengs*, and outside factory buildings, when workers get off their shift and together take their first, protracted draws from the thin, elegant cylinders.

"What are you going to do then?" she asks.

"Quit. Leave." He blows out smoke through his nose. "I've been thinking of joining the police force. Did you know a new recruit can earn as much as eighty thousand a year? I'm lucky if my dad decides to pay me, and it's only when he thinks I've met his standards."

Oi Lin is silent for a while. "I thought of leaving the shop too at one point," she confesses. "I wanted to be a painter. Not calligraphy painting, but oil, contemporary stuff. I even made a portfolio and picked the colleges I wanted to apply to."

"Really? I never knew that. Why didn't you do it?"

"Well, first, my mother would never let me. And secondly, I realized something. Even if I were a painter, I don't think I'd be satisfied."

Hao shakes his head. "Why?"

"I realized . . . that I'm seeing a part of life, every day, that reminds me of how futile it is. Whatever we do, whatever we love, whatever we put our heart into, it all just dissolves in the end. Nothing is solid. Nothing *seems* real." She pauses. "You know, when I was young, really young, I was so confused about why the funeral home was called the big hotel."

"I prefer big restaurant, but okay," Hao says.

"Big hotel. Big restaurant. Anyway, it seems like a joke, so callous, right? But why shouldn't it be? There are the same number of bodies, with plenty of food and beds. The only difference is that while we're all still walking around filling our guts with made-up dreams to fulfill ourselves, someone else isn't around to see the festering of human life anymore. And the better for them. There's something so nice, so calming about not being able to think or see anymore."

"Huh," Hao says. "That's really depressing."

They sit for a while.

"You know, if I became a detective, I would earn a lot of money. You wouldn't have to work at all. Maybe you could be a painter. Even if you feel like you'd be unhappy, at least you would have tried. That's all one can hope for anyway, right?"

Oi Lin is suddenly shaken by the conversation. Is it a coincidence that Hao wants to be a detective? The events of the past few days, with the widow and the detective's funeral, are brought up again in her mind, but why? She asks herself again: *What is happening right now? A dream? A piece of my future or my past?* Her mind races as she frantically attempts to link the thoughts in her head. Is she Oi Lin or the widow?

She turns to look at Hao, his face half-buried in shadow. "You never said you wanted to be a detective before," she says hollowly.

"Didn't I? It's been on my mind for a while. Oi Lin . . . ?"

She feels herself breathing heavily, and then the sky is spinning. She is falling. She feels all logic has been smashed, its pulpy remains submerged in a black pool in which they are spiraling, toward an end that is receding and expanding, as unfamiliar, changing, and desolate as the dark and star-lined edges of the universe.

The nurses at the hospital wear blue face masks; their hair is black and their uniforms are white. Through the opaque veil that surrounds her bed, cordoning Oi Lin off from the rest of the ward, she sees the shapes of these women and men, coming in and out of the room quietly, against the soundtrack of bell-like wheels on the floor and the dim hum of a television set on low. On occasion, shadows overlap as one leaves and another arrives. Oi Lin sits up to look at the large wall clock just above the line of the curtain: it is six p.m.

"Medicine." A nurse is by her side. There is a small needle attached, with surgical tape, to her hand; a second nurse is pressing a tiny vial into this, from which a cold liquid flows, instantly freezing up Oi Lin's veins. "You were asleep for a bit. We called your mother; she'll be in in around a half hour or so, when visiting times open."

The chill in her arms and hands causes a momentary numbness. Oi Lin feels her eyelids drooping; sleep pulls her back into its undercurrents.

When she awakens next, her mother is sitting by the side of the bed, reading a book. There is a lamp next to her, emitting a lovely white glow that she somehow feels she hasn't seen in a while.

"You're awake," her mother says, closing the book and hurrying to the head of the bed. "How are you feeling? The nurses told me not to wake you."

"I'm fine," Oi Lin says slowly. "I don't remember what happened, though."

"You fainted again." Her mother wrinkles her forehead. "Oi Lin, listen to me. Is there something I should know about? Are you on drugs? Are you pregnant?"

A nurse comes in bearing a syringe. "Medicine," she barks as she plunges the syringe into the vial in Oi Lin's arm. A cold sensation spreads through her arm. The nurse checks the chart. "Your medication causes drowsiness. You have to rest." She moves on to the patient next to Oi Lin, an elderly male who croaks desperately: "Where's my son?"

"I'm not pregnant. I'm just very confused," Oi Lin says. "I

feel like I'm meeting all these dead people in my dreams—"

"Perhaps it's the medicine," her mother interrupts. "The nurse was right: you really should get some sleep. Don't talk now."

Just hearing the word *sleep* causes extreme lethargy in Oi Lin. Even though she tries to stay awake, the effort of simply opening her eyes drains all remaining energy from her body. She struggles to remember the events of the past few days; everything escapes her.

Her mother is leaving, or so she thinks; her vision is blurry. "Doctor, I need to speak with you about my daughter . . . She's having visions again . . ."

Before Oi Lin falls unconscious again, she sees before her a procession of images. The shop at dawn, empty and lonely. Her mother watching her write in her journal, lines of worry marking her face, but silent all the same. The funeral home, the detective's widow and her hard glare that day, as if she could see the spirits that live in Oi Lin's head. And then: cold, milky chrysanthemums; serrated-silhouette lilies with rust-hued stamens; tissue-thin globe peonies; creamy roses with rubbery skirts; flowers, flowers, and more flowers, clouding her vision until all is blinding, whiter than white.

ABOUT THE CONTRIBUTORS

SUSAN BLUMBERG-KASON is the author of *Good Chinese Wife: A Love Affair with China Gone Wrong*. Her writing has also appeared in the *Los Angeles Review of Books'* China Blog and China Channel, *Cha: An Asian Literary Journal, Asian Jewish Life*, and several Hong Kong anthologies. She received an MPhil in government and public administration from the Chinese University of Hong Kong. Blumberg-Kason now lives in Chicago and frequently travels back to Hong Kong.

Willem Molesworth

YSABELLE CHEUNG is a writer and editor based in Hong Kong. She is currently the managing editor of *ArtAsiaPacific*, a publication focused on visual contemporary culture, and was previously the arts and associate editor of *Time Out Hong Kong*. She holds a BA in English literature and creative writing from the University of East Anglia in the UK, and is the cofounder of the Hong Kong edition of Liars' League, a spoken word organization with branches in London and New York.

FENG CHI-SHUN was born in Wuhan, China, and grew up in Hong Kong. He graduated from Hong Kong University's Li Ka Shing Faculty of Medicine and found his passion for writing late in life. He is the author of the memoir *Diamond Hill*, as well as the story collections *Hong Kong Noir* and *Kitchen Tiles*. A history book, *A Little History of Sex and Romance in China*, and a novel, *Three Wishes in Bardo*, will be published soon.

TIFFANY HAWK is a former flight attendant with an MFA from UC Riverside. Her debut novel, *Love Me Anyway*, was published by St. Martin's Press. Her short fiction and essays have appeared in the *New York Times*, the *Potomac Review*, *StoryQuarterly*, and on NPR's *All Things Considered*. She has also worked as the travel editor at *Coast* magazine and as a freelance journalist for the *Los Angeles Times*, *Sunset*, CNN.com, GQ.com, and *National Geographic Traveler*.

CHRISTINA LIANG grew up in Canada feeling like she and her sister were the only Eurasians in town. Now based in Hong Kong and armed with a curiosity to discover more about her heritage, she's attempting to learn Chinese and find the best dumplings in town. She also writes for children under the name Christina Matula. Her debut picture book, *The Shadow in the Moon*, was published by Charlesbridge.

Lincoln Potter

CHARLES PHILIPP MARTIN grew up in New York City. After university and music conservatory he joined the Hong Kong Philharmonic Orchestra. He eventually quit bass playing to write for newspapers and magazines in Asia. *Neon Panic*, his first novel featuring Hong Kong police inspector Herman Lok, came out in 2011. Martin now lives in Seattle with his wife Catherine. His jazz radio show *3 O'Clock Jump* is broadcast weekly on Hong Kong's Radio 3 and online.

MARSHALL MOORE is the author of seven books, most recently the novel *Inhospitable* and the short story collection *A Garden Fed by Lightning*. A collection of his translated work, *Sagome Nere*, was recently published in Italy. He has also written dozens of essays, book reviews, and other odds and ends. He holds a PhD in creative writing from Aberystwyth University in Wales, and he teaches English and creative writing at Lingnan University in Hong Kong.

JASON Y. NG is the best-selling author of *Hong Kong State of Mind, No City for Slow Men,* and *Umbrellas in Bloom*—the first book in English to chronicle the Umbrella Movement of 2014. His short stories have appeared in numerous anthologies. Ng is also an adjunct associate law professor at the University of Hong Kong and president of PEN Hong Kong, an advocacy group that promotes literature and defends freedom of expression.

SHEN JIAN is a lawyer and an occasional contributor to the *South China Morning Post*. His writing has been nominated for a Pushcart Prize and recognized as notable in *Best American Essays*.

Alex Trebus

BRITTANI SONNENBERG was raised across three continents and has worked as a journalist in Germany, the US, China, and throughout Southeast Asia. Sonnenberg's fiction and nonfiction have apeared in *The O. Henry Prize Stories, Ploughshares, Time,* and on NPR Berlin. Her debut novel, *Home Leave*, was selected as a *New York Times* Editors' Choice. She serves as a visiting lecturer and thesis advisor for the University of Hong Kong's MFA program.

CARMEN SUEN was born and raised in Hong Kong, where she wrote and edited for *City Magazine*, *Eat and Travel*, and *East Magazine*. She was also a founding editor of the photography blog *Resolve*. After relocating to the United States, Suen has been living a semi-nomadic life with her husband Gary and their boys Genghis and Rohan, moving from the Wild West to the Southwest and the Midwest, until finally settling in New York.

Genghis Arthur

JAMES TAM is a pseudo-scientific realist who regards twenty-first-century Homo sapiens a self-endangered species. His novel *Man's Last Song*, a Proverse Prize finalist, is about humanity facing protracted extinction due to sterility. His bilingual stories have been anthologized by Hong Kong Writers Circle, *Asia Literary Review*, Hong Kong Writers (Chinese), and Ethos Books in Singapore. He regularly writes about an assortment of irregularities at www.guo-du.blogspot.com.

RHIANNON JENKINS TSANG is a British writer whose work focuses on historical fault lines and contains strong international themes. She read Oriental Studies at St. Anne's College, Oxford, and is a nonpracticing lawyer. She speaks Mandarin, Cantonese, French, German, and Spanish. Her second novel, *The Last Vicereine*, was published by Penguin Random House in 2017. Her debut, *The Woman Who Lost China*, was published by Open Books in 2013.

XU XI 許素細 is the author of twelve books of fiction and nonfiction. Forthcoming are *Insignificance: Stories of Hong Kong* and *This Fish is Fowl: Essays of Being*. An Indonesian-Chinese from Hong Kong, she lives between New York and Hong Kong and codirects the new low-residency International MFA in Creative Writing and Literary Translation at Vermont College of Fine Arts.

LeslieLausch

SHANNON YOUNG is an American author living in Hong Kong. Her books include a coming-of-age travel memoir, *Year of Fire Dragons*, a Kindle Single on millennial student debt, and two novellas set in contemporary Hong Kong. She was the editor of an anthology of creative nonfiction by expatriate women in Asia, *How Does One Dress to Buy Dragonfruit?*, and she once won a Literary Death Match.

Also available in the Akashic Noir Series

SINGAPORE NOIR
edited by Cheryl Lu-Lien Tan
240 pages, trade paperback original, $15.95

BRAND-NEW STORIES BY: Colin Goh, Simon Tay/Donald Tee Quee Ho, Philip Jeyaretnam, Colin Cheong, Cheryl Lu-Lien Tan, Monica Bhide, S.J. Rozan, Lawrence Osborne, Suchen Christine Lim, Ovidia Yu, Damon Chua, Johann S. Lee, Dave Chua, and Nury Vittachi.

"Singapore, with its great wealth and great poverty existing amid ethnic, linguistic, and cultural tensions, offers fertile ground for bleak fiction, as shown by the 14 tales in this solid Akashic noir anthology . . . Tan has assembled a strong lineup of Singapore natives and knowledgeable visitors for this volume exploring the dark side of a fascinating country." —*Publishers Weekly*

"Across the book as a whole a picture emerges of Singapore, an image at variance with tourist board literature and with the popular conception of a safe but over-controlled conformist society." —*Crime Review* (UK)

MANILA NOIR
edited by Jessica Hagedorn
240 pages, trade paperback original, $15.95

BRAND-NEW STORIES BY: Lourd de Veyra, Gina Apostol, Budjette Tan & Kajo Baldisimo, F.H. Batacan, Jose Dalisay Jr., Eric Gamalinda, Jessica Hagedorn, Angelo R. Lacuesta, R. Zamora Linmark, Rosario Cruz-Lucero, Sabina Murray, Jonas Vitman, Marianne Villanueva, and Lysley Tenorio.

"While certain cities in past Akashic volumes might appear to lack an obvious noir element, Manila (like Mexico City, which shares many of the same problems) practically defines it, as shown by the 14 selections in this excellent anthology." —*Publishers Weekly*, starred review

"[I]t is Manila itself—its heat and throb, its particular melange of Asia and America, its poverty and wealth, its diverse neighborhoods, the iconic *pan de sal*—that is the main protagonist in the collection as a whole . . . every reader—even those with weak stomachs or no particular affinity for noir—is likely to find some that are intriguing, enjoyable or eye-opening." —*Asian Review of Books*